YOU'VE BEEN WARNED

My room is cool—I've left the window open—and I close it quickly, before I change into my pajamas: oversized, patterned with unicorns. What would Sabrina think of them? Not much, I imagine.

Then I wash my face in the bathroom mirror. I look drawn, a crease between my eyebrows. I am just tired, I tell myself, and I rub moisturizer between my hands and smooth it over my face, the familiar nighttime ritual soothing me, before I rummage in my wash bag. Why can I never find anything in here? There it is, my lip balm—I smear the stick onto my bottom lip in a practiced stroke—

"Ow!" I suck at my lip, tasting copper.

At first I can't understand, as I stare at the smear of red on the white waxy stick, then something glints under the overhead light, and a chill runs through me.

I twist the tube so the stick of balm is exposed as high it goes, and scratch away with my thumbnail, unconcerned about wrecking it.

I can see it now, shining silver and sharp: a needle . . .

Books by Emma Rowley

WHERE THE MISSING GO

YOU CAN TRUST ME

Published by Kensington Publishing Corporation

YOU CAN TRUST ME

EMMA ROWLEY

PINNACLE BOOKS
Kensington Publishing Corp.
www.kensingtonbooks.com

PINNACLE BOOKS are published by

Kensington Publishing Corp.
119 West 40th Street
New York, NY 10018

All Kensington titles, imprints, and distributed lines are available at special quantity discounts for bulk purchases for sales promotions, premiums, fund-raising, educational, or institutional use. Special book excerpts or customized printings can also be created to fit specific needs. For details, write or phone the office of the Kensington sales manager: Kensington Publishing Corp., 119 West 40th Street, New York, NY 10018, attn: Sales Department; phone 1-800-221-2647.

ISBN-13: 978-0-7860-4768-0
ISBN-10: 0-7860-4768-2

First printing: September 2020

10 9 8 7 6 5 4 3 2 1

Printed in the United States of America

Electronic edition:

ISBN-13: 978-0-7860-4770-3 (e-book)
ISBN-10: 0-7860-4770-4 (e-book)

Prologue

The house is framed by the thick dark trees, ink-black in the summer night.

There is nothing to see from the outside yet—just a few wisps of smoke barely visible against the clear starry sky.

No one is trying to stop it, and no one is coming to help.

It is the noises that point to what is happening within, disturbing the quiet of the night. The shatter of glass breaking. The crack of wood under stress. A heavy thud as something falls unseen. And all of it underscored by that deep muffled roar, like a beast is stirring at the heart of the house.

No one is trying to stop it, and no one is coming to help.

Then the stillness of the night splinters, and an orange flower blossoms forth from one of the downstairs windows. The flames are quick and hungry, reaching up into the air like hands clawing at the sky, streaking the white walls with soot. The fire is taking over the house now.

No one is trying to stop it, and no one is coming to help.

Someone is watching, though. And now it is time to go.

PART 1
NICKY

Chapter 1

Ghosts are real.

I should know: I am one.

That's what I sometimes tell people at parties, just to watch them stutter for a second. It livens up the usual and-what-do-you-do conversations, when you tell someone you're a ghost.

They stand there looking confused, and then I relent and smile, and say, "A ghostwriter, I mean."

The conversation, from my side, goes as follows:

"Yes, I ghostwrite books."

"Yes, you'd have heard of them."

"In bookshops, yes."

"No, I can't tell you who. Sorry."

"No, really."

Then I do a conspiratorial lean in: "If I did, I'd have to kill you."

That's a joke, too.

* * *

They say everyone has a book in them. Perhaps they have, perhaps they haven't. What interests me is whether they can get it out of themselves and onto the page.

The reality is most people can't—or won't—or just don't have the time, what with the job and the commute and the kids and the in-laws coming on the weekend, and have you seen that latest Netflix series, it's really very good.

Pile success and a public profile on top of that, a calendar packed with TV shows and award ceremonies, add a thirty-date one-man (or woman) tour, and maybe a collapsing marriage and a rebound toy boy, and it becomes even more impossible.

And that's where I come in.

It's Saturday and I am working again: up against my latest deadline.

I've nearly finished the book I'm currently writing, the memoir of a celebrity chef known for the cheeky twinkle in his eye. Which should, the publisher hopes, help his sales figures to rise as quickly as his Victoria sponge.

This afternoon, I'm finishing off his acknowledgments, that final flurry of thank-yous that I'm never sure if anyone reads (yes, I write them, too, if my subject can't be bothered). I scan what I've got so far:

> *First, many thanks to my agent Gerry. And huge thanks to my editor Frances and the rest of the team at my brilliant publisher. But above all, thanks with a cherry on top to my wonderful wife Tracy, who was so helpful in getting my memories straight for this autobiography.*

Let's face it, some of it was tricky for me to piece together—especially that colorful spell just before rehab! And some of it, of course, I didn't want to mention to my ghostwriter at all.

The truth is, I've really made a cake of myself in more ways than one, not least over my assistant—

With a decisive tap, I press the backspace on the keyboard in front of me and watch the words I've just written disappear off the screen. There's no way I can submit that, I am just letting off steam. I had thought I was finished with the book, until the editor called to ask if I had seen the papers. There might be a little bit of rejigging needed . . .

I should have known. Whenever I visited the chef, there was far too much meaningful eye contact between him and the over-officious Ruby, his PA. Meanwhile, poor Tracy would be hovering in the background, fiddling nervously with her cardigan sleeves.

He is still denying it all officially. His team wants to give it a decent amount of time before he announces the sad news of his separation. And of course I won't really out him as a cheater in his thank-yous. After all, I am nothing if not reliable.

That's what I am paid for: to make sure pages get filled, deadlines are hit, and books make it on to the shop shelves in time for Christmas, regardless of the author's last-minute panto rehearsals or discreet trip to Thailand to dry out. I am a professional.

So I think for a second, then start clacking away again.

A special thank-you, I type, *for the people
who've been with me from the start. I really
wouldn't be here without you.*

That's for poor heartbroken Tracy. Let him explain
to the publisher why he wants it taken out.
I keep going:

*And thanks also to Nicky Wilson, who made this
book possible.*

I stare into the air above my screen, then tweak that:

*Thanks also to the supremely talented Nicky Wil-
son, who made this book possible.*

Might as well give the credentials a little polish—
it's not as though as I can shout about this on a CV. Because that's me: Nicky Wilson. I tell other people's
stories.

You might even have read one of my books already,
though you didn't know it. Remember that not-so-
chatty footballer with the best-selling autobiography?
He didn't actually park himself in front of a computer
to bash it out between ball drills. That TV presenter
busy with three shows whose lifestyle guide is in every
good bookshop? She didn't, either. And that always-
smiling influencer whose perfume, pencil case, and
(rather short) memoir your preteen daughter insisted
on buying? You guessed it . . .
They all talked to someone like me. Talked for hours,

days, weeks—and always with a tape recorder rolling. Then, once we'd covered everything I needed in our interviews—had heard their whole life story, or collected all their thoughts on the subject they'd picked—I went away and wrote their book for them.

Other ghosts might focus on victims of true crime or moving "real-life" tales; I tend to work with celebrities, or people on their way to that—lighter fare. Relatively.

Afterward, the only trace of me will be somewhere in the acknowledgments, if at all. There will be a thank-you "for all your expertise" or for "helping to get my story out there," or maybe—if the person's decided to do the acknowledgments themselves—I'll find my name sandwiched somewhere between their hairdresser and their dog.

I don't care. I'm good at it, even if I do have to say so myself. The authors get the praise, that's true, but I take my money and move on to the next job. And I enjoy it, even if I kind of fell into it. I can set my own hours, and mostly it's interesting work.

Now I prop my elbows on the kitchen table, my makeshift desk, and look out of the window, to the leaves of the trees that shade my little patch of South London. A bumblebee—a lone survivor of the summer—is batting half-heartedly against the glass, and I get up to let it out. I'm glad I'm nearly done with this particular project; this job's much easier when you like the person.

I have promised Frances at the publisher that she'd have the revised manuscript back imminently. For the last few days, her e-mails have been getting shorter and terser, as mine get ever more filled with upbeat exclamation marks. "All going well!" "Getting it back to you ASAP!!" "I will call you back as soon as I can! Thanks!!!"

For the next hour or so, I work hard, doing a few final checks and tweaks to the text. I am concentrating, going as quick as I can, so when my cell phone rings, shrilly breaking the silence, I jump.

I register the "private number" flashing on the screen—like that's going to make me pick up—and watch the phone vibrate, slowly sliding closer to the edge of the table. Then I punch the disconnect button and turn back to my screen.

But after a few minutes more, I close my laptop. My concentration has gone now. Anyway, I tell myself, it's getting late, and I have a date . . .

Chapter 2

"So, Nicky. Do you like working in—uh—what you do?"

I smile at the man in front of me. "I do, mostly. I'm a writer," I add, guessing that he's forgotten. "I ghostwrite books."

"And how did you get into that line of work?" he asks me, raising his voice over the clamor of the bar we're in.

"Well, I started off as a reporter in newspapers," I explain. "Then my grandparents got to the stage where they needed a bit more looking after, so I was going back home a lot to help. Getting into ghostwriting was a bit of a sideways move—I needed to be able to organize my own time—but actually, I found I liked the work."

We met on an app—no flirting by the photocopier when you work from home. He's a lawyer, has been telling me all about it. He seems nice enough, if unable to talk about anything but work. Although I can't really criticize him for that.

I keep thinking about the manuscript I'm working

on. The chef hasn't taken much of an interest in the project, beyond worrying whether the cover photo gives him a double chin. You never know, though, when a subject might choose their moment to become A True Writer, whipping a red pen through half your carefully written words.

"But doesn't it annoy you, seeing someone else's name on your book?" Phil—it is Phil, isn't it?—asks me. "When you've done all that work?"

I smile again. "Not really. It's not my book, you see. It doesn't feel like mine."

"But even so," he says earnestly—his way of making conversation, I notice, is by arguing with everything I say—"don't you ever want to write your own book?"

And maybe it's because he's a stranger, and I am already sure I won't see him again, that I tell him.

"Actually, yes, I've been thinking recently . . . I'd like to do something a bit different."

Tell a story of my own, you could say. I even have an idea, have taken tentative steps toward making a start—though I haven't mentioned it to my agent Barbara, or anyone else.

"My father's writing a book," he says.

"Oh," I say, trying to switch gears mentally. "Well, that's great."

"Military history." He pauses. "Do you know much about military history?"

There's a certain type of person, I've learned over the years, who hears you've written a book—any book—and feels the urge to test your credentials. "No, I couldn't say I do."

"Hm," he says, with satisfaction.

There's another silence between us. Don't fill it, I tell myself, don't—

"So your profile said you're into current affairs." I wince inwardly: *current affairs.*

"Well, up to a point. There's really no need to follow domestic politics."

"There isn't?"

"No, no." He pulls his glass of expensive red a little closer. "It's all about China these days . . ."

He's off, me nodding like my head is on a string. I can't help it: I'm a good listener.

It's not deliberate, not really. I've just had a lot of practice, through my job: listening to people tell me all the details of their lives, childhoods, relationships, careers. People really will tell you anything, if you just shut up and listen.

Sometimes, a person will realize they've just unburdened themselves of all the details of their fraught relationship with their father, or confessed to some minor lawbreaking their boss mustn't know about, and feel suddenly exposed.

"What did you say you do?" they'll ask crossly, like I've just tricked them. "Where are you from again?"

But some people are just thrilled to find an audience. My ex, Rob, was an actor. So it worked well for a while, until we both realized even I had tuned out.

This guy's on a roll now. "It's important to carve out thinking time, you know? I like to set time aside in my schedule. Just to think."

"Wow," I say. "That's such a good idea."

But these days I'm trying not to repeat my mistakes, trying not to get lost in someone else's life again. I pick up my glass and down the last sickly dregs of my rosé.

I paid for our round, so I'm not going to let it go to waste.

"Actually, you've just made me *think*." I smile to signal the weak joke. "I'm going to have to head off, I'm afraid—I've got a really early start tomorrow."

"Go?" He frowns. "Don't you want another drink? It's Saturday night."

"Oh yeah," I say, feeling my eyelids flicker. I forgot for a moment what day of the week it was. An occupational hazard when you set your own hours. "I mean, I know that, of course, but my trainer's coming really early."

"You have a trainer?" he says, a little skeptically.

"Paid up front," I lie. "So I can't back out!" I'm already gathering my bag up from the floor. "So nice to meet you, though. Have a great rest of the weekend, OK?"

I'm indignant as I leave the bar and start the short walk home from the high street. Who does he think he is, casting doubt on my polite fib? Who orders a £12 glass of merlot when you're splitting the bill, anyway?

Still, by the time I near the turn off the main road to the row of town houses where I live, my righteousness has worn off. I wanted a night out to forget my problems; instead it has put them at the forefront of my mind. Because even if I'd wanted to, I couldn't have stayed there ordering round after round.

I rarely indulge in feeling sorry for myself. But as I let myself in through the front door and head up the stairs to my dark, silent apartment, I am feeling small and deflated. And—if I'm honest—lonely. For once, I can't be bothered to switch on the cozy lights and TV to create the illusion of company as I get ready for bed.

It was my ex Rob's idea that we rent this place. He made—still makes, I suppose—a nice living, padding out his theater spots with lucrative voice-over work. I worried that since I'd been having to go home so much, interrupting my writing, we should wait until my finances were healthier. He said that we could afford it together and that I should stop fretting.

Then, after things went south between us, it was too late to back out of the lease. He offered to stay at his brother's. Graciously, he thought; I didn't have anywhere to go. But the rent is steep for just me, and it's a long time until the lease is up.

Before I slide between the sheets, I check my phone. It doesn't help my bleak mood. I missed a call this evening, from an unlisted number—the second today, in fact, after the one I ignored earlier.

I know my editor wouldn't call me over a weekend, however worried she was about a manuscript. So I know who it must be: another brusque call-center operator telling me I owe money on my account, asking how would I like to make repayment?

I always try to explain that I will have money coming in soon, that I am doing my best, trying so hard to get out of this situation. But it doesn't stop the calls.

I pull the duvet over my head. I'll deal with it all in the morning.

Chapter 3

The phone wakes me, shrilling on my pillow. I fumble for the silence button, and toss it across the room, anger flashing through me. These people are relentless.

I'm reminded—as if I could forget—of the state of my bank balance. So although it's Sunday, I make myself get up, make proper coffee, and sit at my laptop, still in my pajamas, waiting for the grogginess to clear.

It doesn't take me long to get the chef's rewrite done and e-mailed off to the publisher. I allow myself a celebratory cookie and sit back down.

I have already asked Barbara, my agent, to put me up for another ghostwriting job. Work is my only way out of this mess.

The celebrity in question is too busy to meet prospective writers, so the publisher is asking us all to submit a writing sample to show how we might capture her voice.

It's tricky to do without meeting her, but not impossible.

This first step is research, as it always is when I'm

prepping for a book: pulling up YouTube to watch clips of the subject's TV show, if they have one; trawling through past appearances on talk shows; combing through old newspaper interviews. I pay for a cuttings service, which lets me access years of past articles.

Along the way, I can check the facts; even discover a few new ones. You'd be surprised what people can get wrong—the names of old colleagues, the years their children were born—and what they might, to put it charitably, *forget*—early career flops, that band member who didn't work out . . .

If I do my research thoroughly, when I sit down for my interviews with the person whose book I am writing, I am ready to ask every possible question that might give me an interesting answer. It means I can avoid repeating the same safe stale anecdotes they like to trot out. And I can challenge my subject, in the politest of ways, if they gloss over things, waffle, or bluster. It makes for a much better book.

Because, yes, I can empathize with someone, build a rapport. I can deliver a manuscript to deadline, I am reliable. But this is the other side of my job: turning over stones, seeing what's underneath. I'm good at it, with my background in newspapers. It's what gives me my edge—it's my niche, you could say. Looking closer.

Of course, I have to be tactful. I always remember it is not really my book, that the person I'm writing for has to be happy with what I write. And no one wants you to show them exactly as they are. They want you to show them as they want to be.

I learned that the hard way. I was writing a rushed-out autobiography for a singer who struck me as a very nice young man. It shone through in the way he talked to me about his family and his girlfriend, the same one he'd had since school.

I knew his fans would lap it up. They liked how smiley and kind he seemed, even in the pressure-cooker environment of the talent show that made him famous. I filed the first few chapters to the publisher, to check I was on track. They loved what I'd got, they just needed to run it by his camp. And then . . . the tone changed.

"We'll get back to you," my editor e-mailed me, "just ironing out a few issues."

I couldn't figure out what they could object to, until she called the next day.

"You know, Nicky, don't feel you have to tone him down. You can let him be a bit rock'n'roll." My confusion was almost audible. "I mean," she finally cracked, "you don't need to delete all the swear words. Or mention the girlfriend."

Aha. So I threw in some not-so-veiled references to a substance-abuse problem, hinted at a string of drunken one-night stands, and deleted all mentions of his long-term girlfriend. She understood, I was told, and everyone was happy.

So who, I wonder, does this next potential project want to be?

I can see why the publisher signed her up. *The Coupon Queen*, her TV show, has been a surprise hit, moving from a morning to an evening slot.

The format is simple: she turns up at someone's home, looking like a cartoon version of a bank manager, in her signature skirt suit, beehive, and cat's-eye glasses. Like a costume really—almost a disguise. Then she goes through your bills and tells you exactly where you've gone wrong. Wonder what she'd tell me . . .

On the screen, she is breezy, upbeat—unshockable. But it's hard to get a sense of *her*.

I turn to the notes I've made for inspiration.

Sally Cooper was working in a bank when she started her *Coupon Queen* newsletter to help other moms save money, I read. Snooze. She has a son, now a student. She has talked about co-parenting with her ex. Nice. But snooze again.

There's nothing juicy, except some rumblings when she jumped ship to her current broadcaster, doubling her pay. *Greedy*, said some media commentators.

I start to type, trying things out on the screen:

If you can't control your budget, you can't control your life.

That's what she always says—but her catchphrase reads so leaden on the page.

Not everyone understands that my job isn't just to repeat what people actually *say*. I have to be more creative than that; I have to tell a good story.

"You mean you put words into their mouths?" Rob asked me once, when things were turning sour between us.

"Well . . ." I hedged, sensing he wanted to pick another fight. "They check it all over . . . they're things they're happy to say."

Now, staring at the screen, I take a swig of cold coffee and try again.

I want this book to inspire others to achieve their financial potential, to take control.

Yawn. I'd fall asleep reading this. I'll have to keep digging.

Of course, you never really know what bit of info you're looking for until you find it. It's curiosity that drives me, more than anything else; that prickly feeling I get, when I might have come across something that could take me somewhere interesting . . .

And eventually—*bingo*. I find my lead in one of the oldest articles about the Coupon Queen, from back when she was plugging her newsletter in her local paper. She was Sally Berrycloth then.

That's how, after a bit of searching, I track down her son on social media. Then, in his friends list, I spot the profile for someone with the same surname—an older man. It is set to private, but a quick Google search turns up some very interesting results.

And, after I check the online inquiries directory I use, to confirm that a Sally Berrycloth was once listed at the same address this man gave in court, I am sure: this is her ex. And theirs is not quite the cordial relationship she makes out, I'd bet.

I start to write, confident now that my sample will grab her attention.

I haven't told anyone this before. But when I was just a young mother, my little boy just starting school, his father went to prison. They got him on an assault charge in the end.

Any money from him—patchy at best—dried up. I was broke. Dead broke.

That's when I told myself: I'll never be in this situation again.

And that's how I know. If you can't control your budget, you can't control your life.

Now that's a story worth telling. Whether she will let me tell it is another matter. But at the least, she and her publisher will want to talk to me, to find out what I know.

I sigh, despite knowing I need this job—desperately. It's exhausting, the prospect of going from one book to another without a break. But I have to do it.

From my bedroom, my phone rings again. I get up, stiff from sitting so long, and go to find it wedged down the side of the dresser.

When I pull it out, it's covered in dust. My place is always a dump by the end of a book.

It keeps ringing, an unlisted number. Probably time to face the music.

"Hello?"

Chapter 4

"Nicky?"

"Hello, who's calling?" I wander back into the other room, and sit at the table again.

"Am I speaking to Nicky?" The woman's voice is clipped and unfamiliar.

"I think you rang me?" I say, pointedly polite. I find it's best not to lose my temper when a collections agency calls. "And you are?"

"This is Julia." Clearly I'm supposed to know who Julia is. "Didn't you get my e-mail?"

"No." Not a call center, after all. I minimize the document on my screen and open my junk file, scanning quickly. Among the dross is an e-mail that isn't trying to sell me Viagra, sent yesterday. "Ghostwriting" reads the subject title.

"Thanks so much, but I'm not actually taking on any more work at the moment." I say automatically, clicking the e-mail open. I prefer people to go through my agent—she's better than me at dealing with people who find my website and think the story of their life in middle management is a guaranteed best seller.

"Are you sure?" Julia sounds sharp. "Have you definitely read the e-mail?"

"Oh." I take my feet off the chair next to mine and place them back down on the floor, as I scan down. "I'm so sorry, long day." I have registered the sender's name now: Julia Levitt. "You work for Olivia Hayes, of course. How are you?"

"That's right, I assist Olivia." She manages to sound both impatient and smug. "So, she's keen to get started. She's very impressed by the projects you've worked on."

"Thanks. All confidential," I add, automatically.

"Naturally. So how's this week looking? Her schedule's just opened up."

"This week? Well, let me check . . ." I say, stalling for time. I don't like surprises.

"We thought you could just blitz it. Get the bulk of the interviews done. That's how it works, right? Otherwise it's difficult for her to commit. She's so busy."

"Right, yes. That's how it works." It's been a while since Julia and I exchanged e-mails over this; so I feel unprepared for her call. "I'd just have to rearrange a few things . . ."

"Well, if you don't have time in your schedule, that's a shame, but I am sure we could always find another writer."

I think for a moment, then speak decisively. "It's fine, let's do it."

"Great. She's in Annersley, on the Cheshire border. If you get there tonight, you can start tomorrow morning, finish up on Friday. If all goes to plan."

"OK, can I just ask—"

"I'll pop all the details and directions in an e-mail. Thanks."

"Sure, but can I check—"

But she has already hung up.

I put the phone down. I don't like being bounced into decisions. Go tonight, start tomorrow? Then I think of my overdraft, the unpleasant call, and letters in the post . . .

For a moment I sit there, wondering if I've done the right thing by saying yes.

But there's no question, really. I know what I'm going to do. The Coupon Queen pitch will have to wait—my mind's already on the new task ahead.

I push my chair back and swing myself up. Better get packing.

Chapter 5

An hour later, I am sweating. My bedroom is in chaos, clothes spilling out of my open suitcase and discarded in piles over my bed. Never mind black tie or winter weddings. What do you wear to meet Olivia Hayes?

I need a break. I flop down on my duvet, picking up my phone, and open Instagram.

Straight away I see a new photo is up: a woman, back to the camera, stepping delicately through a sun-dappled meadow. Barefoot in a diaphanous white dress, one hand clasping a straw hat to tumbling blond hair, as she heads deeper into the grass. Olivia.

She's not a household name yet. Despite hundreds of thousands of followers—from office girls in Newcastle to Midwestern moms in the United States—she's not among the biggest influencers around. She's not quite, well . . . *relatable* enough for that.

This is not a woman who will share her toddler's

latest meltdown, crack jokes about wine o'clock, or offer earnest thoughts under smiling photos, pale flesh spilling unapologetically from a bikini, about sharing #flawsandall. No, the most Olivia might admit to, in one of her to-the-point captions, is the need for some #metime. Maybe.

And yet the women—and it *is* women—that do follow her are remarkably involved in terms of liking and commenting and clicking through to buy a little of her taste. *Engaged*, they call it. So, naturally, over the years, there have been various sponsorship deals (with the higher-end brands), as well as tasteful tie-ins: her recent homewares collection at a department store; that one-off range of bedding that flew off the shelves.

More recently, there have been spreads showcasing her home in interior-design magazines, mentions in Sunday supplements, spots on panels where she and other polished young women tell others how to follow in their footsteps.

A book is the logical next move: how to get a life like Olivia's, step by step.

And who wouldn't want that after seeing her life offered up in these pretty little squares? Yellow glasses of champagne piled high at a party, pastel cupcakes teetering on a frilled café table, a bubble bath nearly overflowing at some new hotel. Endless beautiful shots of shops, parties, vacations, her home. And, of course, of Olivia herself.

Olivia, silk dressing gown clutched around her, posed in the arch of a garden wall. Olivia, in long wool coat, wreathed by leaves in an autumn forest. Olivia, in full-on ball gown (*ball gown!*), framed to perfection by misty water and a weeping willow.

Sometimes there is a suggestion of other people—a hand with a glass caught in frame, blurred figures in the background—but usually it's just Olivia, lovely and alone.

It is not narcissism, I know that. Or at least, if it is, it's business, too.

With some of her rivals, as you look through their feeds, you can see the transformation take place: how the photography becomes more skilled, the poses more practiced, the whole persona hardens and calcifies, as a hobby becomes a job.

But Olivia was slick from the start. Professional.

Still, I keep scrolling back through time, trying to get a better sense of the woman I'm about to meet. Though her captions are brief, I can mark some changes in her life.

She never shows her daughter's face or names her—once explaining that she wanted to protect her privacy—but there are glimpses over the years: a tiny hand to announce the baby's arrival three years ago, an arty shot of candies spelling out the number "1" on a cake, the small figure of a toddler clambering over a distant stile.

And of course, a home like that took time and money to create; a process she has charted along the way.

"Painting all weekend," reads the caption under a smiling Olivia, holding a brush, a smudge of green-gray paint on her cheek. "The job that will never end!"

Her wedding photos date back eight years ago, artful close-ups to showcase details of her dress and ring. Before that, there are discreet references to "Josh, my fiancé." Her followers love it, still, when he makes the odd appearance. "#Mumcrush," they write, "Your husband is #goals!"

And now I've reached the end, or rather the beginning of her photos, shot nine years ago: the house gleaming white under a clear blue sky. "Home," is all the caption says.

Yes, that's her secret, I think: Olivia retains her mystery, even as she shares and shares.

If you do sense anything of the person behind it all, it's the sheer effort that goes into maintaining this aesthetic, through the thousands of photos that she has offered up to strangers, through the months and years, not one veering an inch from her brand.

Tasteful. Classic. Luxurious. And of course, underpinning the whole edifice, rich.

I wonder if that isn't where her appeal lies: as an escape from her followers' daily grind. Because who could imagine anything going wrong for a woman like this?

Still, it's no surprise that sometimes the tone of their comments fails to quite disguise the envy. "You should see the chaos inside my fridge, who even has a pantry these days," "If I tried to take a picture of my toddler it'd just be a blur as she bolted for the door!" "God, did you *ever* take a bad photo in your life?"

It's silly, really, to let this stuff affect you. I certainly don't. Not normally.

But as I toss my phone onto the bed and survey the wreckage of my room—the shabby old suitcase, the tired-looking clothes, the damp patch in the corner that I don't know how to fix—I feel a wave of something that is almost despair.

She's just so together, so immaculate. And I'm . . . not. My hair needs a cut, I haven't bought anything new for ages, and my apartment is a mess. And that's just the surface stuff. But surfaces matter to her: what will she think of me?

My stomach is starting to roil with nerves. I can feel the sweat prickling on my palms . . .

Then I catch myself. What am I doing? I am getting this all wrong.

Remember, I tell myself sternly, I'm a ghostwriter. I'm not trying to prove anything, not trying to compete. I don't need to take all this with me. In fact . . .

More confident now, I tip out my suitcase so it's empty again. Then I throw in T-shirts, soft with washing, a few ancient woollen sweaters—the countryside will be chillier than the city—some comfy pairs of jeans, running shoes.

I stand there a moment with my hair straighteners in my hands, deciding, before I stick them back in the basket by my bed.

Within minutes, I'm packed and ready. No need to panic. It will all be fine.

Right?

Chapter 6

It is dark when I arrive, replaying my excuses in my mind—*The traffic was terrible out of London, I got stuck in construction, I am so sorry*—and I am tense, the slam of my car door sounding too loud in the quiet evening as I get out to press the buzzer at the gate.

No one answers, but someone must have heard, because slowly the iron gates open inward, gravel crunching under the wheels as I roll forward. Gnats dance in the glare of my headlights, tree trunks looming tall and bare in the twin beams, as I navigate the winding driveway, the house just visible over the treetops.

And yet it still surprises me when I round the last turn and there it is, gleaming huge and white out of the darkness like an iceberg. I pause for a second; taking in its tall clean lines, its bold handsome shapes, the dark trees pressing in close all around.

I park my little yellow Fiat on the far side of the circular driveway, to the left of the house, so I don't block in the cars already parked there, a big silver 4x4 and a shiny black sports car that no one has bothered to put inside the garage—a converted outbuilding that looks grander than the home I grew up in.

As I walk up to the main house, my suitcase dragging noisily over the gravel, I can see past one long, low wing, down to the tennis court on one side of the flat lawn. Out of sight, to the right of the house, I know lies the small walled kitchen garden Olivia often uses as a backdrop for her outfit of the day.

Everything is familiar—and yet not. Seen in the flesh, the house is so pristine, a vast wedding cake of a building, there is something almost false about it, like a set mocked up for a period drama.

I feel suddenly disoriented, almost dizzy. I pause a moment to take it all in, push down my nerves. It has just been a bit sudden, that's all, from getting the call to pulling up at her house. Deep breaths.

Then I bump my bag up the shallow stone steps, past the slim columns holding up the porch—portico? the word comes to me—and press the bell.

I don't hear anyone approaching. I find myself imagining that nothing but plywood and glue lies behind the house's eggshell-smooth façade, the dark crawling ivy that drapes over it; behind it is nothing at all—

The door swings open.

"Oh!" I say. It's not Olivia, but an older woman.

We stare at each other.

"Sorry," I say. "I thought you were going to speak first." I laugh, putting out my hand. "I'm Nicky? The writer?" I let my hand drop slowly. "Olivia will be expecting me . . ."

The woman steps aside so I can enter. With her short curly hair, sensible cardigan, and pleated skirt, she could be anywhere between fifty-five and seventy-five.

"You can leave that here," she says, nodding to my suitcase.

"OK," I say brightly, bumping it into the cool, shadowy entranceway, as she pushes the front door closed behind me, then I follow her through glass-paneled doors—and stop.

To my right, a wide oak staircase curves up and around to the open landing, so the space I am in stands two stories high. I look up. The skylight will be spectacular when the sun is out, I know.

I feel a pulse of excitement, despite my nerves. Even Olivia's photos can't quite do it all justice. I want to look more closely, at the paintings, the fabrics, the beautiful lamps, even the roses scenting the air—

"If you'd just wait here a moment."

"Of course," I say, focusing. "And I don't think I caught your name . . ."

She's not the assistant Julia, surely.

"Annie."

At the back, the main hall opens off into corridors on either side, leading to the rest of the house. As Annie heads off slowly, her footsteps sounding down the corridor to the right, I check myself in the hallway mirror.

My eyes are wide; my dark hair hanging limp around my pale face after the long journey. I fiddle with my necklace—spelling "Nicky" in looping gold letters—so it's not askew. I feel off balance, too.

On the hall table under the mirror is a photo in a heavy silver frame. I pick it up to distract myself. I always try look at the photos in a subject's home. They tell you so much about a person's taste, values . . . little white lies. I heard of one ghostwriter who realized only when he saw the eighties perm in his subject's wedding photos that she must have knocked at least a decade off her age.

But there is nothing to alarm here. It's the three of them, Olivia, her husband Josh, and their little girl, in matching chunky sweaters, propped up laughing on the lawn. I haven't seen her daughter's face before, and I scrutinize it for a moment. She is fair like her mother, but I can't decide who she takes after—

"Nicky, is it?"

I twist around, putting down the frame with a clunk. Olivia is standing behind me, her head tilted, watching me. Is she annoyed? But she is already darting forward.

"Hello! How are you!"

I register those familiar fine-boned features, ash-blond hair, blue eyes. As we clash cheekbones, I catch her perfume—vaguely familiar, as if I've tried it in an expensive department store—and we are both smiling as we draw back from each other: I must have mistaken her expression, before.

"Hi! Yes! I'm so sorry," I say, my words tumbling out. "The traffic was insane coming up, even on a Sunday. And then I missed the turn the directions said to look out for after Annersley village—"

"Don't worry at all," she says firmly. Like every famous or semi-famous person I have met, she is smaller than I expected, even a little fragile-looking in her soft, sleeveless top and jeans. "Well, why don't we go into the kitchen . . ."

But she doesn't move, and I see her glance flicker down to the vast velvety rug almost filling the hall, covering the wide wooden boards. It looks old.

I inch back, so I am no longer touching the tassels. "Shall I take off my shoes?"

She smiles again. "Would you mind? Our housekeeper, Annie, will look after them."

So it was the housekeeper who let me in. Of course Olivia has staff.

I feel my face heating up as I step back into the shadows to kick off my Converse, and then I am annoyed at my own reaction. I don't get starstruck, I've met people far more famous than Olivia Hayes, but I've let myself get rattled.

"Thanks so much," Olivia says. "I wouldn't normally ask, but it's been so dry, the driveway gets dusty . . ." She takes a few steps in, then spins round: clasping her hands in front of her. "But forgive me—we are starting tomorrow, aren't we?"

I pause a second. "Yes. That's right. Monday."

She frowns slightly. "So we must be on the way, before your hotel? Where are you staying, the Rose and Crown in Mansford? That's the best round here, definitely."

My expression says it all. *Oh shit.*

Chapter 7

For the second time in minutes, I am falling over myself with apologies.

"I really am sorry. I just thought from Julia's e-mails that I would be staying here. Isn't that what she meant?"

Olivia is shaking her head slowly. "Didn't you see an attachment, about B&Bs?"

I grimace. "No, sorry, I was in such a hurry when I was reading the e-mail. Look, don't worry." I fish my phone out of the pocket of my denim jacket. "I'm not normally this disorganized! But I can fix this—"

"It's OK," she says, rather flatly.

There's an awkward silence—broken as someone walks in from behind her, jangling his keys in his pocket. "Hello, hello," he says, his voice carrying. "Now who's this?"

"This is my husband, Josh," Olivia says politely to me, half-turning to him. "This is Nicky, Josh, the ghostwriter—you remember."

He is tall and tan, in jeans and a blue jacket, somehow filling the big space with his presence. His handshake pulls me ever so slightly forward, but at least I am braced for another double kiss. I had to learn what to anticipate when I moved to London after college. Kiss? Hug? Two kisses? How about a handshake, please?

"Great to have you here," he says. He looks between us, picking up on the atmosphere. "Everything OK?"

"It's totally my fault," I say, before she can reply. "Please, don't let me disturb your evening. Only . . ." I look at them both a little helplessly. "Is there anywhere you can recommend I try at the last minute? I'd better get going before it gets dark. Or any darker."

The hall window, curtains hanging open, already shows a glossy black sky. I can't imagine waltzing into a country B&B at this hour. I am sure they know this, too.

They are silent for a second, as some unspoken communication passes between them. In the glow of the hall's lamps, the pair of them look like one of those black-and-white ads for Swiss watches you see with some twaddle about timeless heritage values . . .

Then Olivia gives herself a tiny little shake. "Of course, you must stay."

"Really, it's no problem—I'm sure I can find somewhere . . ." I look vaguely in the direction of the front door.

But she has decided now. "No. You won't find anywhere at this hour, anyway, you'll just be driving around."

"Well, if you're definitely sure . . ."

Josh is smiling: that's sorted. "Right," he says, clapping his hands on his wife's shoulders. "Got to get to the shop before it closes. Liv, do you want anything?"

She shakes her head and he moves past us both. It

seems very quiet again when the front door shuts behind him.

"I'm so sorry," I say again. "There was a list attached to the e-mail . . . ? I didn't see—I just assumed—the phone call was so rushed."

"Never mind," she says briskly, starting toward the hallway off to our right. "Let's have a cup of tea," she turns round, as I follow her, "and talk about the schedule."

"I'd love a cuppa," I say, trying not to let the relief sound in my voice.

In the kitchen, she fills the kettle. "Mint? Builder's? Earl Grey?"

"Builder's, please." I lean against the central block, taking in the stone-flagged floor, the vast wooden table, the deep old-fashioned sink, the French windows, now covered by curtains. It all looks just as pretty as it does online, and so does she—but different: her hair is pulled back in a ponytail for one thing, no trailing blond locks, and her movements are quick and deft. She is more . . . businesslike.

I feel the need to fill the silence. "So it's called Annersley House after the village?" *No shit, Sherlock.* "I didn't see much of the village in the dark . . ."

"There's not much to see of Annersley in the daylight, either," she says, handing me a mug. "We have to go to Mansford for a lot of things."

"Yes, it's not obvious you're quite so remote. From your feed."

"I don't advertise the name of the house or my address online, of course."

"No, of course not," I say, feeling a little stupid.

"So," she says. "Do you want to talk me through how your week would normally go? I've kept my schedule pretty open."

"Sure. Well, in a week of interviews we should be able to cover everything I'll need for the whole book. I'll go away afterward and finish writing the sample chapters. Then after you've had a look at them, of course, my agent can send them out as a proposal to the publishers, and see who bites—she's already got a few excited." I make myself take a breath. "And we do think it's great that you're doing it this way, going to them with your proposal, rather than the other way round."

"Yes. I thought this way I might retain a little more control." She takes a sip of her tea, watching me over the rim. "I'd be keen to see a chapter or two by the end of the week, though, so I can get a clear sense of the direction it's all going in . . ."

"Of course, I can show you something as soon as we've had a few interview sessions, and you can provide feedback on what you do and don't like, make any changes."

"Thanks." She sets down her cup, her mind seeming to be already onto the next thing. "Now, we've already eaten, but I'll show you to your room, and Annie will bring you a tray, if that's OK. If you smoke, can I ask you to go outside on the terrace? Otherwise we're pretty relaxed. And shall we get started tomorrow at, what, nine o'clock? Annie will leave breakfast out for you."

"Sure," I say, feeling like I am checking in to a hotel.

"Great," she says brightly, and stands a little straighter,

ready to go. Her gray cashmere shell top is the exact same shade as the velvet cushions on the bench behind her.

"Great," I echo. I've barely touched my tea. I try to regain the upper hand. "And I just want to say how pleased I am that I'll be working with you on this book. I think it's such an exciting project."

"You do?" she says, neutrally.

"Well, yes." I think of what was thrashed out over e-mail, and start reeling it off. "Part lifestyle guide, part memoir. Something that goes that bit deeper, not just covering your home and style and habits, but also offering the reader insight and advice based on your own experiences. A book to let people get to know the real you."

"The real me," she echoes. She raises her eyebrows a little, smiling again. Her teeth are perfect, like everything else in this house: even, pearly, not too bleached. "I'm not sure how I feel about that," she says. "If people could see the state of my to-do list . . ."

I laugh to be polite, but she's not so good at the self-deprecating shtick. "Everyone has their share of trials, however wonderful their life may seem."

She just looks at me, her head tilted again in that pose I recognize: watchful and curious, almost bird-like. "Is that so?" She turns for the door. "Let me show you up."

Chapter 8

RECORDING 1 from Writeflash: We will turn your transcription round in under 24 hours, guaranteed.

VOICES:
NICKY WILSON
OLIVIA HAYES
MAN 1 (not identified)
WOMAN 2 (not identified)

NICKY: So, would you mind saying your name for me?
OLIVIA: My name?
NICKY: Yeah. Um, I know what it is [laughter]. It's just what I tend to do, for the tape. And it means they can add our names in when it's transcribed?
OLIVIA: Of course. Olivia Elspeth Hayes.
NICKY: And I'm Nicky Wilson. So, um, I thought we could start with why you decided to

let your followers into your life through a book.
Of course, you do through your social media already, and so well, but an Instagram feed can
only tell half the story. How you want to share
some of the secrets behind Olivia Hayes—
OLIVIA: Yes, that's fine. Whenever you're
ready.
NICKY: [pause] OK—so, why do you want to
do a book?
OLIVIA: Well, as you say, I want to let my fans
into my life. I mean, what you said just then
sounded fine. I have to say, I'm really better on
the practical stuff . . .
NICKY: OK. So, it might make sense to
check—
[phone rings]
OLIVIA: Excuse me, would you mind . . .
NICKY: No, not at all.
[silence]
MAN 1: Hello, hello.
NICKY: Morning, how are you?
MAN 1: I'm so sorry. I've forgotten your name.
NICKY: Nicky. That's OK.
MAN 1: Coffee? If I can find where Annie's put
it . . .
NICKY: Oh yes, please.
[silence]
OLIVIA: Hi. Right. Sorry, I had to take that call,
it's a possible sponsorship deal, and they're in
Korea, the time difference is tricky. So where
were we? Josh, could you please try to keep the
noise down a bit? Is this OK for the tape?

NICKY: We're fine, it's just a kettle.

OLIVIA: I thought he'd be out this morning—anyway.

NICKY: OK, could I check a few things—you're thirty-six?

OLIVIA: I'm thirty-two.

NICKY: Oh. It's just there are different ages given online . . .

OLIVIA: Thirty-two. [pause] I would know.

NICKY: So did you skip some years at school?

OLIVIA: What? No.

NICKY: It's just, I noticed Josh's LinkedIn profile says he graduated from university in 2003. And on your blog, you say you met there in his final year, when you were in your first year. So if you work it all out . . . that would make you about thirty-six today.

OLIVIA: [long pause] I think all the reader needs to know is that after having a great time at university, where I first met Josh, I moved to London. As did he.

MAN 1: Annie! Could you give me a hand here?

NICKY: Let's start at the beginning. Could you tell me about your childhood?

OLIVIA: Well. I was more into sports than sitting in a classroom [laughter]. But I did work hard. I believe that if you put your mind to something, you can achieve it.

NICKY: OK. Um, so what about your mother?

OLIVIA: What about my mother?

NICKY: You're obviously such a great mother yourself. Were there any lessons your mother taught you, growing up?

OLIVIA: [inaudible]
MAN 1: Dying for this, thanks Annie.
NICKY: I know your followers would be keen to
know—oh thanks, let me take that tray, just a
cup of coffee would have been fine—careful—
[Inaudible, noise drowns out conversation]
OLIVIA: Josh, watch what you're doing—
WOMAN 1: Mind that, Mr. Hayes—
NICKY: Oh, it's hot! My recorder—
TAPE ENDS

I groan as I finish reading the transcript of our first
session. Then I drop my phone onto the duvet and flop
back onto the bed, staring up at the ceiling of the room
they've put me in.

It's lovely, really: pale eau de Nil walls, an old-
fashioned brass bed and thick white towels in the
gleaming en suite. It's at the end of a corridor flanked
with solid oak doors, all closed. Mine says "guest," in
a tiny neat script slotted into a brass nameplate.

Last night I was too busy unpacking to take in my
immediate surroundings, getting on the Wi-Fi—Annie
gave me a slip of paper with the password, alongside
my plate of cheese, crackers, and grapes—and falling
asleep early, sinking into the thick mattress topper.

I woke up feeling much calmer than when I'd arrived, ready for the week ahead. My room is at the
back of the house, looking out over the garden. I
leaned out of the window to check: no, I couldn't hear
the road from here, just the breeze through the leaves
and the chirping of birds.

And that view! The wide flat lawn, rolling out to the
water, silver in the morning sunshine—a pond, Olivia

calls it online, but more like a small lake—and big enough to swim across, to reach the grassy meadow on the other side. And all around, the massed trees, oak and beech, lending privacy, before giving way to patchwork fields . . .

The kitchen was empty when I padded downstairs with my recording equipment and notepad. After helping myself to the muesli and juice that had been left out, I put my bowl and glass in the sink.

I was still a little early for Olivia, and wandered round the corner into the adjoining space: a living room, more casual than the rest of the house, with an overstuffed L-shaped sofa and vast wall TV.

I was standing in the corner, when Olivia stopped at the threshold, looking puzzled.

"Morning!" I said, ducking out from behind a bookshelf.

I gestured behind me: "That's a beautiful painting. Is it by someone I should know?"

"Oh," she said vaguely, "I don't think so. Sentimental value only."

She was in workout clothes—her default outfit, I know from her Instagram (it's so much easier to fit in a workout if you're already dressed for it #fittip).

"It's so easy to get up when the weather's like this," I offered.

"I've been up for hours, actually. I've dropped Bea off at a playdate for the morning, so we shouldn't be interrupted." Bea. So that was her daughter's name. "Shall we crack on?" she continued. "We can sit over here."

And that's when I started to roll the tape and we began talking, before Annie came in with a cafetière and cups balanced on a tray, Josh in her wake.

"It's fine," Olivia kept saying afterward. "Accidents happen."

"I'm sorry," I said again, in case they thought it was my fault.

I couldn't quite work out what had happened. Annie had been setting the tray down in front of us, when Josh had taken a cup, a little too soon, so Olivia had reached to steady the tray. Too late, I had thrown up a hand to try to stop the whole thing from tipping over, covering both myself and the sofa in hot coffee.

After that, Josh had disappeared, as Olivia steered me back into the kitchen, handing me paper towels. "Lucky you're not scalded," she said, as I mopped myself down. I'm glad I was wearing jeans, now in the custody of Annie.

At least my digital recorder, a little black oblong, is intact. I could still upload the recording of our brief interview to my laptop and send it off to the transcription service I use, as I always do. That's the first step.

Afterward, I remove all traces of my questions and prompts. Then I start to weave the fragments of memory into a coherent whole.

But I haven't much to work with here. The transcription service turned it round in an hour, the session was so short. On the page, without the veneer of politeness provided by Olivia's measured voice, it is clear that her hackles were up from the start.

She wouldn't be the first person to agree to do a

book, then balk at what it involves. And she isn't really a words person, either. I'm surprised, actually, that she agreed to this . . .

Still, she did agree.

So maybe it's the age thing that made Olivia's hackles rise. I am thirty myself. I am sure now, if I ever was in any doubt, that she is deliberately keeping her real age quiet. It will be a commercial decision, so many would-be rivals coming up the ranks.

Maybe she was nervous, too, I reassure myself. It can be awkward, until you get into a flow.

At least we're over a hurdle: our first session done. And Olivia said we could pick up again before lunchtime.

But another thought occurs to me now, after what she said about her age: we've ticked off another first there, too. Her first lie to me.

Chapter 9

When I come back downstairs in fresh clothes, Annie is still scrubbing—rather ostentatiously for a woman so inexpressive—at the new brown stain on the sofa. At the kitchen table, Olivia takes the initiative: she has a few things she wants to cover.

"For starters, how I run my business, including the rewards and challenges of being a working mother, then we can talk more broadly about how every woman can create a lifestyle that works for her. Is that OK? *After all*"—I shut my mouth, as she overrides me—"It's my book, isn't it?"

"Of course," I say mildly.

So she wants to focus on practical ways to replicate her success, avoiding anything very personal. It wouldn't be the first time that a subject has set out boundaries. I've learned how to handle it: let them get whatever it is off their chest—"Wow. Who knew school geography trips could be so amusing?"—to warm them up for more interesting topics.

But, as we talk, she stays on message.

"Women should never be ashamed to ask for more, I've learned the importance of negotiation . . ."

And every time she says something a bit juicier, she edits herself.

"I don't read every comment on my socials, and I stopped checking the gossip forums. It's not a good idea to seek that stuff out—but . . . that's off-brand. Leave that out."

It isn't really what I'm looking for. Still, I get a sense of the discipline that drives her, as she plows through her mental checklist of topics, from her attitude to life—face each problem as it presents itself—to how she stays on top of her to-do list.

What strikes me most is the sheer effort involved: from managing her calendar, to her careful planning of meals and outfits, down to ranking her favorite Instagram filters.

"What?" she says at one point, catching my expression. "Did you think it would all be make-your-own-flower-crowns and my-favorite-smoothie recipes?"

"No, not at all." That was exactly what I had been thinking.

"I can cover that for the book, too, I know what people expect," she adds, slightly defensively.

"No, it's fascinating. It's just—it's a lot of work," I offer. "To have a life this perfect."

She is silent a moment. "It's not perfect. I'm not perfect." She brightens, flashing me that white smile. "But perfect gives you something to aim for. Right?"

There is only one moment where she seems to get frustrated. We are talking about the jobs she had before all this, the latest in marketing for a major law firm, when she raises her voice. "Josh, aren't you going to the site today?"

He has settled himself in an armchair in the adjoining family room. Normally I hate people listening in, but he seems absorbed in his copy of the *Times*.

"Maybe later," he said, turning a page. "They know what they're supposed to be doing."

Her smile looks a little tight. It *is* Monday, after all: I make a mental note now to check if he is still working for that posh real estate agency. His LinkedIn profile hasn't been updated for a while.

But after an hour, Olivia starts to get fidgety, and says she has to catch up with her e-mails; we'll pick up again at three thirty.

I stay at the table a little longer, checking that my tape recorder is definitely still working and thinking of the session ahead. I will need more than she is willing to give me, if I am going to make this week work. I don't have all the time in the world.

But I want a break, too, after an hour of paying close attention. Off the kitchen is a smaller room with an outside door: through the window by the door I can see the neat beds of the kitchen garden. I am suddenly eager to get out of the quiet house.

I leave my stuff on the table and wander through. Under a rail of coats is a row of green Wellingtons, ordered by size. The Converse I arrived in are here, too. I sit down on the stone floor, feeling the cold through my thin trousers, and start pulling them on.

"Everything all right, dear?"

I look up—it's Annie, a basket of laundry in her arms. "Oh, I'm fine! Thanks."

With another tug, I have them on and stand up to face her.

"Now, your jeans are washed," she says. "I'll leave them in your bedroom when they're ironed."

I'm touched by the gesture. "There's no need to iron them, really."

She ignores that. "Can I do anything else for you?"

"Thanks, I have everything I need. I thought I'd get some fresh air."

She glances at the clear sky through the glass. "If you stick to the path, it will take you on a loop round the grounds." And with a nod, she is gone.

I follow her advice to start with, staying on the stone-flagged path that takes me out of the walled kitchen garden through an arch, skirts the edge of the broad terrace at the back of the house, and down the right-hand side of the lawn.

Despite its size, the garden feels secluded, framed by the trees that hang over beds of shrubs and shade the tennis court across the other side. Up close, the grass is yellowing in places after the long, dry summer, only turning lush and green on the sudden slope down to the reeds. Across the quiet water, ducks idling on the surface, the whole vista opens up: fields, thick hedge-rows, cows in the distance.

When I reach the end of the lawn, the paved path twists left to lead me across and up round the other side. But to my right I can see a little earthen track. I turn and follow it up into the trees, wondering where it leads.

I smile when I see the stone bench in a shady clearing, and sit down on the mossy seat. Whoever put this here placed it perfectly to enjoy the view: the still water framed by the trees of this little copse, pale sunshine slanting through the canopy. In fact, I am surprised I don't recognize this spot from one of Olivia's garden shoots: I can just imagine a picnic blanket spread out here at dusk, fairy lights winking among the leaves . . .

Some of the tension leaves my shoulders. You don't always realize how wound up you are until you get a chance to relax. I'd been more nervous than I thought about this first day. She hasn't given me anything good yet, but I can still make it work . . .

There's a rapid flutter in the corner of my eye. Among the low branches, a bird is preening furiously, ripping through its black and white feathers with its beak.

Slowly, I get up and take a step toward it. It stills, as if it can sense me watching, then in a flurry of movement it is off, tail flashing green and purple.

I wonder what it was. But—what was it perching on? I crouch down closer.

The stone is almost covered by old leaves. I brush them away, expecting to read ROVER, or SPOT: they're mad about their pets, these country types . . .

ALEXANDER VANE
1956 – 1997

I stand up, cold skittering down my spine.

Don't be silly, I tell myself. It's not like I am standing on his grave. You can't just bury people anywhere you like. It's just a remembrance marker.

I twist around, suddenly sensing movement behind me.

"Oh!" I try to laugh. "You startled me."

An old man in cap and waxed coat is standing at the mouth the clearing. "You shouldn't be looking there."

"I was just exploring the garden." I brush my hands on my trousers. He must be the gardener. "It's really beautiful," I add, flattering him—though it's true. I gesture to the stone: "So—what do you know about this guy?"

But he just says again: "You shouldn't be looking there." And then he actually jerks his head away, the message clear: *beat it.*

"How was I to know anything was there?" I say, crossly. "Excuse me."

I force myself not to hurry as I brush past him out of the copse, cutting across the grass back to the paved path. I feel his eyes on me, all the way back to the house.

Chapter 10

I shift on the bed, the small of my back aching: I have been hunched over my computer too long, the sandwich Annie brought up untouched on its tray.

It doesn't take long to find the story if you know what to look for: searching for "Alexander Vane" and "Annersley House" has brought up all the details in the online newspaper cuttings service I use.

MANSION INFERNO

reads the first headline, which is dated Wednesday, August 27, 1997.

Not all the papers had the story as it broke. Those that did repeated much the same details.

> Neighbours raised the alarm in the early hours of Tuesday to report a fire at a mansion in Cheshire. It took six fire crews to contain the flames.

Certainly no reporter was here at the house in the dark heat of that night, as the embers flew into the sky.

Whoever arrived, as the village woke up after the Bank Holiday weekend, only had time to speak to a few locals.

The Vanes were on vacation, according to neighbors.

> "Thank God they were away," said Mary Bryant, owner of the local pub, the Bleeding Wolf. "But we can't bear to think how they will feel when they see what's happened to their beautiful house."

Indeed, while police were keen to reach the Vanes, concern seemed focused on the family's reaction when they realized their home had gone up in flames. It wasn't so strange then to be unreachable, to not have your cell phone on at all times.

> Officers have so far been unable to enter the property.

But then the authorities found Alexander Vane's Aston Martin, parked on the side in a quiet country lane near the house. He would have stopped there to walk his dog home through the fields, locals suggested; he was often seen out walking.

Still. Wouldn't you move your car before going on vacation?

The discovery—or, more, the feeling that it had surprised police—signaled a major shift in tone in the second day of reports, a step up in the level of coverage.

DID FAMILY PERISH IN BLAZE?

> The Vanes have not been seen since fire-
> men were called to a fire at their eighteenth-
> century manor house.

By then dramatic photos had emerged of the firefighting effort. It is odd to see them, to see the hoses
pouring water into the very same building I am sitting
in now, the bright flames belching from its windows in
the light early hours of the morning.

Today, the exterior looks identical to that burning
shell, but the damage was clearly devastating. They
must have rebuilt this place almost from the ground up.

I keep reading. More background had been uncov-
ered, too.

> The ivy-covered Georgian mansion,
> situated amid farmland on the Cheshire
> border, has been in the family of
> Marlborough-educated Alexander Vane
> since 1861, when it became the home of
> Sir Patience Vane, a former Lord Mayor of
> London. During the First World War, the
> sprawling Grade II–listed house was used
> as a military hospital . . .

I skip ahead.

> Mr. Vane and his wife Elsa, 36, a former
> model, have established themselves as pil-
> lars of local society since relocating from
> London, following the death of the elder
> Mr. Vane.
> After working in finance at [*I skim*

through various firms I've never heard of]
Mr. Vane, 41, known to friends as Alex,
has adopted the role of squire, embracing
countryside sports . . .

There was less about Elsa, who lacked the same society pedigree: it was said she had dropped out of art
school to model before Alex had swept her off her feet.
But several papers had got hold of a photo of the two
of them at a gallery opening, caught in the flash against
the press of bodies.

He is smiling at the camera, tie pulled loose; her expression more hesitant, her dark good looks the perfect
counterpoint to his golden fairness.

Worse was to come in Friday's papers.

A body was recovered yesterday in the
main part of the three-story mansion destroyed by the blaze.

Though it had yet to be identified formally, the papers made much of the discovery of Mr. Vane's abandoned car, inviting readers to draw the link.

But where was Alex's family? Were they still inside
the house? No one seemed to know.

The shell of the building has been left so
unstable that it could take forensics inves-
tigators weeks to pinpoint precisely how
the fire began . . .

Mrs. Vane, Alex's widowed mother, was said to be too upset to comment, while Elsa's parents were being comforted by friends.

The Saturday papers offered better news. Police had located the rest of the family: not in the rubble, thankfully, but living and breathing.

> Officers broke the news of the tragedy to Elsa Vane in the early hours of Friday, after she was located at a vacation cottage in Cornwall.

Apparently, after spending the weekend together at home, Alex had waved his family off on the Bank Holiday Monday. He planned to shut up the house and go to London, where he often went for business.

He was supposed to join his wife and two children at the end of the week, to spend a final weekend together before the school term started. But he never made it.

> The death of a man found dead in a country house fire is not being treated as suspicious . . .

reads one of those final articles, as the family—what was left of it—put out a short statement via the police, asking to be allowed to grieve in peace.

On Sunday, some of the earlier editions carried breaking news from Paris: Princess Diana had been involved in a car crash.

And then there was no more coverage of the mansion fire.

Only a regional paper sent someone to report on Alexander Vane's inquest a few months later:

MANSION BLAZE CAUSED BY CIGARETTE

The hearing seems to have been quite brief.

> The fire investigation officer told the coroner that the blaze broke out near or inside the sitting room, not far from where the body was found. A silver cigarette case belonging to Mr. Vane was discovered nearby.
> Although the extent of the damage was severe, the fire investigation team are confident in their conclusion: the source of the blaze was a smoldering cigarette.

The inquest also heard how the mansion's heating-oil tank, used in the old-fashioned central heating system, had been inadequately insulated in an outhouse. When the flames reached it, it exploded, accelerating the fire.

The body, badly burned, had to be identified by dental records (the firefighting efforts—code for firefighters' boots, I remembered from my reporting days—causing additional damage that meant a postmortem could not identify further injuries). However, on "balance of probabilities," the hearing was told, Mr. Vane had fallen asleep in his chair, and succumbed to smoke inhalation. For a moment I can almost see it, the nodding head, his cigarette dropped or forgotten . . .

Whether he had been woken by the flames and stayed in the house too long to search for his dog, as some newspaper reports had speculated, was impossible to say. The animal, a gun dog, was later discovered whining for food at a neighbor's, unhurt.

The whole thing wrapped up quickly: the coroner's verdict was accidental death.

I click on the link at the end of the article. It leads to the investigation report from the fire service, which says much the same in a wordier way. It finishes:

> In conclusion, the approximate time of the fire starting was 24:00 hours.
> The probable cause was a discarded cigarette catching fire which was not contained through adequate fire compartmentation, spreading quickly throughout the entire building.

So that was the official word on the incident: a tragic accident.

And that's it. Almost. There is just one more mention, easy to miss, had I not, out of habit, set the dates as wide as possible for my search, from before the fire to the present day. You never want to overlook any detail.

And that's how I found it, the final link chaining the dead past to this house's living present. It is not a news story but a marriage announcement, dated eight years ago.

Mr. J. C. Hayes and Miss O. E. Vane

> The engagement is announced between Joshua, eldest son of Mr. and Mrs. Charles Hayes of Richmond, London, and Olivia, daughter of the late Mr. Alexander Vane and Mrs. Vane, of Annersley, Cheshire.

And that's why I am sitting here, flicking through the cuttings before the session ahead, my stomach twisting in anticipation of what I must address.

She is Olivia Hayes. But once she was Olivia Vane. This is her house. Her family. Her story.

Chapter 11

When I head downstairs for our next session, I can hear the sound of a child laughing down the corridor; Bea has been picked up from her playdate.

My mood is not so lighthearted: it's always awkward when you have to bring up sensitive topics with the subject of a book. *Now, could we just address how it felt when you went bankrupt/got arrested/turned up drunk on breakfast TV?*

But by the time my phone tells me it's closer to four, I am not so much anxious as annoyed, as I wait in the family room by the kitchen.

Annie has been in to see me: "Olivia will be down in just a minute." She gave me a slightly apologetic smile; at least she seems to be warming to me. The Julia who e-mailed me must be away, or perhaps she doesn't work from the house.

I try not to bristle at Olivia's lateness. Her time is more important than mine: she is the talent, I am her ghost, who will help her to more success. I can't argue with that. But I only have this week. It is a reminder that time is limited—and steels my resolve.

* * *

"Sorry I'm late," she says, when she finally appears. "Bea was acting up a bit, and it wasn't fair to hand her over to Annie."

"No problem." I'd have thought she'd have a nanny. "I'm glad the coffee stain is gone," I add, to appease her. "Annie has worked wonders."

"Oh, that . . ." She waves away my concern, then squares the design magazines on the coffee table. "Are you set—would you like a glass of water?"

"Nope, all good," I say; my recorder already out in front of me. "Ready if you are."

"Of course." She sits, tucking her hands between her knees. For a second, I can see the girl she once was: posture born of ballet lessons, hair neatly tied back. She smiles.

I smile back. "So, I thought this afternoon we could address your life from a more—personal aspect. What has shaped you, what has led you to this point."

She tilts her head, listening.

"Obviously, you're known for your perfect life"— she nods, not attempting modesty—"but of course, social media shows only half of the story." Her smile is still fixed in place. "So that's why," I plow on, "it's so helpful when someone like you does agree to draw back the curtain on your experiences. Your hardships."

She frowns. "Well, I could talk about how I manage stress. Fail-safe tips for everyone."

"Uh, definitely. We should definitely cover that." I let my eyes drift to the bay window: the September sky a glorious blue above the line of trees. "But actually I was thinking of the particular adversity that *you've* been through, Olivia."

She's not smiling now.

"I want to address what happened when you lost your father in that terrible fire."

She looks at me blankly.

"And by sharing your story, I know you will be able to help so many of your followers. Of course," I say, a little uncertainly, as she stays still and silent in front of me, "you'll see the final version to make totally sure you're hap—"

She stands up.

"How dare you," she says, flatly, and for a stupid second I wonder if she's joking. "How dare you?" Her soft voice has grown even quieter, and yet when she steps closer, I flinch. She almost seems to expect an answer—but I just stare, openmouthed. Then something in her face shutters: she turns and walks out of the room.

Chapter 12

I am curled up on my bed, talking on the phone, when the knock comes at my door.

"So what do you think," I say, "do you think publishers will still go for it, if she doesn't seem to want to talk about anything personal?"

Whoever it is knocks again, though the door is ajar.

"OK, I won't do anything for the mo—hold on one sec."

I go to the door and open it fully, my phone still in my hand.

"Hi." It's Olivia, her face neutral.

"Uh, hi," I say warily. "Let me call you back, Barbara," I say into my handset, and click the off button.

"Shall I come back?"

"No, no, come in. I was just on the phone to my agent." I stand back to let her past. "Listen, Olivia, I—"

She puts up a hand, her wedding ring flashing in the sunlight through the window.

"Please." She takes a deep breath. "First, I want to apologize. I was surprised. You see"—she starts to smooth down the rumpled white duvet—"not a lot of people know about . . . that time in my life. I reacted badly." I am struck suddenly by the note of formality: she has prepared this. "But I'm ready to move on, if you are."

"Oh." I let her words sink in. "Well, apology accepted. I was too blunt, I should have . . ." What? Not mentioned it? This is a book about her, her life. But I don't say that.

She starts fluffing a pillow. "And I'm sure any publisher will understand that I would rather keep some things private. I'm someone who lives in the present, not the past."

"Of course," I say carefully. She is still not looking at me. "After all, it's your book."

She puts down the pillow. "And however you found out this information about my family—I would very much prefer if you kept it quiet." Finally, she turns to face me properly. "My personal life, I keep very separate from my public . . . existence."

"I understand totally." I nod for emphasis. "And it's really important that you feel you can trust me. And vice versa."

I follow her eyes and realize I'm twisting my hair round one finger, my tell that I'm uncomfortable. I stop.

"Look," I say, "no one would talk to me if they couldn't trust me to tell their story in a way that they're happy with. That goes without saying."

"And you signed an NDA weeks ago," Olivia adds baldly. "You e-mailed a copy over."

I try not to react, feeling slapped down. "That's true."

Nondisclosure agreements can help to set a subject's mind at rest: I can't divulge what is told to me without their consent.

"But you know," I try again, tentatively, "it really could make it a better book: powerful, emotionally true, if readers were to know how you have faced your past—"

"No. My mind's made up."

"Olivia—"

She talks over me: "And if it *is* really essential to getting a publishing deal, then I'm prepared to walk away from the book entirely."

Checkmate.

"OK then," I say. "We move on."

She leaves after that, saying we can pick up our sessions the next morning. I'm free for the rest of the afternoon.

Out of nowhere, one of the first ghostwriting jobs I ever did comes to mind.

It should have been easy, whipping up a daytime-TV darling's reminiscences into something for the Christmas market, taking her from her start in Saturday morning TV all the way to her primetime hosting gig. In her private life, she had finally come through a painful battle with infertility to secure one doted-upon baby.

Only, that wasn't true, she told me.

"So, the baby thing, we thought that was a good way to get the press off my back once I got married. I had just signed up for the show, Frank was mad busy, too, we weren't even sure if we wanted kids then.

What, Pippa," she directed that toward her manager, busy telegraphing STOP signals with her eyebrows. "Nicky signed an NDA, she can't tell anyone. And we're not going to put this in the book, obviously. But what do you think we should do?"

And I almost saw the logic of what she'd done: as she put it, "I just couldn't face five years of Is-she-isn't-she pap shots every time I breathed out."

Still, wasn't it my job to get the full story out there? It could be really interesting, revealing the pressures that we place on women in the public eye . . .

But the editor, an old hand, had laughed off my earnest concerns.

"Darling, you're not the truth police. Write the story she wants to tell, so long as you make it a good read. It's her name on the book."

So I did the job. And in the end, we sidestepped the whole mess by glossing over the topic in a few vague paragraphs, citing respect for the privacy of her young family.

I've remembered that lesson, for every book I've worked on since.

Normally it's not that dramatic. Maybe it's just skating over that failed first marriage in a few brief sentences, or omitting that embarrassing West End flop, if they insist.

But the principle is the same. As much as I excel in digging for details, prodding and probing, my job at heart is to tell *their* story—albeit with some negotiation round the edges to make sure it has some life to it. Not to expose what they want kept hidden.

*   *   *

So I know what that old editor would say: *It's Olivia's story.*

It is what anyone would say, really. That I have already trespassed in Olivia's life, her history, as much as anyone should.

And, really, there is no need for me to keep pushing. I could keep it straightforward, get this week wrapped up, and get back to my life.

For a second I am overwhelmed with longing for the sirens and bustle of my South London neighborhood. I've barely been away long enough to be homesick.

And yet . . .

I can feel the story here, just under the surface, like an itch I need to scratch.

You never know, Olivia might change her mind and agree to address her past in the book. And if I know all the background, I will be prepared.

So if that's the case, what's the harm in looking into it, outside of our sessions?

That's all, I tell myself. She doesn't even need to find out.

And I know just who to talk to first . . .

Chapter 13

There is no one else in the pub garden when a lanky figure arrives on a bicycle, wheeling it through the gate. At first I assume it's a teenager arriving for his shift. But when he heads straight toward my table, I see he is older than I realized, perhaps twenty-four, twenty-five, tall and thin in a heavy navy parka and too-short jeans, exposing pale ankles.

"Nicky?" he says, as I stand.

"Joey, how are you?"

"All right." He gives me a nod, propping his bike beside the wooden table.

He had suggested we meet at the Bleeding Wolf, a long low building. Inside, it's all heavy wooden beams and shining horse brasses, but quiet this Monday evening, like he promised.

It took me just a few minutes to get here from Olivia's house, turning left out of the driveway to head back into the village. She was right, there isn't much to Annersley. After the church and village hall, I passed a convenience store and a few other shops strung in between houses to reach the pub. It sits by a tiny railway station, barely more than a platform and a bench. Beyond that, the road races out to join up with a bigger road, then eventually the highway.

"I think that was the one you asked for," I say back outside, as I set Joey's pint down.

"Oh, it's all pretty dire. I have to go to Mansford for a proper drink, I'm a craft beer man myself. But thanks," he adds, manners kicking in.

"Right," I say, taking a sip of my watery cola. "So did you have to come far?"

"Nah, I'm based just on the edge of the village," he adds. "My parents live in Spain now, and after college finished I needed somewhere to crash. Got to build up the portfolio . . . And this way I can keep an eye on Gran, too."

So he has no job and is living with his grandmother, I translate.

"I see," I say, wondering where to start.

The idea came to me when I was sifting through the articles I found about the fire.

"Chilling pictures reveal scorched remains of tragic mansion," read the headline on the piece, published on a newspaper website a decade ago—a full thirteen years after the fire, I calculated. The brief text mostly recapped what had happened there, while the photos themselves had not been archived. I continued on.

But a little later I realized I might have missed something interesting. I read the last few paragraphs again:

*The photographs were taken earlier this year
by urban explorer Joey Crompton, shortly before
the house underwent redevelopment. He said he
was struck by "the scale of the devastation" and
that it gave it a different perspective to the headlines. See more photos at his website
nobarrierz.co.uk.*

So he got *inside* the house. I'd seen no photos of the interior from the time of the tragedy: the building would have been full of police and forensic scientists, cordoned off.

But the original article published online seemed to be down, so I checked his site: lurid orange text on a black background. "This project is an exploration of the boundaries in our society," it began: nothing to do with teenage kicks, no sir. But there was nothing much besides some nighttime cityscapes taken from a roof he probably shouldn't have been on. The last photos had been uploaded years ago.

So I clicked on an e-mail address at the bottom, Joey something 95. I told him I was a writer interested in the photos he took of Annersley House. Would he be willing to share them? I gave my number. The barer the details the better, I felt: stoke his curiosity.

To my surprise, he got back to me quickly, the beeping of my phone signaling a message. "Happy to chat."

Then another: "Off the record."

Then: "It's Joe Crompton, the one with the photos, by the way."

I sighed. But he was the nearest thing I had to a lead.

* * *

And arranging to meet was fairly straightforward, once I'd made contact to tell him I was in the area. He could grab a drink this evening, if I liked.

I hesitated, but Olivia had made no mention of dinner; I didn't feel expected—or encouraged—to join her and Josh.

After a while, I went downstairs to the kitchen, where Annie was wiping down the surfaces.

"I thought I'd grab some food in the village." She just nodded. "Could you let Olivia know? I won't be back late."

Even then, I had braced myself for him not to show. But here he is, fiddling with his phone, foam from his pint on his upper lip.

"So Joey—" I start.

"It's Joe nowadays, if you don't mind."

"Joe. So, I was wondering if I could take a look at the photos?"

"Ah," he says meaningfully, "the photos." He stretches out his long legs. "What newspaper did you say you work for?"

"Actually I didn't. I'm a writer: I'm working on a local project."

"Oh." He takes a sip of his drink. "Just as well . . . vultures." He says it without rancour. "Anyway," he adds, with a trace of pride, "none of *them* made it inside."

"No, exactly. It must have been really tricky to get in." I'm never ashamed to try flattery.

"Well . . . no one really cared by the time I took the photos," he admits. "It must have been, what, twelve, thirteen years after the fire? Kids used to go in as a bit of a dare. I'd done it myself, the summer before. But we weren't supposed to, it did have signs up, 'danger.' "

He stops talking as a teenage girl brings out the sandwich I'd ordered. I hear another car roar past. They go too fast through the village, because it's the only way through to the highway.

"Anyway," he continues after she's gone, "I was just starting to get into photography, back then. I heard they were about to start the rebuild, so I thought, if not now . . . They had new scaffolding up, but no one was about. I went under some plastic sheeting." He tucks his hands in his pockets. "But why are you so interested?"

"Look," I say, "I'd just like to find out a little more about the fire. For a project."

"What kind of project?" he says, doubtfully.

I'm going to have to tell him. "Between you and me, I'm a ghostwriter—I'm working with Olivia Hayes, who lives there now, on a book about her work, her life, all that."

He snorts. "Her work . . . you mean that Instagram stuff? I suppose a Vane was never going to end up stacking shelves, was she?"

I ignore his jibe. "That's right. She's a big influencer." So he knows who she is.

And then I explain how I am here for the week, how I saw the marker for her father, asked her about what had happened with the fire—

"You're in luck," he says. "I worked it out."

"You have?"

"Mm-hm." He lowers his voice, despite there being

no one around now. "All that money sloshing about, then his house burns down around his ears? That guy Vane had pissed the wrong someone off."

"You think the fire was deliberate?"

"Oh yeah. City boy, got mixed up in something he shouldn't, owed someone money. And maybe they just wanted to give him a scare—they thought he'd gone away, too. Only," he adds, unnecessarily, "he hadn't."

"I see . . ." I am trying to imagine—who? money men? gangsters?—driving up here incognito to wreak havoc.

"These things do happen," he says, a little huffily.

But perhaps my reaction works in my favor, stoking some need to impress me, as he is already getting a brown envelope out of his rucksack and tipping its contents onto the table between us: what must be a dozen big color printouts.

"Where did you . . ." I start, before they register.

Then I don't say anything at all. They're so much worse than I expected.

Chapter 14

At first I just see blackness: the soot. "There was a drought," says Joey. "So it went up like a firework."

The walls are streaked with red, too, the bare brick showing through what was once plastered. Here and there I see splashes of green—shoots of grass, tiny plants, curling over the debris covering the floor. Higher up, the dark ivy has grown through the windows and down the walls, like the house is sinking back into nature.

"I mean, I was years late," he says. "There'd been the fire, then the water from the hoses. And they'd cleared anything valuable out. But there was some interesting stuff. Look, this was the kitchen—you can still see the labels on some tins on the shelves."

I spread the pictures out across the slats of the table, trying to map the wreckage onto the house as I know it now.

Here is a cracked mantelpiece pulling away from the wall. Here the remains of the grand staircase, spiraling up to nowhere. And here an upturned—what?

"Isn't that a bed?" I say.

"The upstairs had collapsed," he says. "Everything ended up on the ground floor."

"Oh." Now I see: I am holding a photo he has taken to show the carcass of the house from a wider angle: the walls are still standing, but above them is sky. It looks like a giant's dollhouse with the roof pulled off.

"I didn't realize the damage was this bad," I say. "They had to completely start again."

"Oh yeah," he says, seeming pleased at my reaction. "Did you know, the air at the top of the room can get hotter and hotter and then—bam!—everything on the ground just catches fire at once." He laughs and shakes his head, animated. "I'd love to see that."

I put down the photo I'm holding. "Would you?"

"Well," he looks abashed. "I don't mean . . ."

I flick through the rest of photos quickly, more businesslike now, at least on the surface. But what kind of person would trespass in a place like this?

Maybe he picks up on my changing mood.

"Some people think it's morbid, but really it's not," he says, rubbing the side of his face with his sleeve. "You could say it's a way of paying respect."

"Really."

"I mean, it's not just that. I've always been interested in spaces where you're not supposed to be—there are lots of people like me," he adds, giving me a cautious look. "And I didn't think anyone round here would care. I should have just put them on Reddit or somewhere, harder to find than my own website," he says glumly.

"Oh? I couldn't find them anywhere online."

"Oh no," he says knowingly. "I'd told the newspaper they had to embed them from my website. So when I took the photos down, they disappeared off their site, too." He laughs, pleased with himself. "They'd paid me £150 for that privilege."

"But why did you take them down? Did you think you'd get done for trespassing?"

He pulls a scornful face. "Trespassing? I'd got in more trouble than that before. Anyway, I was only fifteen, the police weren't going to do anything."

"What then?"

He hunches his shoulders. "Well . . ."

I wait.

"I hadn't been living with my gran very long, by then. And she got upset when she heard about my photos."

I stop myself from smiling. Nothing dramatic then.

"I thought it would be all right, if the paper only put them on the website." He mutters: "She didn't even have broadband then, but the way she went on, about how it wasn't respectful to a fine local family. It did my head in."

I take a bite of my sandwich, then push it away—my appetite has gone.

"Of course now she's always online," he continues, "she's just got herself a new iPhone. An iPhone! I told her what I think about Apple—"

"Joey, sorry, Joe—one thing," I interrupt. "How did your gran hear about the photos? If she didn't have Internet then."

He shrugs. "Everyone knows everyone round here."

I think. It certainly doesn't support his theory that the fire was not an accident. And I can see why his gran wouldn't welcome him posting photos like these online for anyone to see. Despite time passing, they might still feel intrusive to a grieving family. Even so . . . I wonder who let her know about them in the first place.

"Would I be able to take these printouts?" I say.

He looks at me, frowning a little.

"I'm happy to pay." I get out my wallet and count out five ten-pound notes. "That cover your costs for, say, printing? They're just for my reference. And no need for everyone in the village to know I'm looking into it."

"Uh. Yeah, sure," he says, looking at the money. "But—"

"All right, make it sixty," I say, adding another note. "Honestly, you've been so helpful." I start gathering the photos up before he can reconsider. "Well, I mustn't keep you."

"But I thought . . ."

He looks a little wounded. I wonder briefly if I have misjudged him, if he is not just out for money or kicks, but is genuinely interested in what happened. Or perhaps just a bit lonely out here.

"Sorry," I say, more gently. "But I really do have to go."

Chapter 15

In the cold light of Tuesday morning, Joey's theory seems still more unlikely. Gangsters. Dodgy money. A cover-up.

The house was silent when I got home the night before. It wasn't that late, but I had a text on my phone before I drove back, with the code for the gate: *Key for you under the doormat. Please don't ring the bell, it will wake Bea. Olivia x.*

Inside, I was careful not to tread too loudly. Back in my room, I slid the photos from Joey into the zip-up compartment in my suitcase. I didn't want to leave them lying around. And yet I keep thinking of them anyway, unwelcome images in my mind.

I need to focus, as I get ready for my next session with Olivia. I want to ask her about her style, her taste—the Olivia look. It is what people love most about her.

More importantly, it will be an antidote to the intensity of our last encounter. I can't have her shut down on me completely.

* * *

And I'm right; when I suggest what we could cover today, she relaxes visibly.

We are back in the living room off the kitchen. Josh has gone out; his car isn't in the driveway. Annie has Bea in the garden; before, through the kitchen window, I saw a small figure heading down the lawn, little legs pelting along, as the housekeeper followed.

I am quietly braced for a mind-numbing morning, as Olivia starts to talk about every aspect of fashion and interiors that I can imagine. But her enthusiasm carries me along, as she shares all her tips and tricks. She has some clever ideas about how to develop your own personal style, though I doubt her fans want to do anything but replicate hers.

When she finally comes up for breath, I tell her we should cover what first established her as a tastemaker in this area: her own home.

"Where do you start with something on this scale?" I gesture around me.

"Well," she begins. "In many ways a new home offers the chance for a fresh start. But this was a house with a lot of heritage. I had to respect its history."

"And you were committed to coming back here," I say a little nervously. "After . . ."

"There was no question," she says briskly. "It always goes to the eldest. My father was an only child, then it was my responsibility." She gives herself a little shake, as if to rouse herself. "We don't need to go into that, do we? Perhaps we could take a break."

"Well . . ." I am calculating how much time I am likely to get with her this week, but I am talked out myself. "How about you give me the tour, instead?"

"The tour?"

"Of the house. I know there are so many photos on-line, but it's different seeing it in person—you can talk me through your design choices, for the book."

"OK, that's really quite a good idea. Let's go."

She seems cheered to be out of the hot seat, as she starts to lead me through her home.

"So the TV room and kitchen you've seen: it's where we live really; now *this* was the original pantry"—im-maculate, all the labels on the jars facing forward—"as this would have been the working end of the house. This door opens to the cellar"—down a flight of stairs I glimpse bikes hanging from a wall—"it's just storage," before I follow her quick steps along the corridor to the rest of the house. "The building itself is mostly Geor-gian, added to over the years . . ."

I get just fleeting impressions of rooms as she pulls opens doors to either side: a dining room with long shining table, tall windows opening onto the terrace; a study full of wood and leather; a stately "morning room," all creams and pale stripes, with a vast gilt mir-ror. And here is the *library*, look at all those books—

"And this is our library," she says pointedly, as she follows me in.

"Oh, sorry." I turn away from the shelves, and let her lead the way out. "After you." I forgot myself.

"Now, the conservatory was part of the later addi-tions, Victorian we think . . ."

And we are off again, our footsteps sounding in between the rugs and runners. My head is spinning. The house is so beautiful, grander than it seems on her feed—maybe even a little oppressive, for just the three of them . . .

"I won't show you the garage, that's Cav's domain, but it used to be the carriage house, interestingly enough."

I tune in again. "Cav?"

"The gardener. Now upstairs—" Olivia has one foot on the staircase already.

"What about in there?"

We've missed a room off the main hall, just to the left as you enter the house.

"Oh yes." She steps toward it and opens the door. "This would have been the drawing room originally."

It is another formal room, darker, all rich velvets, tartan throws and a pale marble mantelpiece as its focus. The air feels stale.

"This is beautiful," I say. "Do you use it much?" I don't remember seeing it on her feed.

"Not really. There's not as much light on this side."

Too late, a phrase sounds out of memory, like a warning: *the blaze broke out near or inside the sitting room, not far from where the body was found.* No wonder she doesn't use it.

And suddenly I feel pitched off balance, realizing I have let myself fall under the spell of this house, its beauty and patina, so I almost forgot what happened here . . .

She pulls the door shut again.

Chapter 16

Upstairs, I don't get time to linger, either, as she opens one door after another into more stunning rooms: four-poster beds, silk eiderdowns, fresh flowers spilling out of tall vases. One is different: toys all over the floor, a colorful jungle mural covering the walls.

"Wow." I see a tiny painted tortoise peeping through green foliage. "This is not what I expected—"

I catch myself, as she looks at me sharply.

"I know it doesn't really go with the rest of the house," she says. "I don't show it online. But it was fun to do. I got an art student in to help."

Then she leads me to the bedroom next door, at the end of the house. "And this is ours," she says. It is a little bigger than the rest, but just as immaculate.

After that we head back onto the main landing, where she pulls open another door, onto a flight of back stairs. "Mind your head," she says, as she climbs the narrow stairway. "So, this floor would have been the servants' quarters originally. I have my office here now. That's Annie's bedroom there, and I use this one as a dressing room."

In contrast to the rest of the house, the low-ceilinged dressing room has an air of organized chaos, clothes spilling from huge bags on the floor, more jammed onto metal racks that have been dragged in front of the full-to-bursting wardrobes.

"Do you buy all this stuff?" I ask, amazed, and then regret it.

But she doesn't take offense. "God no. Some is sent to me, some I request for shoots."

"And do you take all your own photos?" Somehow I can't imagine Josh clicking away patiently while she poses.

"A lot. These days I have photographers I use if I need to be in the shot. They'll come up to get a batch done. And I've got interns, fashion students, who come every few weeks and help me with call-ins and returns."

Again I am struck by how different the process is from the end result: that dreamy, effortless life captured in the photos.

"I have an idea," she says, cocking her head at me.

"About what?" I am wary.

"How about we give you a new look?"

I look down at my worn jeans and sludge-colored sweater. "Fashion's not really my thing."

She raises her eyebrows invitingly. "Oh, let me." She laughs. "It will be good for the book." She knows I can't argue with that.

Before I know it she is talking at me rapid-fire, leafing through a rack of clothes. I am confused by the change in mood: it's Olivia the influencer in front of me, as though she's in one of her style videos. Her appeal doesn't translate as well as you might think to video, she is a little stiff, but the fashion ones do very well.

"Now this would look great on you, just with the jeans you have on—and this jacket might be worth a try, why not . . ."

I let her talk, as she rifles through the rails with practiced speed.

"I'm not so sure about that on you." I have a soft pink mohair sweater slung around my neck, "just for the color." She has put me in front of the full-length mirror. "But see this? This is perfect. Go on, try it," she says, handing me the next item.

"Lilac *fur*?" I say, swinging it over my shoulders. "I look like a Muppet. Literally. Like I've just wandered off *Fraggle Rock*."

She laughs. "I used to love that program."

We both look at my reflection, and she shakes her head. "But you're right, I thought you might do that boho glam thing but—maybe not . . ."

Next I shrug on a navy peacoat with flashy brass buttons, a swingy red trench, and a structured jacket in yellow tartan, each of which looks increasingly bizarre on me.

"They don't look quite right," I say. *You've lost your mind*, my tone conveys.

"I know!" she says. "That's the thing, right? You should be going for a classic look. I just wanted to show you. You've similar coloring to me, actually.

Try this, I just got it," she says, pulling a long loose camel coat off a hanger and draping its weight over my shoulders. "See how the color makes your eyes pop? That really suits you."

She's right: my teeth and eyes look whiter somehow, the tailored coat transforming my nondescript outfit into something pared back and chic. I turn a little, half-heartedly striking a pose in front of the mirror. "I guess."

"Oh come on, admit it! You've got the Olivia look," she says with a grin, wisps of fair hair escaping from her ponytail. She puts her hands on her hips to assess me.

For the first time since I met her, she seems genuinely enthused and happy.

"It is lovely," I admit. I run one lapel through two fingers, feeling its velvety thickness. I've seen this coat in a magazine. The price was a penny less than a thousand pounds.

"Have it if you want."

"I can't take it!"

She shrugs. "I've got one just like it."

I feel my mood sour a little. She has so much.

She gives me an appraising look. "Have you ever thought about cutting your hair?"

"My hair?" I touch one frizzy strand.

"Don't worry, I won't get the scissors out. But what about just pulling it back maybe"—and she's already sweeping it all back to my crown, away from my face—"this will show off your bone structure, keep you from hiding away. See?"

For a moment our eyes meet in the mirror, our faces framed side by side, both of us with hair up; her fair, me dark. Then I duck my head down, shaking her hands away, laughing embarrassedly.

"Oh gosh, it's just—just not me," I say, already sliding the coat back onto its hanger. "I'm not really into appearances."

That last word comes out with more emphasis than I intended, hanging in the air between us. Shallow, I might as well have said. Superficial.

Olivia looks surprised, then collects herself. "Well, of course," she says quietly. She starts to hang the rest of the clothes she'd pulled out for me back on their hangers.

"Thanks, though," I say awkwardly.

"You're welcome," she says, not meeting my eyes.

I hesitate a second longer, then hang the coat that I'm holding back on the rack.

"Actually," she says. "I've got to take Bea to the dentist—and my goodness, is that the time?" She looks at her slim gold watch. "I can give you a lift into town, if you want."

Her tone suggests she'd rather not.

"Oh no, I'll get on with writing if that's OK."

"It would be great to see something soon." *To make sure I'm happy with what you're doing.* "Now, help yourself to milk and tea, there's food in the fridge. You know where the spare key is."

"Annie won't be here?"

"She needs a break, she's been helping out so much at weekends—but we'll be back before six. Right, sorry to rush."

I'm dismissed. "Sure. See you later."

* * *

I messed that up, I think, I should have found some way to go along with her gesture of friendship, however uncomfortable I felt. But I just . . . got spooked, under the scrutiny.

Never mind, I tell myself, as I follow the back stairs all the way down; as I suspect, the door at the bottom brings me out into the corridor by the kitchen, so the servants could once creep about the house unseen.

Fitting, really. Because now I wait in the family room until I hear them leaving—Bea's piping voice, Olivia's measured responses, I can't make out the words—and check through the window to make doubly sure: there are no cars left in the driveway but mine.

Time to get to work.

Chapter 17

It was the mantelpiece in the sitting room that gave me the idea: it is almost an exact replica of the one I saw in Joey's photos, if that were not blackened and cracked by the heat beyond repair. Really, you would never know the difference.

That got me thinking. I'm going to go around the house with his photos, comparing what is in them with what I see now.

Maybe they got taken down simply because Joey's gran felt they were intrusive—that would be totally reasonable. But maybe I will see something in them in a different light.

At the very least, I hope it will mean I can stop thinking about them.

I start on the ground floor, shuffling through the photo printouts: I see now that there is another page, too, that I gathered up as I left Joey.

Applicant's name: VANE it reads at the top, phrases

jumping out: "Demolition of remaining interior walls . . . Listed Building Consent . . ."

This must be from the planning documents for the restoration. Everyone seems to have been roped in: "Westcott & Westcott, architectural practice," "G. Rafferton, specialist heritage consultant," "Hayden Ltd, specialist contractor" . . .

Below the text is a floor plan of the building, ground and first floor mirroring each other, with smaller shapes for the attic and cellar. On the ground-floor diagram Joey has drawn little numbers that match numbers written on the back of each photo, marking where he took them.

I start to wander through the house, mapping the photos from its burned-out carcass onto the luxury of today. This photo of the ruined staircase was taken here, in the main hall; the tall boarded-up windows match these in the dining room, now showing the terrace outside; this damaged panelling belongs here, in the study.

The family did a fantastic job with the restoration. It is just a little . . . spooky to think how much of what seems to have been here forever was wrecked and replaced.

But soon I am done with Joey's map and photos. He kept getting distracted by details: a rusted metal fork still in the rubble, an umbrella turned to blackened spokes, a thick airport thriller with a curling cover. They tell me nothing new.

And yet after that, I find myself wandering through the rooms upstairs, too, even with no photos to compare them to. It was all so rushed when Olivia showed me round, I just want to see everything properly.

This time around I go into bathrooms, pulling open cupboards to look at toiletries, sniffing at a bottle of expensive liquid soap. No stolen hotel miniatures for Olivia. I pull open drawers, lift out a pillowcase, unfold it, put it back.

I am haphazard, not sure what I am looking for—despite my digging, I wouldn't normally go this far. But this place, Olivia's refusal to give me anything of her past, is getting under my skin. I've that prickly feeling I get when I might have come across something that could take me somewhere interesting . . .

And so I keep going, up to the top floor into her office, ignoring the closed silver laptop on her desk. I am not interested in the present so much as finding some trace of the past, some proof that something happened here.

Of course, I know the place has been rebuilt and redecorated, with huge care. It's just a little unsettling somehow, that you'd never guess. I've been over the whole house now. There is just the cellar left.

Downstairs in the kitchen, I flick on the switch by the cellar door and hear bulbs blink on below. The wall to my right is chilly to the touch as I follow the steps down; then duck to avoid the decorations spilling from a shelf above my head. Olivia always goes all out for Christmas, Easter, Halloween.

At the bottom of the stairs, the little hall is filled with family stuff, a surfboard or windsurfing board propped in a corner, I can't tell. On one wall is a vast wine rack, full of bottles, stretching almost to the ceiling.

Down here, the air is cooler, and I can't hear anything from the house above or the outside, nothing but the very faint buzzing from one of the bare bulbs overhead, as I wander through the windowless rooms.

The biggest has a table tennis table and a dartboard, but the dust suggests no one uses either. The second is full of metal shelves stacked with trays of screws, old cans of paint, stuff left by workmen I'd guess. The third room, smaller, is empty, bare brick showing where the carpet doesn't quite meet the painted walls.

I have hit a brick wall—literally. There is nowhere else to go.

Back in the kitchen, I make myself tea, feeling like an intruder as I look in the cupboards for sugar—silly, really, when I've just been over their whole house.

With my mug in hand, I head into the family room and slump down on the floor, leaning against the sofa base. I used to get told off for sprawling over the furniture, kicking my legs over the arms of armchairs and teetering back on kitchen chairs. You'll crack your head open, they said, but I kept doing it.

I tip my head back against the seat cushion, feeling the ache of tight muscles in my neck and slowly roll it from side to side. I blink and think of nothing for a second.

To my left, on the bottom shelf of a bookcase, big coffee-table books have been lined up, perhaps to be rotated on to the table at a suitable season. I stretch out a finger and run it along the smooth spines. It comes away with a thin film of gray dust, I note with bitchy satisfaction: nobody reads them.

And then I see the untitled one at the end, a little smaller, more worn.

I pull it out an inch. Not a book, a photo album. I open it up. The inscription just says "Olivia Vane" in rounded letters.

The first few pages are given over to school photos of Olivia: chubby-cheeked at four, in a too-big blazer; serious at eleven.

But it takes me a moment find her in the next few. It's almost a puzzle, spotting a young Olivia in the groups of children pictured: slick-haired in a swimming pool; in white Aertex shirt and shorts at a sports day; pretty in a paisley party dress as someone else blows out a cake.

And then I realize the reason she is always off to the edges, never the focus . . . The original albums can't have survived the fire. That's why I'm seeing Olivia's childhood pieced together through the eyes of other people's parents, coaches, and camp helpers. I imagine the school photographer asked to check his archives, "it's a very sad story"; the rest collected from friends in the aftermath . . .

I look up at the arch linking the living room to the kitchen. I had a sense, just then, of being watched. No one is there. But something disturbed me; did I hear a car outside? I am exposed, sitting here with the album in my lap.

Hurriedly, I straighten the photos that weren't stuck down—those are footsteps in the house, definitely—and now I try to slide the album back into its space on the shelf, but the heavy books have shifted in place and my hands are sweating.

The footsteps are closer now, coming down the hallway, unhurried but steady. I am still trying to get this stupid album to fit—and I do, suddenly. It slips back into the shelf, and I slide myself back to where I was sitting, against the sofa.

Whoever it is is in the kitchen now, dropping something on the table, and I grab my phone out of my jeans pocket and stare at it, like I am engrossed.

I wait a beat, then look up slowly. But it's not Olivia, it's Josh in the archway.

"Oh hi. Did you want to watch something on TV? I can go—"

"No, no," he says, giving me a nod. "You stay there."

And he ducks out: I can hear him in the kitchen, pulling open the fridge. "Can I get you anything? We've food, drinks . . ."

"No, but thanks," I call back, "I'm fine, really!" Before he goes away again.

I hug my knees. I am a little disgusted with myself, prying all over their house, going through old photos. But underneath that, I am still curious.

That scrappy photo album can't be all that she has left of her life before. Can it?

Chapter 18

After lunch, some bits from the fridge that I take back up to my room, I get a phone call from Joey Crompton.

Joe, I correct myself. But he feels more like a Joey.

I wonder if he is already regretting giving me the photos, but he sounds excited.

"So what did you find out?" he says. "Did the photos help?"

"Oh, right. Hi. No, I'm afraid not."

He doesn't seem abashed. "I have an idea. We should talk to Pete Gregory, the policeman."

I register the "we." "What policeman?"

"He's my gran's neighbor. That fire was the biggest thing that happened round here in years. He'd know all about it."

It's not a bad idea. "So you could introduce me?"

"Well, ah. He's retired now, he's getting on. I don't think he'd like it if we just went round. I've already asked Gran to put in a good word."

I think for a second: Joey's a bit presumptuous, but

it's going to be a pain to track this policeman down without him.

"Why not? Thanks."

"Uh, Gran wants to meet you first. Make sure you're nice."

"I'm very nice," I say. "But that's fine. When would be good?"

"Now? She's going out later, she has Zumba—you don't need to know that. Have you a pen to write down the address?"

"Yes, and yes," I say, scrabbling for a pen. I have mostly been in my bedroom since Josh came back, trying not to get in the way. "But what will you tell her? I don't really want anyone else to know I'm working with Olivia. If it gets out that I've been asking around— it could look a bit . . . unprofessional." That's an understatement.

"No worries. Say you're writing a local history book. She'll love that."

"So you're the young lady writing this book about Olivia Vane. Hayes, I should say."

It's almost the first thing Marie Crompton says, after Joey's introduced me and the three of us are sitting in her cozy front room, a plate of shortbread in between us.

I pause with my shortbread halfway to my mouth and look at Joey.

He looks at me, surprised: *I didn't say anything.*

Joey's grandmother must be in her seventies, small in a navy tracksuit with immaculate pink sneakers, pale hair cropped in a bob. She lives a couple of turns off the main road that runs through the village.

Hers is one of a row of neat little cottages of mottled red brick, straight out of a period drama. Inside, however, her home is bright and modern.

"You're right," I say now, "I am writing a book."

"So you want to know all about that fire," she says.

"I'm just trying to fill in a few gaps, without upsetting Olivia. I didn't mean to be less than straightforward."

"It's all one to me," she says, in a tone that suggests it is not.

"And of course she'll see the finished book. Can I ask who mentioned it?"

"A little bird told me."

There's a short silence. I should have known that me being here would get around. It's a village.

"Well," I say, "Joey thought it might be an idea to speak to your neighbor, the policeman. Do you think he might talk to me?"

"He might," she says. "He might not. It's a tricky thing, stirring all that up again."

I've made a mistake by not being honest; she's annoyed.

"And you were living round here yourself, at the time of the fire?"

She nods. "But we were on vacation ourselves, thank goodness. Awful business. I made my Derek get rid of our heating tank after that. Theirs exploded in the fire, you know—fuel to the flames."

"Did you know them? Alex and Elsa Vane?"

"Just to say hello to in the street."

"What were they like?"

"He was always very pleasant. And good with the children, too. Olivia, of course, and, what was it, little Alex. Named after him, of course."

I try to interpret her tone. "So people didn't like his wife so much? Elsa?"

"I didn't say that," she says, snappishly. "Lovely family."

Time for another tack. "What about the people who called the emergency services that night? For background—"

"I know who it was," Joey interrupts. "The neighbor who lived in the barn then, you said, Gran. What was the name—Gibbons, something, Simon—Si—"

"Sam Gibbons," Marie says, after a pause. "He's gone now."

It takes me a second. "You mean—he died?"

She nods. "I'm afraid so." She gets up and puts her cup of tea in the sink. "There are really not many people left round here who remember all that. People move away, they get older. . . . Now. I've got to pop out. But Joey, do look after our guest."

"And you'll put in a word with your neighbor, Pete?" I say.

"I'll certainly see what he says, dear." I have the distinct sense I am being fobbed off. "What have you planned for the rest of the day?"

I get the message. Joey walks me out not long after that. He looks a little deflated.

"She might still ask him," he says.

"I won't hold my breath. Thanks, though."

* * *

But before I set off again in my car, I pull up the browser on my phone. I search for Sam Gibbons on the directory inquiries website I use. He might be dead, but maybe he has a widow who remembers the fire.

Searching for Sam Gibbons and Annersley brings up an entry for the Old Barn, Back Lane, Annersley. He is listed on the electoral roll for 1995–1999, and a Marjorie Gibbons for the very same dates—so that that must be his wife. There is also an Edward T. Gibbons listed at the same address, just for their first year there—their son, I'd guess.

So I just need to find an up-to-date number for Marjorie if I can.

But while several entries for Marjorie Gibbons come up when I search in Cheshire, they are not promising—all out of date. However, I do find an Edward T. Gibbons currently living at an address in Chester. Better yet, the phone number isn't ex-directory.

When I dial, it goes straight to voice mail, an anonymous automated message:

"Hi, my name's Nicky Wilson," I say. "I'm trying to reach Edward Gibbons regarding his late father. I'd be so grateful if you could give me a call back."

I leave my cell-phone number. "Thank you."

Chapter 19

Back at Annersley House, for want of anything better to do, I take a shower. I hear Olivia returning, then noises from the rest of the house that I interpret as Bea's teatime, bath time, bed.

I throw on jeans and another sweater, and I am sitting on my bed toweling my hair when out of the corner of my eye I see a slow movement. The door to my room is open now, ever so slightly. But no one's there.

I look down. Two small hands are hanging off the doorknob, then a small girl swings into view, bare feet pushing herself along.

"Hello," I say. "You must be Bea." She does look like her mother, the same silky ash-blond hair and determined chin. "Are you looking for Mummy? Or Daddy?"

She drops off the handle and stands still, eyeing me cautiously.

"No," she says finally. "Why are you in my house?"

"I'm Nicky. I'm staying here this week." I think about what I know about three-year-olds. "Um, shouldn't you be in bed?" She's in a long blue nightie.

"No," she says, firmly. "I'm tree." She tries again. "Tree. I stay up later now."

And she starts heaving herself up beside me, but the silk-lined throw at the foot of the bed is slippery.

"Do you want a hand, Bea?"

She assesses me, then reaches out a small hand.

"But are you sure?" I say theatrically. "Are you sure you want the hand . . . the *monster hand*?" And I whip up my hand and bracelet my wrist with the other. "Oh no," I say, "I can't stop it, it's going to get you. It's the tickle monster hand!"

This is my default move with all children. Soon she is shrieking in delight, as I pretend the tickle monster hand is going for me now, but then she stops, looking to the door. I am laughing, still tossing the damp hair out of my eyes, as I do the same.

Olivia is standing there, white-faced.

"We were just—"

"Come on, Bea," she says in a controlled tone. "You should be in bed. I heard the screams all the way down the corridor," she says to me.

"Sorry," I say. "I didn't realize we were so loud."

"She'll enjoy it now," she said tightly, "but she gets scared later."

"I'm really sorry," I say again, at a loss.

Bea looks between us uncertainly. "Mummy cross?"

At that Olivia seems to collect herself.

"Well, I'll get this one back to bed. Why don't you come down in half an hour, have supper with us? You can use it to ask a few questions, if you like."

*   *   *

I know parents can be strict about routines. Still, I don't quite understand why Olivia was so angry. I am braced for an awkward atmosphere when I go downstairs.

But everything is calm and tidy, soft music playing, the kitchen table set for three: a roast chicken, plump little cheeses, a fresh green salad.

"This looks amazing," I say.

"It's nothing fancy," says Olivia, pulling bowl-sized wineglasses out of a cupboard.

I realize I am twisting my hair round one finger, and stop. "Can I help at all?" I need something to do with my hands.

"No, just relax," said Olivia, coming to pour a glass of white wine. "Help yourself."

I can't read her that well, but she doesn't seem annoyed anymore.

After we have both filled our plates, I hesitate, conscious of the third place.

"Please start," says Olivia. "Josh is running late. Anyway, about the rest of the week . . ."

"Sure," I say brightly.

"I won't have much space in my schedule, I'm afraid, probably can't do more than a session a day. Annie's helping me with Bea, but she's not as young as she was . . ."

"OK, we'll do what we can . . ."

"But I hope you can use the rest of the time to work, too," she says. "Did you get much done today?"

For a tense moment I think she knows what I've been doing, then realize she means the writing.

"Well . . ." I start.

"I'm keen to get a sense of the shape it's taking," she says, as behind me I hear noise, and turn round.

Josh is coming through from the utility room in his blue jacket, rubbing his hands theatrically, though it's not cold. There is a woman following him in, tall and rangy with long caramel hair.

"So sorry I'm late, darling," he says, leaning down to kiss Olivia's cheek. "But look who I bumped into in the village."

Olivia stands to greet her—"Sabrina, how are you? No Leo?"—and the woman waves her back down, heading toward the cupboards over the sink.

"Oh, don't get up, Liv," she says over her shoulder, opening cupboard doors until she finds what she wanted and fishes a large glass out. "No, no, I won't eat with you. I told Josh I'd just come and say hello, I really had to talk to you both about—"

As she turns back to the table she seems to notice me for the first time.

"Sabrina, this is Nicky," Olivia says, adding to me: "Sabrina's an old friend."

"Oh. Hi," she says, her light eyes skimming over me, before she leans forward. "What does that say— Nicky. Haven't seen one of those for years. Sweet."

I reach up, automatically, to touch my necklace. She is closer to forty, a bit older than Olivia.

"The ghostwriter—remember?" says Josh, rooting through the fridge.

Sabrina's brow clears. "Oh yes," she says absently, sitting down, as Josh joins us with a chilled bottle in his hand.

"This looks great," he says, enthusiastically, pulling

out his chair with a screech. "Darling, the garden's a bit of a mess. What's that man doing?"

"I'll check," Olivia says.

"Pay him enough to sit in his shed and glower at me all day," he says.

"I'll check."

For a moment there's silence. I feel like the interloper I am, but Josh charges on jovially. "So, Nicky," he says. "You're a writer."

"I am." We haven't really had a chance to talk properly yet.

"And have you written many books?"

"Yes, quite a few."

Josh shakes his head and laughs, like I've made a joke. "And now Liv's getting a book!"

"Who would have thought it," says Sabrina coolly. "That Liv would have all these—*fans*." She makes it sound like a rash.

There's another pause. Whatever Sabrina wanted to talk to them about, she's not going to do so in front of me. I didn't think Olivia's invitation included my digital recorder, but I might as well use this dinner.

I clear my throat. "So Josh. What do you do these days?" I ask, then wonder if that is some sort of solecism.

"Property mostly," he says easily. "I kept doing stuff for my old company for a while, after we moved up here, but it wasn't practical. I'm doing up a house over in Allerton at the moment."

"You're doing it up yourself?"

Sabrina snorts.

"Certainly feels like it sometimes," he says politely.

"Builders wouldn't do a thing if you're not there to keep an eye on them."

"Tell me about it," says Sabrina. "Always on a coffee break, that lot."

"You were at the site?" says Olivia. She takes a sip of her wine.

"Just passing by." She shrugs.

I plow on. "And are you from round here originally, Josh?"

"God no, not me," says Josh. "Middle of nowhere. Very strange bunch of people. Just look at the locals." He jerks his chin at Sabrina, who rolls her eyes at his joke. "I grew up near London. And you drove up from there, Liv said?"

"You don't sound like a Londoner," says Sabrina, before I can reply.

"I'm not really. My apartment's there. But I mostly grew up in the Midlands. Outside Wolverhampton?" I catch myself sounding doubtful, like I can't imagine them having heard of it.

"And are you . . ." Josh glances meaningfully at my ring finger.

"Nope. Just a recent ex."

"Josh!" Olivia scolds.

I smile. "I don't mind."

"And have you done many, uh . . ." Josh wiggles his fingers toward Olivia, reaching for the word.

"Influencers?" I finish. "Olivia is my first."

"And last, I bet," Sabrina finishes.

I laugh, genuinely. "I doubt it. It's the way things are going."

"Seriously?" Sabrina grimaces, like she's bitten into a lemon. "How depressing."

"Seriously," I say. I wonder if she realizes she's just insulted her host.

"So who else's book have you done?" she says. "Anyone really famous?"

"Sorry, I can't say," I reply.

"Oh, go on. You can trust us."

"Really, I would, but I can't . . ."

"Or wouldn't I have heard of them?"

"She can't tell you, Sabrina," says Olivia, evenly.

"Fine." Sabrina purses her lips. "I suppose you're not one for the limelight yourself," she says to me then, her tone a little pointed.

Suddenly I am conscious of my shabby outfit and frizzing hair, sitting next to these three gleaming people. But I look back at her squarely, my chin up.

"No, I suppose not."

Chapter 20

Sabrina seems to feel snubbed by Olivia backing me up just now; she goes off into the house to "powder her nose."

But the rest of the meal is not too bad, really, as Josh talks about life in the country, the excitement of finding out their favorite supermarket delivers ("civilization!"); he seems to like an audience. Olivia is the grown-up in their relationship, I'd guess, but I can see how they work together. Sabrina is quiet, clearly not interested in my attempts to find out more about my hosts, and eventually fishes a pack of Camels out of her bag.

At Olivia's look, she stands up—"OK, OK, I'm going outside."

When she comes back in, I am asking them about when the house was first built—

"God, you really do want to know everything, don't you?" Sabrina snaps, slumping back down into her chair. "Now Liv, has Lucy spoken to you about that weekend? I'm happy to leave the kids, they're old enough, but Leo was digging in his heels, so I said . . ."

She launches into a long, involved account of some trip that's being planned, not bothering to explain the background to me.

I concentrate on my food as they talk. It's not personal, I tell myself, until I look up and catch Sabrina's pale gaze on me; her expression is not friendly.

I am wary of overstaying my welcome. I yawn theatrically, a hand over my mouth. "Excuse me! I'll head up. Thanks so much for a lovely dinner."

We say our good nights—Olivia and I agreeing to meet in the morning at nine again—then I leave them there in the warmth of the kitchen.

As I walk down the corridor to the main hall, I pause for a second. Sabrina is still talking, but she sounds different now—hushed, more urgent, perhaps?

I wait, trying to make out what she's saying, before she stops, and I realize they might be able to hear my footsteps—or lack of them. I start off again.

In the main hall, I can't find the lights, and make my way up the staircase in the dark, replaying the meal in my mind.

I think of Olivia just now, telling her friend that I couldn't talk about who I'd written for before; that was nice of her, I suppose. Then I wonder what Olivia would do if she knew I'd been looking into the things *she* won't talk about. I don't know . . .

But whatever lies hidden in her past, this evening has left me sure of one thing: that this woman has moved on, built a new life, a new family. Sitting at Olivia's table, being hosted by her and her husband, meeting her daughter earlier—it made it all real to me, in a way it wasn't before. And suddenly I wish, quite clearly, that I hadn't started any of this. I don't want to pry anymore.

My room is cool—I've left the window open—and I close it quickly, before I change into my pajamas: oversized, patterned with unicorns. What would Sabrina think of them? Not much, I imagine.

Then I wash my face in the bathroom mirror. I look drawn, a crease between my eyebrows. I am just tired, I tell myself, and I rub moisturizer between my hands and smooth it over my face, the familiar nighttime ritual soothing me, before I rummage in my wash bag. Why can I never find anything in here? There it is, my lip balm—I smear the stick onto my bottom lip in a practiced stroke—

"Ow!" I suck at my lip, tasting copper.

At first I can't understand, as I stare at the smear of red on the white waxy stick, then something glints under the overhead light, and a chill runs through me.

I twist the tube so the stick of balm is exposed as high it goes, and scratch away with my thumbnail, unconcerned about wrecking it.

I can see it now, shining silver and sharp: a needle.

Did the top of the balm come loose in my wash bag? I cart all kinds of things about in there, headache pills, a sewing kit. I am ready for anything . . .

Or Bea was in here earlier, wasn't she, maybe she has been playing around in here while I was out, too. Kids get into everything.

But as I twist the stick up and down again, I think: you'd have to press the needle in very carefully, so that the sharp end was just below the surface . . . wouldn't it have to be deliberate?

I shudder and throw the thing in the trash. I don't want to look at it anymore.

No, it could have been an accident. It *could*. It would be easy for things to get mixed up in my bag. . . . But I keep picturing Olivia's white face earlier this evening, when she found her daughter in my room. She seemed so unlike herself. So *angry*.

And I'm still standing there thinking about that, growing cold in my thin pajamas, when my phone rings on the dresser.

"Nick Wilson, please." It's a man's voice I don't recognize.

"That's me. Nicky."

Whoever it is digests that.

"Well, Nicky"—the voice is thin, almost a whisper—"I must say, I don't appreciate you trying to kill me off."

Chapter 21

"**B**ecause I can tell you right now," says the voice on the phone, "I don't think it's very funny at all."

"I think there's been a mistake—"

"Did you leave a message with Gibbons, zero, one, two . . ." Slowly, he starts to reel off a phone number.

"Ah yes, I left a message for Edward Gibbons, I was trying to reach him about Sam Gibbons." I go to blot my lip with tissue paper. The scratch is really starting to sting.

"Well, I can tell you, I certainly am not—"

In the background another man's voice cuts across: "Who are you on the phone to so late? Dad, it's not good for you to get worked up."

"Just a minute Ed!"—as I realize what's happened. "Now, I may have one foot in the grave, young lady," he says to me. "But you can't push me in there yet."

After I apologize repeatedly for accidentally killing him off in my message to his son Edward, Sam Gibbons mellows.

"No harm done, let's hear no more about it."

Did I misunderstand Joey's gran? I can't remember completely, but I'm sure she said he'd died. . . . But now Sam seems interested more than angry, as I tell him I'm working on a book about Olivia Hayes, daughter of Alex Vane who died in that awful fire—his former neighbor, I understand.

"A book, hm? What kind of book?"

"A memoir. I'm Olivia's ghostwriter There are just a few blanks I'd like to fill in."

"A few blanks, I like that." He chuckles darkly.

He doesn't mind telling me about what happened that night. "It's the recent stuff I'm a bit shabby on nowadays." He sighs comfortably. "Now, we were living in the barn, we'd just finished doing it up . . ."

"And had you ever met the Vanes—your neighbors?"

"I'd seen him about. You know, we'd wave when we were out walking the dogs. But we weren't neighbors, really. It was a bit isolated out there. Too quiet for my wife, Marjorie, though it was her idea to move in the first place, God rest her soul." He laughs to himself. "That's why we didn't stay that long."

"So what do you remember of that night?"

"Now," he says, "let me think."

I make myself stay quiet. I sense he has to tell it his way to get the story out at all.

"So. The dog we had then, Bess, she was called, lovely nature. On the night in question"—he spends some time trying to remember the date—"Bess had decided to have her puppies and I'd stayed up with her, until they were all nice and settled. Then I'd gone up, trying not to wake Marjorie—it was late, after midnight. And I had got into bed, I was falling asleep myself, when I heard this great big bang.

"*Crack*—it echoed. So I went to the window and opened the curtains, but everything was quiet. I remember that: it was a bright night, the moon was out, and everything was still, the fields and the trees and the big house behind them.

"But I didn't go back to sleep after that, it gets harder as you get older—you'll learn. I went downstairs to make myself a cup of tea and sat at the table, keeping Bess and her puppies company. Eventually, I thought, I'll be shattered in the morning, I'd better head up again. And as I got up, I looked again out of the kitchen window.

"I thought, how is it morning already—and then I knew. The light was wrong. I called 999 there and then. And, well, you know the rest . . ."

"Thanks so much." I can't think of much more he could add. "Can I ask—what sort of time did you say you heard the explosion?"

"The explosion? I didn't say it was an explosion."

"But—the bang. That must have been the fuel in the heating tank going off?"

That was what the articles had said: the tank had exploded in the fire.

He snorts. "I know what gunshot sounds like. And that was a gun."

And he won't be budged: that was what woke him, nothing to do with any poxy fuel tank.

"Some twerp from the police told me I'd misheard," he is getting a little indignant now, upset by the memory. "Embarrassed they still hadn't done anything about the poachers, no doubt. That was my very first thought when I heard it, you know, that someone was poaching in the woods again. Some idiots set snares the year before, and Bess nearly got caught in one. Nasty."

I don't want him to get distracted: but what about the fuel tank, I say, everyone agreed it had blown up . . .

"No doubt it did, no doubt it did. There were all sorts of noises out of the big house later; glass shattering, things falling—bangs, too. But that was *later*."

I think for a second, pondering all this. "The woodland comes so close to the house," I say. "A poacher could have been right in there."

"Oh certainly," he says. "They were very bold. Now—what, Ed?" He speaks back in the handset. "I'm going to have to go, dear, it's getting late."

I am about to hang up when something occurs to me. "Just one thing, sorry. You said your first thought was that it was a poacher. But did you think something else after that?"

"Oh, that." He sounds a little embarrassed. "Marjorie always said I had an imagination."

I wait.

"Well, I did wonder," he says. "Vane was a big name round those parts. People don't like to rock the boat. And how could they tell, really, what had happened to the body, after a fire like that?"

"What do you mean—what did you think had happened to it?"

He stops for a second, as if he's deciding whether to tell me.

"All right. After I heard they found him in there, the whole place going up in flames, the family out of the way—you want to know what I thought?" He waits a beat. "That he'd run out of money and shot himself."

"Really? Why?"

"Well. It was just the things you'd hear. That car of his, that house, the parties they'd have. Big spenders, to keep it all up."

"But how would he even have got hold of a gun?"

He puts on an affected voice—"Huntin' shootin' fishin,' what ho"—then switches back. "Vane was the county type. He could have got hold of a gun."

"Then why burn down his house, too?"

"To cover it up, maybe, to make sure the life insurance paid out for the family? Or he didn't want the bank to get the house—"

"But the papers didn't say anything about any of that," I insist. "No one, official or otherwise, suggested it was suspicious at all. Even at the inquest."

The mention of the inquest, making it all real, seems to make him collect himself.

"Well, you certainly mustn't put that in any book—it just crossed my mind. No, I was right the first time," he says more firmly, "I heard a poacher, whatever the police said."

He is quieter now, speaking almost to himself. "All the same, it's only natural that I of all people would wonder if something else had happened to him . . ."

"It is?"

"Because I made the call, you see. *I* called 999. Oh, I know what they said, about the speed of the fire and smoke and all that. But I always asked myself—why didn't he?"

Chapter 22

I am groggy when I walk into the kitchen on Wednesday morning.

It is another bright day, and I can smell fresh laundry from the utility room, where Annie is moving around. I call good morning and busy myself making a strong milky coffee. After what I heard last night about a gun . . . well, it took me a long time to fall asleep.

I take my hot cup into the living room, settling on the sofa. Soon Josh follows me in, a slice of toast in his hand.

"Liv says she won't be long, she's just getting Bea ready."

"Sure," I say lightly, expecting him to go. Instead he sits down, on the sofa with me, clearly intending to wait for his wife.

"So. All going well with the book?"

Overnight, I had decided what to do—with regard to Olivia, at least. Fall back on my experience, like I would with any other ghosting job: work on building a rapport, getting things on an even keel, so my subject will open up.

I don't need to tell her husband that, though.

"Yes," I say, "thanks. We're getting there. So are you off to the site today?"

"Mm," he says. "Probably will head over there."

Then we are both silent; last night's ease, fueled by wine, now gone.

"That's beautiful," I say, gesturing to the painting that had caught my eye before. It really is: the small canvas glowing with oils, showing a silver streak of water among high grass and a young green willow. "That's your lake, isn't it? I just realized."

"It's getting a bit wild down there. Cav needs to do something about it."

"Well, the painting's gorgeous, at least."

"Doubt it's worth anything. But Liv likes it."

There's so much loveliness in this house, despite its past.

"Sorry to interrupt." Olivia has one hand on the frame of the arch into the living room. "But I've got to go to Mansford with Bea this morning. Nicky, I thought you could interview me as I drive. Save a bit of time."

"Uh, sure," I say. She is already dressed to go out, in a buttery soft leather jacket. "I'll just grab my bag."

As we leave the house, Bea in her mother's arms, I see another car parked next to Olivia's gleaming silver 4x4.

"Is that Annie's?" I ask. I can't quite picture the housekeeper driving the mud-splattered Land Rover.

"No." Olivia pauses, before politeness presses an explanation out of her. "It's Sabrina's. She didn't want to drive after drinking."

I nod. I thought I heard noises in the corridor outside my door last night; Sabrina must have stayed in one of the rooms near me.

Olivia drives in silence down the driveway. No small talk, then.

"OK," I say, as she clicks a button on her key fob to open the gates. "I thought we could cover relationships today, starting with the workplace?" An innocuous opening.

She checks for traffic as she pulls out, turning right for Mansford. "Sure."

Half an hour later, we are still barreling through the countryside. I am trying to focus on the question prompts I've written in my notebook, my recorder balanced on my lap.

To be fair, Olivia has talked fluently all the way, covering everything from her first boss to how to deal with tricky colleagues.

Even Bea, as immaculate as her mother in a soft gray dress and pink socks, has been quiet after Olivia gave her a box of raisins: strapped in her seat behind us, she has been contentedly dropping them on the floor one by one.

The problem is me—after bombing down the winding roads, breathing in that sickly-sweet new car smell of plastic and air freshener, I am fighting the urge to throw up.

I focus my gaze on the white line in the road in front of us, and force out my next question.

"How about romantic relationships? I thought we

could do a section on how to choose a good man. Or partner, of course."

"I suppose." She straightens slightly in her seat. "Well, it's about communication, isn't it? Respect and trust . . ." She trails off. "You can do something with that, can't you?"

It wouldn't be the first time an author has expected me to magic up a book out of nowhere.

"Yes, that's great. I wonder if we can get just a bit more personal detail. Your followers are so interested in your relationship with Josh, how you make it work."

She lifts her eyebrows a little, waiting for me to ask a specific question.

"So," I say, annoyed—this is supposed to be a collaboration; she doesn't need to act like a politician cornered on TV—"how did you know that he was the man for you?"

"How did I know . . ." she muses. "Because he made me feel safe. Like nothing could go wrong." She glances at me. "Does that make sense?"

I nod. "You know, it really does. And what else?"

But the shutters are up again.

"Oh gosh," she says politely. "Why don't you have a look at the website? I've written a little bit about it on there. When I used to blog."

I've read that blog: beautiful pictures strung together by sugary captions as short as they are sweet. I'm not going to get anything from that.

"What about . . . nightmare boyfriends," I say chummily. "Any horror stories?"

"I'm afraid not. Josh was my first serious boyfriend."

"The first?"

"I went to a girls' school," she says flatly.

"Would you send Bea to one?" I ask, curious.

"Depends what she wants." She checks in the mirror on her daughter, now singing to herself quietly. "It was my home from home after . . . But no, not if she didn't want to."

"And do you want Bea to have a similar childhood to yours? I mean"—I add hurriedly, of course she doesn't want a repeat of what happened—"a country-side upbringing?"

"I do. I loved growing up here, all the space to run about in. Swimming in the lake, playing hide-and-seek in the meadow. That's what I like to remember."

I see my chance to get at what's on my mind. "What about the other side of country life—foxhunting and all that. Would you ever have gone on, say, a shoot, growing up?"

Even as I say it, it sounds clumsy, and I worry I'm giving my secret interest in her background away, but she just glances at me. "God no. I had my pony phase, but I never tried anything like that. Bea won't, either."

I see her eyes flick down at my list of questions: her answers are so short that we tend to whizz through them. "And would you like a big family?"

"We'll see. Josh is the youngest of four, there's a whole tribe of them. But it's just me. And I'm fine."

I'm still absorbing that—that she's calling herself an only child though I know that's not true—when something makes me look up. We are heading over a small humped bridge, too fast. My stomach lifts and swoops, and I close my eyes as a cold wave of nausea washes through me.

When I open them again she is looking at me, amused, before her gaze flicks away, her face wiped clean of expression.

Anger flashes through me. She's driving like this on purpose.

"So, I wanted to talk about your parents," I say smoothly.

Her attention is now fixed on the road. "I said, I'm not talking about what happened."

"No, but there's no harm in talking about them a little, is there?" I say sweetly. "It'd be strange not to mention them at all. Just whatever you're comfortable sharing."

"What do you want to know?" she says stiffly.

"Why don't you tell me about your father?"

She thinks for a second. "My father—OK. Daddy was great fun, charming, handsome. And generous, too. The life and soul. Everyone liked him."

"And your mother?"

"She had an artistic temperament. Great highs and lows. Fantastic taste."

She talks like they're people she met at a party. "And were you much alike?"

"I got my eye for color from her, perhaps. She made a beautiful home."

I press on. "Are you and your mother close now?"

"Not exactly." She checks her side mirror. "She's dead."

"She's dead?" I echo.

"Road accident. A while ago now. And that's not going in the book. It's not relevant."

"Not relevant?"

Maybe it's because I'm feeling sick and angry, but

something breaks in me: I am filled with frustration—with upset.

The stories we tell ourselves, about where we've come from, who we are, the things that have shaped us, they do matter: without them, we're just hollow people—ghosts.

I hear myself saying, aloud: "But you do realize, Olivia, you can't just erase the past—"

"Nicky!" She glances over at me, with a shocked little laugh.

Oh no, did I go too far? Forget myself? Be professional. I take a deep breath. "Sorry. I shouldn't have said that."

"Mum-meee . . ." Bea's small voice, cranky with sleep, breaks the silence between us. We must have woken her. "Mum-meee . . ."

"What is it, darling?" Olivia says. "Do you want the shark song?" She presses something on the steering wheel and music bursts out, too loud for any more talking.

The conversation's over, anyway.

Chapter 23

I am relieved to step out onto solid ground by the time we reach Mansford, a picturesque market town with narrow roads and the odd black-and-white half-timbered building set among the redbrick shop fronts.

"The main street is just over there." Olivia jerks her chin to the exit of the car park, and starts hauling Bea out. "No, Bea, shoes on. We're going to the shoe shop." To me: "You've got my number, but see you back here in, say, an hour?"

"Sure, see you in a bit."

So that was the essential task that meant we couldn't have a normal session: new shoes. Annoyed, I don't wait for them, but head off onto the narrow high street.

In the fresh air, I soon start to feel better, and my spirits lift. It's pretty here, little triangles of bunting strung overhead for no obvious reason, and cute twisting side streets that I follow at random.

Eventually I want to check where I am, and stop to pull up my phone map outside another little stretch of shops: a boutique full of overdecorated knitwear, a tea shop, and an antique place, a single vase spotlit against green velvet in the window.

Standing on the pavement, I look at the antique shop again: George Rafferton, reads the sign above the glass. Why does that ring a bell?

Then I realize: it was on that piece of paper from Joey, part of the planning documents. G. Rafferton was one of the names who worked on the rebuild of Annersley House.

I glance around me. Then I go up the steps and push open the door.

The shop bell tinkles as I walk inside, and a rheumy-eyed Cavalier King Charles spaniel shuffles up for an obligatory pat before heading back to its bed by the register.

I see no one else in here, among the chests and cabinets and shelves full of objects. In front of me, a pretty wooden box catches my eye, inlaid with—shell? I take a closer look: that stuff looks suspiciously like ivory.

"Hello hello, can I help you?"

I straighten up. It's a neat little man in a cardigan and tie, with white hair and sharp blue eyes behind his glasses.

"I was just having a look."

"Ah," he says with a wave. "There's no price for that."

For a moment I admire a chest of drawers.

"Actually," I say, "The name on the sign was familiar. I wondered if you are the G. Rafferton involved in the restoration of Annersley House . . ."

His face lights up. "Annersley House!"

And he seems genuinely delighted to hear that that I am working with Olivia Hayes, formerly Vane, on a book that will cover her work and life as an "influencer" but also, I add tactfully, address her home, its history . . .

"Of course," he says. "Of course. Well, given the extent of the damage, it could never be a *true* restoration, more a very careful facsimile. In which I played a small part, advising on the cosmetic, rather than structural, questions—plasterwork, wall finishes, furnishings. And yet I do feel my advice was valued, all the same," he adds modestly.

I'm sure it was, I tell him, and I would love to hear all about it.

He blossoms like a hothouse flower under my attention.

". . . with listed houses there are obligations, but even so, they aren't always saved. The expense of it all—the insurance money only goes so far."

But soon I am slightly regretting coming in, enthusiastic though he is. I can't imagine him being interested in any sort of gossip among the builders or in the village.

". . . so much was lost, all those beautiful hangings, statuary, rugs—and oils on canvas are so flammable. Then the water from the hoses . . ." He spreads his hands ruefully. "But we did our best to re-create the spirit of the house, just as it was."

"Just as it was?"

"Much of it from her memory, because the photos that might have helped us had been destroyed. But Miss Vane updated the mod cons, and let the style of the house *evolve*."

"Mrs. Vane," I correct, almost automatically.

"No," he says, slightly puzzled. "Miss Vane. Olivia Vane."

"But . . . wouldn't Olivia's mother, Elsa Vane, have handled the rebuild?"

He looks at me appraisingly. "Ah. Well, now. The house was tied up, you see, so it went to the firstborn, not the widow. But confidentially, I understand she simply couldn't face it—moved away soon after. Never came back.

"So there was a long period where no one quite took responsibility," he adds, a little disapproving, as I stay silent. "Vane was an only son: he had inherited after his father died, and his own mother was elderly and based in London. There was no one else."

"I suppose I just assumed . . ."

I just assumed, somehow, that Olivia's contribution to the house began at the point when she started charting it on her Instagram, a dream project, painting walls and buying knickknacks. Not putting a wreck back together from the ground up.

"Well," says Rafferton cheerfully, "now you know what it does to assume: makes an ASS out of you and me. You as in the letter 'u.' But I do agree," he adds kindly, "not many young women would have the drive to see a project like that through to the end."

At that the bell rings, and a customer enters, a well-upholstered woman closing her umbrella noisily for attention.

I bend down to give the dog a good-bye pat. "Thanks so much."

And promising that if I need any more details about the cornicing or wainscots, whatever they are, I will certainly be in touch, I push my way out of the shop, my mood more somber than when I went in.

It doesn't matter—not really—that I was under the impression that other people had fixed the house up for Olivia. The grown-ups.

But it is a warning to me, a reminder of something I already know. If I don't ask the right questions, I won't get the right answers.

And I can't help but wonder: why didn't Elsa stay, step up?

She just left the place to rot.

Chapter 24

As always, the journey back home seems to be shorter than the way there, and either Olivia's driving is a little more restrained or I have gotten used to it. Bea is tired now, getting restless in her seat, so we have her music playing all the way back.

When I recognize the approach to the village, just before Olivia turns off for her driveway, I speak up. "You know what—why don't you drop me here? I'll do a bit of work in the village and get out of your hair."

She glances at me. "You sure? I'm tied up the rest of the day, I'm afraid, but you're fine to work at the house."

"No, I quite like a change of scene when I work. I've brought my laptop in my bag."

"But how will you get back?" She's not coming out to pick me up.

"I'll walk," I say. I want a break from Olivia and her house.

*   *   *

There is no coffee shop, and the bakery only has one rickety table, for customers waiting for their orders to be wrapped up, so I end up walking along the grass shoulder to the pub, the Bleeding Wolf.

Inside, my eyes take a second to adjust from the brightness outside. Behind the bar, a man in a checked shirt eyes me warily. "No hot food till one."

"That's OK. I'll just have a sandwich."

"Knock yourself out." He hands me a menu. I pay for my sandwich and a coffee, then pick a table by the window—the place is empty—and open up my computer.

The Wi-Fi is slow, but I have gotten on it by the time a teenage girl in black skirt and white shirt appears with my coffee and puts it down carefully, concentrating. It spills anyway, slopping onto the table.

"I'm so sorry!" she says.

It's the same girl who served me and Joey on Monday night. I recognize her now: little red curls escaping from her ponytail. She must only be about thirteen.

"I tipped a whole plate into someone's lap when I was a waitress," I say, helping her clean up with a paper napkin. "This is nothing."

She laughs and checks over her shoulder, to make sure the boss isn't about.

"This is my first week helping out," she says confidingly. "The real test will be Sunday lunch, Dad says, so he's letting me do some shifts before school starts."

"I see," I say, realizing the man behind the bar must be her dad: her vibrant red hair has faded to strawberry blond on him. "I'm sure you'll be great," I add, automatically.

Because I am itching to get on now. I want to look into Sam Gibbons's theory about Alex Vane running out of money. . . . I know Alex worked in London before moving up here, but I have a vague sense that his type always keep a finger in some pie.

And *bingo*. After a quick search on the Companies House website, I find Alex listed as a director of a company called Vanguard.

"Company status," I read, "Liquidation."

There is another name also listed as a former director, a Neil Stone who resigned on October 11, 1997—a couple of months after the fire. There is an address for him, too, in Yorkshire, and it doesn't take me long to find a phone number.

I call it on my cell—noting as I do that I have a missed call from Joey—and listen as the phone goes to voice mail. I leave a message, mentioning Olivia Vane, daughter of Alexander Vane, that I am working on a book . . . and hang up to see the waitress hovering over me again.

"Here you go." She has my sandwich on a tray, tuna salad between two thick white slabs of bread. "So you're working for Olivia Vane?"

"What?"

"I wasn't listening," she says, as she sets the food down in front of me. "I just heard. Are you staying with her? What's she like? Is she nice?"

"Yes, I am. She's very nice." What else can I say? "So you don't see her in here much?"

She shakes her head, her freckles blurring. "I suppose she must be busy going to fancy parties and things."

"I suppose," I say.

She sits herself down in the chair opposite me: someone's clearly a fan. "It must be so exciting. I've got a YouTube channel myself. I only have twelve followers so far, but you have to start somewhere. Has she told you about the fire?"

She brings it up so casually. "I'd have thought you were too young to remember that . . ."

"Oh, I wasn't born. But Dad's the one who saw the car," she says proudly.

"The car?"

"The one that her mother was driving that day, when they were leaving for their vacation. Dad had to talk to the police!" she says. "He was only my age, and his dad—my granddad—had the pub then. But my dad was the one who saw them. He—"

"How are you getting on with laying those tables, Emily?"

She stiffens at the hand on her shoulder: he's light on his feet for such a big man.

"I was just chatting. This lady's staying at Annersley House. She's a writer."

"A writer—a journalist, you mean?" He has white lines by his eyes, like he's spent too much time smiling in the sunshine. He's not smiling now.

I shake my head. "A ghostwriter."

"Well, you mustn't distract the customers, Em."

She hurries off with an air of innocence.

"I'm working with Olivia," I volunteer, "she's writing a book." Working *with*, not against, her, is the unspoken message.

"Oh." He nods and turns back to the bar. I follow

him over, collecting cutlery from the rack at the end—
Emily has forgotten to give me any.

"Your daughter was telling me about the fire, at Annersley House." He tosses me a paper napkin, reading
me correctly. "Thanks. She says you saw the car that
day."

"Whose car?"

"Olivia's mother's. Elsa's." He knows whose car.

"Yes, I saw the car." He starts putting glasses away.

"I don't mean to sound nosy. It's such a sensitive
subject for Olivia, I don't like to ask her all the details.
And nobody wants to discuss it, as you might imagine."

He thinks for a second. "All right. It's not a secret—
yes, I saw the car go past. About midday. Big blue
Range Rover, before everyone had one. You have to go
this way to get to the highway, and I recognized it."

He rattles off the details: they are practiced and familiar.

"When did you find out about the fire?"

"The morning after, when I woke up, it was noisy—
we lived above the pub then. Money was tight. Mum
and Dad had opened up early: they gave cold drinks to
the fire crews, the police. And half the village turned
up, too. People want to get together when something
like that happens. Though no one realized how bad it
was, then."

"Why not?"

He puts down the glass he's holding. "Well. Everyone was already talking about the family being away.
They would have told people, or their staff would have
known—been given time off. But when I told, uh, a
police officer what I'd seen, he said it was useful. It

could help them confirm that the family were absent. Thank God."

"Except for the dad. If they had known that Alex was still in there . . . ?" I trail off, realizing it sounds like I might be blaming him.

But he replies evenly: "They couldn't have done anything. It was far too late when the fire crews arrived."

I want to change the subject. "Would you see the family around? Before, I mean."

"I was just a kid, I didn't really pay attention."

"What about Olivia—did you know her?"

He shakes his head. "Then they all moved away. She didn't come back for a good few years, to fix up the house. Everyone was glad—it was an eyesore."

He looks up as the door swings open, walkers arriving for lunch, and I sense my time is up. "I'm Nicky by the way. Nicky Wilson."

"Paul Bryant."

I spend a couple of hours there in the end. I pick out a few phrases that catch my eye from the transcripts I've got back so far, pasting them into a new document. Olivia is keen to see something, but it's too early to do much more, really.

Outside again, I wonder if I could cut across the fields, but I don't fancy trying to clamber through hedgerows. I stick to the side of the road, my thoughts starting to wander, as they always do when I walk.

So Paul in the pub didn't tell me anything that interesting, really. But he was still more helpful than Marie, Joey's grandmother.

What was she doing, anyway, telling me her old neighbor, Sam Gibbons, was dead?

Maybe she had heard about Sam's wife dying and got mixed up. You might, if you had lost touch.

But she could have just told me, if she didn't want me to bother him.

Chapter 25

Sabrina's car is still in the driveway when I get back, and from the hall I can hear voices in the kitchen. I hesitate, then go straight upstairs.

It is not long before there is a knock on my bedroom door. I grab my notepad and voice recorder: Olivia must have found half an hour to squeeze me in again.

When I open it, Josh is standing there, dressed in shorts and a T-shirt. "Tennis?"

"Tennis?" I look up at him, confused.

"Do you play?" he asks, a little impatiently. "Leo couldn't make it, so we need an extra body."

"I did a bit at school. Not really." Leo . . . Sabrina's husband?

"It's just a knockabout, before it gets too dark. We can lend you a racket."

"Uh . . . will Olivia mind?" I say, thinking of her reaction when she found Bea in my room; thinking about her careful protection of her boundaries. "I don't want . . ."

But he brushes away my protestations—"We always play on Wednesdays! See you down there in five."

And so I fall into line.

"Run for it," barks Sabrina, as I find myself way behind the bright yellow ball, legging it to the back of the court. With supreme effort, I hit it—right into the net

"Sorry," I say. Sabrina has already told me to stop apologizing.

"Game," says Josh.

Bending down to pick up a stray ball, I blow my slick bangs out of my eyes. Just a knockabout, he said. I could almost laugh. Why did I say yes to this?

When I came down, in the comfy sweatsuit I write in at home, the three of them—Josh, Sabrina and Olivia—were already hitting around. Without discussion, I was somehow paired with Sabrina, who clearly plays a lot. They all must.

Josh is managing not to lob the ball too hard in my direction, and keeps rallying with Sabrina, lean and brown in her pleated white tennis skirt. But Olivia has no qualms about hitting to me—low, fast balls that I struggle to touch with my borrowed racket, let alone return. My ankles are sore from sliding about on the artificial grass.

It gets worse when it's my turn to serve, the late afternoon sun shining in my eyes. I am so rusty I either hit the ball way out, sending it bouncing back against the green wire fencing, or straight into the net.

"You can serve underhand if you want," calls Olivia, sounding bored, after I double-fault again. Across the net from me, she is a sleek figure in a black tank and leggings.

Gritting my teeth, I serve overhand but with extra care, and just about manage to get the ball into the serving box before it is slammed back to me.

"Out," calls Olivia, as my final attempt to return the ball fails. "Game."

Now Olivia and Josh have won four games, Sabrina fighting them valiantly over every point, I am hoping it is all over. But—

"Round-robin?" says Josh. "We can swap partners every time we've all served, see who gets the most wins overall."

"Good idea," says Sabrina. She must be itching to be paired with a better partner.

"But why?" says Olivia to Josh, resentment in her tone. "Just because we're winning?"

I suppose no one wants to be so rude as to state the obvious: because it's only fair they all take a turn with the bad player: me.

I feel the familiar urge to smooth things over. "That's OK," I say brightly. "I'm happy to swap, the sun's in my eyes this side anyway." Too late, I realize that it sounds like I am making excuses for my poor performance.

"Fine," says Olivia. "You go with Josh," she says to me.

I head round to the other side of the net, bristling at her high-handedness, as we swap places.

But something shifts as we start to play again.

I am still confused by their scoring system—"No advantage, to sudden death," Sabrina had announced, bafflingly—but I am starting to get the odd ball back. Now I can actually see, no longer blinded by the low sun, it really is much easier. And some old muscle memory is kicking in, despite the years it has been since I picked up a racket.

Josh serves first, then Sabrina for the other side. Josh and I win the first two games.

Now it's my turn to serve, to Olivia first.

At the back of the court, I bounce the ball a few times.

"Do you want to get a move on?" calls Olivia sharply. "We haven't got all day."

"Jesus, Liv," says Josh with a rueful chuckle.

"Well, I need to check on Bea. She may have woken up."

I ignore her. I throw the ball up in the air, against the sky, my racket swinging back and up. For a second, everything is quiet. Then I connect with the ball, re-membering to finish through, the momentum pro-pelling me forward over the line.

And, thank the stars, the ball rockets down over the net and into the serving box, bouncing up low and fast right by Olivia. Primed for yet another of my weak, nervous serves, she is in completely the wrong place, as the ball shoots straight past her.

"Ace," says Sabrina. "Wake up, Sticky!"

Josh is coming to my side of the court and I don't understand why until he palms my hand. "Well played."

"Thanks." I am laughing, and even Sabrina has a smirk on her face.

And then I see Olivia, marching up to the net.

"Fault! I saw her foot. She was inside the line."

"Oh c'mon," says Sabrina. "Does that really matter? It's just a knockabout."

"Nicky was over the line when she served. That's a foot fault. Are we playing by the rules or not?"

No one answers, so I just go back to the baseline and, in silence, get ready to serve again.

Of course I don't repeat my ace.

Still, Sabrina and Olivia just can't seem to get in sync; both chasing the ball at the same time, or neither of them attempting to go for it. Josh seems to have realized this, as he keeps sending the ball right down between them.

"Mine," shouts Sabrina, dashing forward from way at the back of the court. Instead there is a clash of rackets, the noise shockingly loud, as she and Olivia almost run into each other. The ball hits the ground just inside the line at the back of the court.

"In," I say, pettily.

"I said, that was mine," says Sabrina, squaring up to Olivia.

"Didn't hear you," says Olivia, her face a blank.

I think Sabrina is going to say something more, but she just turns on her heel to position herself on her side of the court. They don't gel anymore as we keep playing.

After this latest round, I do a mental tally. Of course, Josh is leading, having won each of the eight games, but due to his skill I, like Olivia, have four wins. Sabrina— yet to be paired with Josh—has yet to win any, to her evident annoyance.

"Time to swap," says Sabrina. She's already heading round to Josh's side, and I'm walking over to pair with Olivia, who is collecting the balls on her racket. She has that teenager's trick of scooping them up with a bounce.

"Can't," she says in a carrying voice, not looking up. "I have a conference call scheduled—I'm going to have to call it a night."

"Oh, come on, Liv . . ." says Josh.

"Sorry," she says briskly. She won't meet any of our eyes. "You're all welcome to keep playing." The invitation is clearly not there. "I'm just going to check on Bea first, she's been waking up a lot, and she wanders about now."

It's the explanation that makes it so clear she wants this over. She is already walking off the court.

Sabrina and I stand by the net, my damp T-shirt cooling against my skin.

"She's a bit of a sore loser," says Sabrina. And she laughs, like it's funny.

"You're not kidding," I say. There was nothing jokey about Olivia's show just then.

Josh is lingering at the back of the court, smashing balls into the net to collect them.

I lower my voice. "Is something up with her?"

"Well, we all like to win."

"I know, but—she seemed *angry*."

She raises her eyebrows. "You really do want to know everything about her, don't you? Oh, don't tell me—you're not just a writer," she says loudly, so Josh can hear as he walks over to us. She smiles unpleasantly. "You're a *fan*."

"Never mind." I turn away, annoyed. I don't know what was up with Olivia tonight, but Sabrina's not my ally. It was just a stupid tennis game, anyway.

"Well," says Josh, tapping his racket against his leg, and he looks at Sabrina. "Drink?"

She brightens. "I'm gasping."

"I'll just . . ." I gesture to nowhere, but I don't need an excuse as the two of them set off back to the house, the wind carrying their voices away from me.

Finally I breathe out. Thank God that's over.

Chapter 26

I don't go straight back inside the house, looming against the darkening sky. I don't believe in bad energy, anything like that . . . only, it is hard not to think about what happened inside its walls, after seeing Joey's photos of the ruins. It looks so stately and permanent, as if it's been there forever. But it's just a fake, really.

So instead I leave my racket and wander down to the edge of the lake. I stand there, feeling the evening breeze, admiring the great sweeping willow, its long branches reaching down to touch the water. Then I pull my phone out of my pocket.

I had brought it down with me to the court, out of habit. And no one else is out here. So I am going try that number again, the one I found for Neil Stone, who was in business with Alexander Vane.

This time, someone picks up on the third ring.

"Hello?" Whoever it is sounds irritable.

"Hi!" I say, too keen. "I mean, hello. I'm hoping to talk to Neil—"

"This is he. I'm not buying anything from you—"

"About Alexander Vane."

"Ah yes. I got your message. I wondered when some-one would want to talk to me about that."

I have my spiel down pat by now. "I'm writing his daughter's autobiography and doing research. She doesn't like to look into it all herself. It's such a painful subject."

"Is it?"

"Uh, yes. Her father died."

"I didn't mean anything bad by that, love. I didn't know the family. Just him."

He doesn't live locally, Neil Stone explains; he's a Yorkshireman born and bred, and is there full-time now that he's retired. A mutual contact had recommended him to Alex Vane, who was thinking about setting up a consultancy after leaving London.

"He asked me to be a director of his company, thought I could keep an eye on the accounts side of things—the boring stuff." This guy is more down to earth than I'd imagined—perhaps that was why Alex thought he'd be useful.

But the business didn't come to anything, he tells me. "Alex seemed to spend more time having lunches and meetings in London than getting any actual work done. No skin off my nose, once I realized I wasn't expected to do anything for my salary."

Because they weren't friends, I feel able to be direct. "I heard that some people thought he might have got in some kind of financial trouble before the fire?"

"Financial trouble? No, no," he says firmly.

"But would you have even known?"

"Thankfully, yes. I used to play golf with his personal accountant. And I made sure to check it wasn't all fur coat and no knickers, as my dear old mum would have said. No, he was the real deal—not all down to his own efforts—there was the property, various other assets. Poor sod," he adds.

I am disappointed—and then feel bad for feeling so. What was I wishing for?

"What was he like?" I continue.

"Oh, charming—they must teach them that in private school. Very good with people. He could have made a go of his business, if he had really wanted to."

"When he died, did you ever think he might have, well, done something?" I press on. "Because I did hear that some locals wondered . . . he had access to guns, I heard."

"I don't doubt he did. But I wouldn't have pegged him as the type to self-destruct."

We keep talking, but he hasn't anything else to tell me. After a while, I thank him, starting to wrap up.

And it's a funny thing I've noticed: as soon as someone knows that you're bringing the conversation to a close, it can change the dynamic. They finally relax.

"You know," he says, "I always thought someone might want to ask me about him. I didn't think it would be an author."

I don't correct him. "So the police never spoke to you?"

"No. I didn't have anything to tell them. And I didn't see the point in talking to the press, at the time. But it's funny that you asked about money."

"It is?"

"Well, it's hardly worth mentioning—but now you've reminded me, he *was* worried about money once, though in a very roundabout way. It was at one of our meetings. Nice dinner, lots of wine. Alex always liked to pay cash—easier to impress the waiters with a big flashy tip." Stone laughs. "But he didn't have what he expected when he got out his wallet. He seemed annoyed. Into appearances, stiff upper lip and all that."

"So Alex might have been under financial pressure, after all?" Joey's theory about him getting mixed up with the wrong people comes to mind.

"No, no. It would have been a drop in the ocean for him. He thought it was somebody who worked for him, who'd been lifting a few notes here and there. Even so . . ."

"Even so?" I prompt.

"I read all the newspaper reports to see if there was anything else going on, after it all happened. But I never saw anything mentioned about money. It was just a terrible tragedy."

"Just a terrible tragedy," I repeat.

"It was only a little thing," he says, cheery to have unburdened himself. "I don't know if I would have mentioned it, if anyone *had* got in touch back then . . . but it's funny what stays with you, isn't it?"

*   *   *

And I am still thinking about this practical man, and this detail that stuck with him all these years, as I go back in and up to my room.

It has been a long day, and not all that pleasant. But never mind about a stupid tennis match, I have much bigger things to do here, starting tomorrow, I—

The crash is loud, coming from inside the house.

Chapter 27

I take the stairs two at a time—the noise seemed to come up from below. In the main hall I almost collide with Josh, coming out of the corridor to the left.

"What's going on?" I can't see over his shoulders. "Is everything all right?"

It sounded like a pane of glass shattering, but heavier. I am thinking of screws holding shelving coming loose, a rack of plates smashed across the floor. Is someone hurt?

"Don't worry," he says, grim-faced. "Olivia just had some bad news."

"Oh God—has someone—not her . . . ?" But who is left for her to lose?

"Nothing like that. Something on the gossip forums. Information that she, *we*, didn't expect to get out," he says shortly. "She just needs a moment by herself."

I can hear nothing from the hallway behind him. "But—"

"This really isn't a good time, sorry. Good night."

He brushes past me and I watch, dismissed, as he

walks down the other corridor to the kitchen. Then I start down the hallway he came out of, seeing the door left ajar—

"And just where do you think you're going?"

I swing around. Sabrina is behind me; one hand still on the banister. Did they tell me she was staying another night? But then, why would they?

"Olivia's had some bad news," I say. "She's upset . . ."

"I get that." She walks toward me. "What I don't get is why you think it's any of your business."

"No, I mean—go ahead." I am suddenly wary.

"Thanks," she says, sarcastically. "You know, I've known Olivia a long time. I'm very protective of her."

"Of course," I say. She's taller than me; I have to tilt my head back a little.

"And I'm not sure I much like how you're going about your job."

"Look," I say firmly, "I was worried, that's all. I'm going to bed."

And I walk past Sabrina and back up the stairs, refusing to hurry—but my heart is pounding.

What did she mean about my job: that I was crossing a boundary just then? Or has Olivia complained to her about my questions? Or—and I almost stop on the stairs—has someone told Sabrina I've been asking around about the past?

On the landing, I look down to check which way she went, in to comfort Olivia or following Josh into the kitchen?

She is still standing there below, watching me.

*   *   *

Behind my bedroom door, I talk myself down. So Olivia's friend is territorial. Surely she can't be that angry about just me; she must be pissed off about something else. Still, it's not ideal . . .

Anyway. I can't think about that now. It doesn't take long to check what Josh was talking about: just searching for "Olivia Hayes" brings it all up.

The site is one of the biggest of those dedicated to discussing influencers, their choices, lives, personas. The thread about Olivia Hayes covers all sorts: speculation about her earnings, whether she'd really wear the clothes from all the brands that sponsor her, whatever details they can glean about her husband.

Yet compared to other threads on there, there is not much—not for lack of interest, I'd guess, so much as lack of information. It's all pretty tame, until a post that appears a few dozen pages back.

"This is her, right?" it reads. "So this is why we never hear about her background. Guess who her dad is? Or should I say *was* . . ."

And then there is the marriage announcement, which links the Olivia of today to her family—and one of the articles about the fire.

The post is recent, just a couple of weeks old, but the thread has blown up since then, placing it among the site's "most commented." In its wake, half the comments are about the tragedy, sharing links and details, while the other half argue for Olivia's privacy. It got heated before a moderator froze the thread for a few days.

Not that that will put the genie back in the bottle, I

think, as I click around similar sites and forums. The story has been spreading across the Internet.

Olivia is even tagged in a tweet about it on Twitter, from earlier today: *@TheOliviaHayes so sry to hear about your dad so sad babe can't believe it x*

The tweet—not so tactfully—links to the thread on the website. That must have been how she learned about all the gossip, prompting tonight's crisis. I know she avoids the forums. She said so.

And yet part of me wonders, even knowing how private she is, what's so bad about it, that she's been linked to something horrible in her past?

It's a demonstration, as if I needed it, of just how tight-lipped she is about her personal life, how protective of her image.

But Olivia is not stupid: she will reach the same conclusion as me, if she hasn't already. This won't go away. Whether she likes it or not.

After that I get ready for bed and climb in between the covers. But when my phone tells me it is one a.m., I am still awake, staring into the blackness of the room.

It's too quiet out here, in the countryside. And I am hungry, too, after tennis knocked out dinner. I get up, straightening my twisted pajamas, and open my door.

The empty corridor is black and white in the moonlight—no one has closed the curtains to the clear night sky—so I don't need to take my phone to light my way, as I pad down the hall and stairwell as quietly as I can. Olivia's room is the other end of the house, anyway, so she won't hear me.

But as I enter the kitchen, I see there is a light on: someone is in the living room. It's too late to go back, so I round the corner.

Josh is sitting in an armchair, still fully dressed.

"Sorry to disturb you," I say, my voice coming out croaky. "I was getting some toast."

He nods, not lifting his head. Something brown and smoky sits in a squat glass in front of him.

"Well, good night," I say, turning away.

"Don't go on my account." Then he looks up, and seems to switch back into host mode. "Sure we can do better than toast. Can I get you a drink?"

I try to think of a reason why not. There are lots, I suppose.

But I say: "A G&T please, if you've got it."

He comes past me and starts to clank around in the dark kitchen.

"Here you go," he mutters finally, handing the drink to me.

It is cold and punchy, burning my throat. I wince. "So if you're drinking through the night—I take it this evening was a bit of an ordeal."

"Tomorrow will be worse," he says, his tone sour.

I sip my drink carefully. "Can I help at all?"

He looks down into his glass, swishing the liquid around. "How could you help?"

I just said it automatically. "Well, I don't know. But what about Julia—her assistant? Couldn't she come up this week to help Olivia, if she's upset?"

He pauses a second too long. "No, I don't think so."

And then I get it. I should have guessed: there has

been no sign of any assistant, remote or otherwise. Really, she barely bothered to disguise her voice on the phone.

"There is no Julia, is there?"

His face is in shadow. "Olivia likes to be in control, if you haven't noticed. Even got rid of the nanny. Poor old Annie's rushed off her feet."

I digest that. "But what about friends, family—support?"

"Olivia?" He is quiet for a moment, before his tone hardens. "You know she wouldn't even go to the funeral? Has she told you that?"

"Whose funeral?" I can't follow his train of thought. "Her father's—Alex's?"

"No . . ." He looks down at me. He is much drunker than I realized; I can smell the alcohol on his breath now.

"Sab thinks you might have had something to do with it all coming out, you know," he says lightly.

For a moment that sinks in, then I react with anger: "But that post went up online before this week! I hadn't even got here, I can't help that she only found out today—"

"Oh, don't worry. I told her that. Anyway," he says, "plenty of people round here know about what happened, it was going to come out online one day. Olivia just hates for people to think anything about her is less than perfect. And I've had enough of it."

He throws the glass back with a decisive movement, downing the rest of his drink, and leans past me to leave it on the side of the sink. In the darkness, I can feel the warmth of his body and his smell, cotton-fresh and a tang of sweat. Suddenly we are far too close.

"I'd better go up now," I say, too loudly, and quickly step round him and away. He stays where he is, staring out of the window, the blinds up to the night outside.

I climb the stairs as quietly as I came.

Chapter 28

Despite my lack of sleep, I am up early on Thursday, dressed and ready for my morning session with Olivia.

It is my second-to-last day, and I have decided: I am going to convince her that she must talk about that night—that the gossip on the forums means that she must rebut any hurtful speculation and set the record straight with a definitive, dignified account of what happened.

Surely she can't argue with that.

I go downstairs with my recording equipment, taking my laptop, too. The radio is on in the empty kitchen, where I help myself to breakfast.

Still she doesn't appear—no one does. And we haven't actually arranged a time.

Eventually I get up and start to look around the ground floor, pushing doors open cautiously—"Olivia?"

Every room is empty, everything in place, but in the morning room something makes me linger in the doorway—in fact, this was the door open behind Josh last night—and then I realize what is different: the big mirror over the fireplace is gone.

There is nothing else to show that anything has happened, until I kneel down and see the splinters glinting in the empty hearth, where they haven't quite all been cleaned up. The whole thing must have shattered in its frame—no wonder it made such a noise.

A glass was thrown, I'd guess, or something heavier. Bad luck to break a mirror.

I go back into the kitchen, wondering what to do. It is balmy this morning, the summer flaring out in a blaze of warmth.

I push open one of the French windows. There is a big wooden table and chairs, where I sit, opening up my laptop. I can jot down some more thoughts for the manuscript, in case Olivia asks again.

But I soon start to feel drowsy. I let myself slump back in my chair, feeling the sun on my face. I can hear the trickle of the radio from the kitchen and the rustle of the trees all around. It's so peaceful out here. I feel better than when I am in the house.

I drift off, and when I come to I can hear voices.

". . . no. That's just unreasonable." Olivia.

I hear a deeper voice reply—Josh—but I can't make out the words.

". . . you've decided to care about the cost now," says Olivia, "there's a very simple answer."

She must have woken me: her tone is irritated, sharp. They must be in the kitchen. No: overhead, in the upstairs hallway that looks over the terrace and garden.

I can't hear his reply, but then they must move close to a window again.

". . . lift a finger to help," says Olivia, "but you won't . . ."

Should I go in? But I don't want them to see me move and think I was eavesdropping.

". . . past it, if you ask me." Josh is clearer now, anger making his voice loud. "Just because someone knew your family doesn't mean you . . ."

I lose the rest. I wait a few more moments, keeping still.

It sounded like they were arguing about money. It must cost a lot, the upkeep on this place, and the staff. There is Annie, of course, and that man I saw the other day. Cav, the gardener.

I wake up my computer and start to type.

After a while, I am aware of people moving around in the kitchen, then someone pushes open one of the doors behind me. "Oh. Morning."

I turn round to see Josh, barefoot in jeans and a rumpled shirt.

"Morning. How's Olivia doing?"

"Fine," he says. "I think." He looks tired—hungover—and less than pleased to see me.

"Will she be down soon, do you reckon . . . ?"

"I don't know." He registers my laptop, remembers I am here to do a job. "Sab's just gone up to her office, wanted to see how she's doing. Best leave it for now, I'd say."

"Of course. Her call," I say to his departing back.

Bloody Sabrina. I turn back to the document on my

computer, trying to focus again on the few words in front of me, but my concentration is shot.

The sun has moved behind a cloud, too, and everything seems dimmed, as if the lights have been turned down. I think I'll go in myself now . . .

I see it in the corner of my vision: just a shape moving, before a clap loud as gunshot.

I jerk back, scrambling out of my chair so fast it goes flying, clattering sideways over the gray shards now scattered across the terrace.

My heart is thundering and I have to lean against the table. It was so near me, if it had been a few inches closer . . .

I hear footsteps running in the house.

"Are you all right?" Josh bursts onto the terrace and takes in the pieces of roof tile shattered around me. "It didn't touch you, did it?"

"No. No, I'm fine, honestly." I am breathing like I've run a mile.

Annie is out here now, too. "My goodness. I'd better get you a Band-Aid for that." She nods at my ankle—I reach down to touch the blood: a sharp piece must have nicked me.

"That looks nasty," says Josh, grimacing.

"Really, I'm OK. They're always so much bigger than you expect, roof tiles, up close," I say nonsensically. I feel a little shaky.

I look up at the roof. It isn't even windy.

Chapter 29

After Annie has brought me a Band-Aid and made me a cup of sugary tea, I am persuaded to lie down for a bit in my room. I look far too pale, she says.

But I don't fall asleep. I wait until everything is quiet, then I head out of my room. The upstairs hallway runs across the back of the house, its windows giving a view of the garden. They open over a small decorative roof that juts out a little over the terrace.

It's at the third window off the hallway that I see that one tile on the short roof below is oddly exposed because its neighbor is missing.

So I was right. That tile didn't fall from the main roof, it fell from here, within an arm's stretch of the open window.

I stay there a second, thinking. The pin in my lip balm, and now this . . .

I lean forward, lifting the iron strut that holds the window open, and pull it shut in its frame.

"Should you be up already?"

I turn: Annie is hovering behind me.

"I'm fine really," I say. "I don't want to make a fuss."

She nods. "If you're sure." But she doesn't go anywhere.

"Mrs. Hayes is very sorry," she says, as if by rote, "but she can't see you today."

"You mean right now, or all day?" There's a definite edge to my voice.

"All day, I think." She looks worried. "Should I check?" She half turns, as if to go back into Olivia's room, the door ajar down the other end of the hallway.

I shake my head. "Sorry—it's just tricky. Here I am . . ." I sigh. "It's a difficult situation."

Annie's professionalism thaws, just a little. She lowers her voice. "She doesn't seem right today. And she's getting all these phone calls. 'Business as usual,' she says, but . . ."

I sense an opening. "It must be tough. How do you find working for Olivia?"

"She's a wonderful employer," she says loyally. "Of all those I've worked for. This place is one of my favorites, the house, the family. Bea is a little poppet. Why, the other day, she said the funniest thing—"

"It must be hard though, for you, such a big house, and helping with the childcare, too. Olivia said something about it being difficult to get a nanny out here?" It is a little white lie—I am thinking of what Josh said in the night. "That the last one left."

She tuts. "Oh, these young girls." So she won't blame Olivia.

"And what about the gardener I saw around—has he worked here long?"

"Mr. Cavendish? If you call standing about with a rake 'work,'" she says primly. "That lawn is getting to be beyond a joke. But I suppose someone had to keep an eye on the house, while it was empty. Which reminds me," she says, turning to go, "*I* mustn't stand around wasting time."

I nod, distracted. I am thinking of what I heard Josh say, when he and Olivia were arguing before. *Just because someone knew your family* . . . He implied she was keeping someone on the payroll out of loyalty. And now I learn Cav has worked for her for years, at least since the house was empty. I wonder just how long exactly?

But then another thought occurs to me.

"Oh, Annie?" I call after her. She turns round slowly. "One more thing, sorry. Would you mind shutting my window if it rains when I'm out?" It's not going to rain, I know. "I want to leave it open to air the room— I'm so sensitive to smoke."

Annie frowns. "Now you haven't been smoking inside, have you?"

"Oh no. I'm not a smoker."

"Because we don't even have candles in the house," says Annie.

"No, I know. It's just"—I grimace—"I think someone *has* been smoking, down this end of the house?" Annie's eyes follow mine to one of the doors off the hallway. "Maybe in one of the other guest rooms. I didn't want to bother Olivia . . ."

I don't know if Sabrina made that tile fall—or that anyone did, for certain. It would hardly be the act of a normal person.

Now Annie sniffs the air, testing.

Although, Sabrina was staying in the house on Tuesday night, too, when I got scratched by that needle in my wash bag. And I'm almost sure she had slipped away earlier when we were having dinner with Olivia and Josh . . .

"I can smell it myself now," says Annie, her mouth a grim line.

But what I have no doubt about is that Sabrina blocked me from talking to Olivia, when I wanted to go to her last night. That woman is getting in my way.

"Leave it to me," says the housekeeper.

I nod. That's just what I hoped she'd say.

Chapter 30

I know my way now to the lane where Joey Crompton and his grandmother live. But I drive straight past their cottage and park at the end of the row.

With no prospect of talking to Olivia today, I am going to try Pete Gregory, the policeman Joey told me about. I couldn't find a phone number, so I am going to do what I should have done already, rather than rely on Marie Crompton. Knock on his door.

On the doorstep, I go over again what I know, what is driving me forward. Not much, on the face of it. The sound of a gunshot. The fact that Alex Vane didn't call the emergency services. His money problems—of a sort.

But it's more than that . . . it's that feeling I have about that house. That something bad happened there.

And that I am not wanted. It is easier to admit, when I am out of there. That I am getting scared . . .

The man who opens the door is tall and solid in a blue sweater and old cords, if starting to stoop a little. The house behind him feels more traditional than

Marie's, with dark wood furniture and a doily under the tulips on the hall table.

"Mr. Gregory? I'm Nicky Wilson. I wondered if I could have a word. About a fire that happened around here a long time ago . . ."

He looks at me, then steps back from the door.

Sunk in a soft floral couch, I am giving my usual spiel about working with Olivia. I mention that I met Joey Crompton, Marie's grandson, who told me that Mr. Gregory was the police officer—I am not sure of his rank then—in charge around here at the time of the fire. The old policeman, sitting opposite me in his arm-chair, nods at that.

I am being more open than I have been, conscious of his background. I tell him the truth: there are things about the fire that seem odd to me, that I am struggling to understand.

I can't read his expression. Some things must stick when they leave the police.

"Well, I don't mind answering a few questions," he says finally, "best not to quote me though."

"That's fine," I say, "thanks so much." I pull out my notepad and pen; I doubt he will want to be recorded.

I couldn't find out much about him online. The most recent mention was in the Mansford paper—he was doing a half-marathon for charity—which gave his potted bio.

The former police inspector spearheaded
Mansford Rural Watch during a career that
spanned more than three decades. Since
retiring, he has held voluntary roles with
organizations advising them on rural crime-
fighting schemes and worked on domestic
violence campaigns . . .

But I couldn't find anything linking him to the fire,
and I tell him as much, in case he thinks I have not
done my research.

He just laughs. "The big boys took over when the
cameras turned up. Old Albright kept giving press con-
ferences outside, when there was nothing new to say."
He harrumphs. "But he ended up chief constable, so he
knew how to play the game, didn't he?"

I smile. "So what would your role have been at the
time?"

"Well, let's see . . ." He rubs his shiny freckled head
with one hand. "It was before I was moved to Chester
for a few years. So back then I was the PC looking
after things around here, pretty much on my own."

"So you would have been the first police officer on
the scene, being based nearby?"

"Ah, one of them, maybe. No one could get near the
house for hours, of course. And then they had to secure
the walls, I remember, before we could enter . . ."

And he's off, explaining the process, giving me
snippets of gossip about the personalities under the
uniforms and white suits. But soon I have the impression he is more interested in settling old scores than
sharing details of the fire.

". . . truth is, the major investigation lot can be a tad
high-handed. They didn't want me anywhere near. As-

sumed all I dealt with out here was the odd stolen pony—"

"And Olivia's parents, Alex and Elsa? Did you know them well?"

"What?" He doesn't like my interruption. "No, but I knew of them. Nice couple, good-looking, everything going for them."

"It must have been a difficult scene to investigate."

He snorts. "Standard house fire. Clear as could be."

"It was?"

"Bloke fell asleep with a cigarette in his hand—maybe he'd had a drink or two, the family away—and it went up like a tinderbox."

"But didn't they consider it could have been started deliberately?"

"Of course. That was checked out, as standard. By the insurers, too, who paid out. Which tells you something." He chuckles. "You see, there are some telltale signs when a fire's no accident—if it starts in more than one place, if you find traces of accelerants . . ."

"Accelerants?"

"Petrol, something to speed the flames up—but there was none of that. And no motive to burn the place down," he adds, pointedly.

"OK . . . but didn't some money go missing, at the house, around that time?"

He looks at me, his head cocked to one side. "There was a bit of unpleasantness with one of the staff, now you mention it, but that all got smoothed over."

I lean forward. "Did anyone get sacked? Might they have had a grudge against Vane? Set a fire maliciously, that got out of hand . . ."

"No, no," he says easily. "The money turned up, all

a misunderstanding. Certainly never got to be a police matter."

"How did you know about it then?"

He looks amused at my effort to catch him out. "It's a village. People talk."

I press on, trying not to get flustered. "I also know that the body was very badly burned, that they couldn't work out exactly what the cause of death was. So no one would have been able to tell, say, if there was a gunshot wound."

"A gunshot wound?" he asks mildly. "And just who's shooting who, here?"

"Well, if Vane killed himself, let's just say." That's what Sam Gibbons assumed when he heard the gunshot.

"Why on earth would he do that?"

"Or even," I hesitate, thinking about Joey's suggestion Vane upset someone he shouldn't—I might as well say it—"if someone else was present . . ."

He sighs tiredly. "Of course there were rumors. Always are. But that doesn't mean they're not cruel and unnecessary." He pauses. "And unwarranted."

It's the moment to pull out my trump card. "Well, I appreciate that. But I know that Alexander Vane didn't call for help that night—that the 999 call came from a neighbor, Sam Gibbons—and that Vane could have had access to guns. And Sam is absolutely certain that what he heard that night was a gunshot."

The old policeman is very still. As the silence stretches on, he keeps looking at me, his pale eyes unblinking, and I feel my heart start to race.

"All right," he says finally, and I realize that I am a little afraid of what he will say. "I might as well tell you, after all these years."

He pauses, and suddenly I know that this is it, at last. I am getting somewhere.

"Yes, we found a gun."

Chapter 31

"**Y**ou found a gun?" My voice is filled with horror.

For a terrible moment, I think Pete Gregory is crying: then he leans back in his chair and I see he is shaking not with tears, but with silent laughter.

"Oh," he wipes his eyes with his handkerchief. "I am sorry. Your face . . . Yes, there were guns. I could tell you even now, Alex Vane had four, including, let me see, a lovely Purdey 12-bore." I try not to look blank.

"I'd have to check the rest," he continues comfortably, "but everything was documented just as it should be. He liked shooting, nothing wrong with that. I've bagged a few pheasant in my time, too." His look seems to challenge me to object.

"But did you check if any of the guns been shot recently?"

"Course we checked." He holds my eye contact. "They were still locked in their cupboard fixed to the wall in an outhouse, but forensics were all over that."

"Sam Gibbons was very insistent that he heard a gun go off. *Before* he saw the fire."

"Ah well. Far be it from me to suggest that a man could be confused about what woke him up in the middle of the night . . ." his voice drips with irony. "But we knew what the bang was: the heating oil stored in the garage went up when the fire reached it. I saw the thing it was kept in—the whole side was bent out. As for Sam hearing it *before* he saw the flames—well, the houses weren't that close. Makes sense that he couldn't see the fire until it had really taken hold."

I am frowning, making sure I follow. He has answers for everything.

"Of course," he says, more quietly, "there were things that weren't made public then. That man shouldn't have died." He sounds angry, for the first time. "Why didn't Alexander Vane call 999? I knew why."

"You do?" Finally, am I getting somewhere?

"Because the fire engines had to come all the way from Mansford—he knew his house would be gone before they even got there. I'd bet he tried to put it out himself. The state of the resources out here." He shakes his head regretfully. "But that's all done now . . . Sam Gibbons!" he says more cheerfully. "Now that's a name I haven't heard for a while, anyway. How is he? Not much of a countryman," he continues without a break. "Got on to me about the cockerel down the road when they moved here, wanted me to 'do something about it.'" He laughs softly. "Townies."

I feel like the insult could be directed at me, as much as Sam.

I stand up. I am done now, all my leads frustrated.

"Well. I really am grateful." I might as well be polite.

He gets up, relaxed as ever. "Not a problem." Relaxed and yet somehow . . . watchful.

Yes that's right, I decide, as I put away my notepad. I just got the sense he was paying more attention than he let on. Once a policeman . . . old habits die hard.

And for me, too, as a ghostwriter. Hoisting my bag over my shoulder, I scan the photos lined up on the mantelpiece behind him, register a row of young smiling faces, his grandkids surely, so he's a family man . . .

He stands up in front of them, breaking my sight-line.

"There is something else I should mention, before you leave." His expression is grave. "You mentioned Joey Crompton. Everything all right there?"

"Yes," I say, surprised. "I know he's a bit—awkward . . ."

He nods. "Now, I hope I've cleared a few things up for you, and that's why I agreed to talk to you. But I'm going to give you a friendly word of warning about that young man, if he has encouraged you to think there was something untoward about that fire. Did he tell you why he had to move out here in the first place, to live with Marie?"

My face says no, and I know I am not going to like this at all.

"Arson. Joey likes to set fires."

I walk down the path quickly, as the door shuts behind me.

"Hey, Nicky!" I keep going, my head down, and there's another shout from the road: "Nicky!"

It's Joey. I can see him out of the corner of my eye as he jogs over—he must have seen me, or my car, from his house.

He catches up with me as I reach my car door. "Didn't you hear me calling?"

I look away, then at him. "What do you want, Joey?" I say neutrally.

"Have you just come out of there? Pete Gregory's?"

I nod.

"I thought we were going to see him together," he says, aggrieved.

"Yes. That was the plan, wasn't it?"

He looks unsure, picking up on my tone. "So, did he tell you anything good?"

"Not really. But is there anything *you* want to tell me?"

"What's that supposed to mean?"

"Do you really have to ask?"

For a moment we bristle like two dogs ready to fight, then he starts to back away. "Sod this," he mutters, and turns round.

At that my temper flares. "Because he did tell me something about you!" I call out. "That you're an arsonist."

He stops. "Oh, that," he says weakly. His shoulders droop a little.

"Oh, that," I mimic. "You didn't think you might mention it? I don't know, before I tell an ex-policeman that you said I should talk to him about a massive house fire?"

He turns back to face me. "I wasn't sure he'd know about me. That all happened when I was still at my mum and dad's. And it's not like . . . I mean, I never hurt anyone." He lifts his chin, defiant. "I don't see what that has to do with anything. It was ages ago."

"Oh no. Nothing at all. Except it made me look like a crank. And when I said I didn't believe him, he told me I could check with your grandmother!" After the session with Gregory, that amused dismissal on his doorstep was the final, humiliating straw.

"I'm sorry," he offers. "Don't say anything to her. I could talk to him, explain you didn't know . . ."

"For God's sake," I say under my breath. "I'm not wasting any more time on this."

"Hey—no—I *did* think that fire was weird! That something else happened there that night. I do have history in that area, I know . . ."

I say cruelly: "I bet you wish you started it."

He looks crestfallen.

I make an effort to be adult. "Look, Joey. If I'd known . . . it's my fault as much as yours. I shouldn't have gotten you involved."

"We can sort this out . . ."

"Good-bye, Joey."

I get in my car and slam the door. In my rearview mirror, he just stands there, a tall, thin figure by the side of the road. I don't look back again.

My anger stays high as I set off for Olivia's house. No wonder Joey didn't want to just turn up on the old policeman's doorstep without his gran putting in a word. I was lucky he didn't kick me out as soon I mentioned Joey's name. And of course! Another knot in this tangle untwists. That's why Joey's grandmother has been so unhelpful. Marie must have thought it was a terrible idea, to pique his interest in fires again.

But I am upset with myself as much as with Joey, for listening to him in the first place, letting myself get carried away.

I really thought I was getting somewhere for a moment, before the policeman laughed at me. But I've gotten nowhere, have I? I've hit a brick wall.

And, if I am honest, I am increasingly embarrassed.

Because what did I have to present to Pete Gregory, really, but rumors and half-baked theories and a *feeling* that there is a story here? The whole sorry mess collapsed like wet papier-mâché after just one sensible conversation.

Even Olivia's coldness, her hostility . . . yes, she is protective of her past, her pain. But that doesn't mean there is any mystery here.

It is time to be rational. Sensible. The truth is I have conjured a story out of smoke and ashes—and now it is drifting away with the wind.

By the time I arrive back at the house, I am too fed up to try to persuade Olivia to talk to me again. What a waste of time this week is turning out to be.

Chapter 32

The rest of Thursday stretches dully into the evening, as I sit hunched over my laptop in my bedroom. There is no point in moping. I need to get something together to show Olivia before I go. But the writing is a struggle. Something is not clicking . . .

When someone knocks on my door, I am surprised to see Olivia with a tray of food: crackers, paté, a glass of wine. I didn't realize what time it was, but it is getting dark outside.

"Thanks," I say. "That's thoughtful of you."

"Annie thought you would be hungry. I won't bother with a meal myself, Josh is out . . ." She looks tired, blue-gray shadows under her eyes. "I'm sorry that we've not had another session today."

"That's OK," I say. "Do you think you'll be ready for one tomorrow?"

"Let's make a call in the morning. If you don't mind."

I nod, resigned. "Of course."

Tomorrow is Friday, the end of the working week. If Olivia doesn't want to give me any time, I'll be off first thing, promising to continue our sessions over Skype. I can be home by the afternoon.

The thought soothes me, as I get ready for bed: this is my last night in this house.

When I wake, sweating, it takes me a second to realize where I am.

I was dreaming, I am almost sure of it, but I never remember my dreams. I breathe into the darkness, waiting for my pulse to slow, and glance at the screen of my phone: 3:14 a.m. I shouldn't have had that wine: I always sleep badly after alcohol.

Or was that definitely what woke me?

I still, straining to hear. The house is old—or its foundations are, at least—and it is always settling and groaning at night. I've had enough of it. I can't relax.

I try to make my mind go blank, to lull myself back to sleep, but it's impossible, the day's events crowding in on me—and my thoughts start to run on familiar paths, replaying the interview with Pete Gregory, that encounter with Joey outside.

Maybe I shouldn't have been quite so harsh. But if it hadn't been for Joey, telling me how he'd had to take his photos of the house down, suggesting that there was something more to the fire, loving my interest, the attention . . .

I should have known he was unreliable. Unstable, even.

All that effort, only to hit a brick wall.

In the darkness, my tired mind starts to wander, making odd dreamy connections.

Joey's photos showed bare brick walls, before they

were covered in plaster and paint and wallpaper again, so you'd never know . . . *if these walls could talk.*

I prop myself on one elbow, the thought not yet fully formed.

Then I flick on the bedside light, swing myself out of bed, and go over to my suitcase. I unzip the pocket, pulling out the sheaf of Joey's photos that told me nothing.

But that's not what I'm looking for now. I want the piece of paper at the back, the floor plan, from the planning application for the restoration work. The one that Joey annotated to show where he had taken his photos in the wreckage of the house.

I barely glanced at it before. Why would I? I was there in the house. Everything was right in front of me. But I wonder now if he might have posted the floor plan on his website along with the photos.

Yes, on balance, I think he would have; he is thorough. So this is the floor plan that the Vanes got him to take down, along with the photos.

No, not the family, I correct myself, Olivia was the one rebuilding. She would have been the Vane named on the application. Of course she wouldn't want those horrible photos made public. But was there anything else she didn't want strangers to see?

I stand there for a moment, in the dim light of the lamp, looking at the neat little diagrams of each floor—just the walls and spaces, very basic. Squares and lines.

Then I start to walk to the door. Because I see it now, what I missed before.

* * *

It is darker than the other night, the moon behind clouds. I know my way, where things should be, but still my mind makes strange shapes out of the shadows around me. So I am already tense as I try to creep down the stairs without a noise.

I relax, just a little, when I finally make it to the kitchen at the end of the house, knowing any sounds I make will be more muffled from those sleeping above. I turn to check behind me, but no one is there in the dark hallway. No one has woken.

I'd better not turn on the kitchen lights, though; I don't want company.

And now I pull open the cellar door, because this is where I have been going all along, take another step— and my foot connects with nothing but air.

Idiot. I steady myself on the doorframe, my heart pounding. It's so dark in here that I misjudged where the stairs were. I could have broken my neck.

I fumble for the cellar light switch, flustered now. Wasn't there one just this side of the doorframe itself, on the kitchen wall, and—

Yes, there it is, just where it was supposed to be.

I click it on, the brightness so dazzling that it takes a split second to focus on what's in front of me.

The face is white as paper, eyes like black holes, hanging three feet from my own.

Chapter 33

I recoil, throwing myself backward so I hit the open cellar door, sending it banging against the wall with a thud, even as I am realizing what I am looking at.

It's just a clown mask, Halloween gear, hanging by its elastic from a shelf in front of me. There is a Santa hat, too, a loop of fairy lights, other decorations stored down here—I saw them all before. I just forgot they were here and my brain translated the face as something quite different, a threat.

My heart is still thundering, the pulse beating in my ears, and I take a moment to re-compose myself, listening to see if anyone in the house has woken.

I hear nothing. But I make myself wait a little longer.

Then I take the first step, pulling the door to behind me, so that just a thin strip of light from the cellar cuts across the kitchen floor. I can't quite bring myself to shut it. Then I go down the stairs, gripping the banister to my left. At the bottom, under the bare bulb, I look at the paper in my shaking hand.

* * *

It is easy to miss at a glance.

The sheet of paper shows four shapes: the first two—the main floor and the upstairs floor—follow the same sprawling footprint. The attic space is a smaller set of boxes, while another diagram shows the cellar layout: three rooms, off this little hallway.

And that's it, but for a little detail—a line of dots in a square that someone has barely bothered to mark on the floor of the biggest cellar room. A place like this is full of nooks and crannies, after all.

But I understand what it means now. That there is another space down here, deep in the heart of the house. I just have to find the way in.

I know there are no stairs or doors or anything like that, from when I looked around before. And as I go into the room, the one with the table tennis table and dartboard, I still can't see how . . .

Then I remember how I noticed before that the carpet doesn't go right to the walls. And when I bend down to lift its edge, it comes away easily. I roll it back a few yards to expose an old brick floor: small thin bricks in a herringbone pattern, so smooth and shiny with age that I am sure they were not part of any rebuild.

I'm inside the old house, I think, the house that burned down.

The door should be about here, but the plans are rough. So I shuffle the table back, to clear the way—I am sweating now, despite the chill in the air—then roll the carpet back farther until I see the dark wood blackened by age, or perhaps smoke. *Age*, I tell myself.

I haul the carpet all the way off it. There is a metal ring set toward one side of the trapdoor, cool to the touch.

I expect resistance as I pull, but it swings open easily, the hinges silent. I stop it from banging against the table, resting the open door against one metal leg.

I can smell earth and damp inside, but can't see anything except steep wooden steps, almost a ladder, and a patch of bare earthen floor. I wish I had brought my phone with me for its flashlight setting. I didn't think this through.

But this is OK. There will be plenty of light from the bulb overhead. Before I can spook myself further, I turn around and descend the wooden steps as quickly as I can, feeling the grain of each smooth, flat board under my hands.

As my bare feet touch the ground I spin around, braced for another surprise, as my eyes adjust to the dimness—but find nothing but bricks and the earthen floor.

It is cold in here. It's just a little space, the arched walls the same neat herringbone brick as the floor above: I could almost touch the sides if I stretched my arms out wide.

An old wine cellar? There is nothing in here now but an old cardboard box, pulled an inch or two away from the walls so the damp can't seep in.

A wide strip of brown masking tape holds the top folds down. I unpeel it carefully, but it has long ago lost its stickiness . . .

The light overhead flickers for a second.

I look up, holding my breath.

Everything is still. But I want to hurry, I am going have to bend the cardboard folds a little, they are slotted around each other . . .

And I can smell something—can I be imagining it? But it is there, so faint. The acrid tang, thin as a ghost, of smoke and fire.

Careless now, I tear open the box.

Chapter 34

There is not much in it. Just junk, on the face of it. But my heart starts to thud as I sift through the contents.

A set of small wooden bowling pins. A small badminton racket. These must have been kept outside. A white mug printed with a Disney princess has come through almost unscathed, but for the long cracks in its glazing—it must have been found among the rubble inside the house. And here is a book that I pick up carefully: a children's Bible, its blackened edges stuck together.

I knew that photo album, pieced together by other people, couldn't be all Olivia had left of her life before. This is what I couldn't find when I searched the house above me—these old secrets, hidden below . . .

I freeze, lifting my head. Did I hear something, feel something in the air—a breeze? All the hairs on my arms are standing up.

But nothing changes.

I turn back to the box. I suppose the focus after the fire would have been to retrieve any valuables that survived, jewelry, or silverware. So I wonder who collected all this, things with only sentimental value, if that. It's like no one has looked at them since . . .

Gingerly I lift up one of the bowling pins: underneath is an old soccer ball, still holding air. But there is something else under that, chunky under my fingertips.

I pull it out: it's a small silver frame. The glass protecting the photo is smeared with dirt, but I can see the family inside. Why isn't this in the album upstairs?

I fiddle with the metal fastenings at the back, stiff with age, and open it up.

It is a lovely family shot, as they all were before the fire. Elsa and Alex, him smiling, golden, her all big dark eyes; and between them a young Olivia, maybe ten or so, a black velvet bow in her hair, and—

It must be a movement in the corner of my eye that makes me look up, because I didn't hear a sound. The trapdoor swings toward me, shutting out the light.

I shoot my hands up to catch the underside of the trapdoor before it slams shut completely, stretching to hold it open. For a second, I expect to feel pressure against it. Then, driven by instinct, I clamber up the steps quick as I can, one hand keeping the door open, to see . . .

No one is there.

I shouldn't have left it propped open like that, leaning against the table leg. Lucky I caught it—I don't know how easy it would be to open from the inside.

I shiver, wanting to get out of there right away. But I make myself arrange the door so it can't swing shut again, then go back down to replace things as they were.

I dropped the frame when I caught the trapdoor, and

the glass cracked—so I thrust it to the bottom of the box facedown, then fold the soft cardboard back into place, arranging the tape on top as if it came loose. It's the best I can do.

Then I scramble up the steps again, shut the trapdoor, roll out the carpet, and push the table back. I am standing back, checking how it all looks, when I hear it: the faint moan that I register as the hinge of the cellar door at the top of the stairs as it swings slowly back toward its frame.

But that's OK, too. There wasn't a Yale lock or anything that would click shut . . .

And then, with the softest of plinks, all the lights go out.

The darkness is total. I can't see anything, not even the hand I bring to my face. The switch was on the wall outside the cellar, to control all the lights, but did I see any down here, too? There must be one in each room, surely . . .

I start to walk around the edge of the room, one hand on the cold wall to orient myself. I just need to find the doorway, and then I will be in the hall, the stairs over to my left.

Who turned off the lights?

Don't think about that. Maybe they were on a timer.

But my breathing sounds too loud in the pitch black, and it takes longer than I expect to find the doorway out of the room: wasn't there just this one wall here, not this corner, too? I don't feel a switch anywhere.

If only I had left a light on above in the kitchen, to signal where the edge of the cellar door might be. But it's OK, I've found the doorway of this room now, so it's just a few steps more to the cellar stairs.

I slide my feet forward carefully, remembering the stuff stacked in the little hall, but still I knock into something, the jangle of gears and chains telling me it's a bicycle.

They surely can't hear me, upstairs in their bedroom, but I am fast-forwarding to my embarrassment, my cheeks flushing, as Olivia and Josh listen with polite bemusement to my excuses . . .

Better that than getting stuck in here.

Shut up, shut up.

I stop for a second to try to figure out where I am. But I hate this darkness, so thick it's almost a living, pulsing thing against me.

I put my hands out a little in front of me, and shuffle to the left. I can't bring myself to stretch them out properly, afraid to touch something I don't expect . . .

Then—*oh thank you God*—one foot hits something hard: the bottom step. I put out my right hand and fumble for the banister, and there it is, relief is flooding through me, *I'm nearly out of here*, and I relax enough to let out a shuddering sigh, almost a gasp. I didn't want to admit how scared I was, lost in the bowels of the old house—

And that's when I hear it: soft, but crystal-clear.

Someone sighs back at me.

Chapter 35

I break—*someone is in here with me*—and I am running headlong up the flight of steps and reaching for the door, fumbling for the handle.

It isn't locked; I slam it open and I am out of the dark kitchen and through the hallway, round and up the main stairs as quick as I can, my speed born of sheer fear, and I am almost at my room when—

"What on earth is going on?"

Olivia is behind me, wrapping her dressing gown around her, feet bare, her hair mussed by sleep.

"What's all this noise?"

I can't think for a second, adrenaline still driving me.

"I was downstairs—getting a drink—and I heard something."

"You heard something?" she says.

I make an effort to control myself, out of breath. "I thought I heard something."

"Well, do you think someone is down there? Should I wake Josh?" She sounds confused.

I look at her, a pale figure in the darkness. The moonlight from the hallway windows is behind her, so I can't see her expression.

"No, don't wake him," I say finally. "I'm sorry. I must have been mistaken."

And then I go into my room, shutting the door on her. There is a key on the inside, I haven't bothered locking it before.

Now I do.

I check the bathroom and the wardrobe, old habits I thought I'd left behind in childhood, then climb into bed, huddling the duvet round me.

Now that I am safe in my room again, I am angry with myself, even ashamed. Because I lost it. I was only on those cellar stairs for a second before I bolted. It *felt* like longer, as I waited to feel a cold finger reaching for me, breath on my neck.

Did I really hear what I thought I heard?

Yes. Whoever it was must have been right up next me, close enough to touch.

And I know what I should have done. I should have turned round at the top of the stairs, I should have switched on the lights and exposed whoever followed me down there, whoever was trying to scare me, whoever—because this is what I think now—shut the trapdoor, and left me in the dark.

That was my chance. I could have faced my fears and maybe even got to the heart of what is happening in this house. But I didn't.

And now images flash through my mind: Olivia, a

white figure on the landing; Josh, drinking alone in the dark; Sabrina, standing over me, *I'm very protective of her*; and, hidden in the garden, the stone marker for Alexander Vane. *You shouldn't be looking there* . . .

I shudder, thoroughly spooked now. Someone *died* in this house.

No. Stop it. The dead can't hurt you. And there is that back staircase, isn't there, so someone could move about the house unseen . . .

And I have what I wanted. I pull the photo out, from where I tucked it in my pajama pocket, before I hid its smashed frame at the bottom of that box. I wanted it to look at it properly, in a good light.

The colors are faded, but it is intact. It was in a bedroom upstairs, maybe, protected from the falling debris and water hoses by its metal frame and glass cover. So did she forget it was in that box? I think again of that patched-together album downstairs, and hold the photo under the bedside lamp, wanting to take in every detail.

It must have been taken at Christmas. To one side a huge dark tree is just visible, wrapped in beads and baubles. And they're standing in the big formal sitting room just off the main hall, I recognize the mantelpiece now, thick garlands of greenery sweeping from it over the fireplace. That's a fire risk—not that that would matter, in the end . . .

And that's when I realize exactly what is hanging over the mantelpiece, in the room where they found the body. And now I see why this photo is not in any album, or on show anywhere. Because it is clear what that is, the only thing it could be . . .

Not locked away in a cupboard. Not checked by forensics. Not accounted for by police. Not accounted for by anyone.

Yet there it is, hanging over the family's heads: its two long barrels shining, its wooden stock gleaming. A gun.

Chapter 36

When it starts to get light, I get up and slip the photo from under my pillow and put it into my suitcase, with Joey's photos and the floor plan. I haven't slept yet, still full of adrenaline, but, reassured somehow by the lightening sky, I drop off for a few hours.

When I wake, the same thoughts are still running through my mind, as if on repeat.

The gun looks old: rich shining wood and decorative metalwork. An heirloom—it could have been in the family for years. But old doesn't mean broken, does it?

You might even like to keep a gun in the house, loaded for pests and . . . anything else.

Sam Gibbons thought there were poachers about, but then I think how *Mr. Vane*, the newspaper said, *has adopted the role of squire, embracing countryside sports . . .*

I keep thinking, too, of Rafferton, in his antiques shop, explaining how after the fire, Elsa had never come back. *Simply couldn't face it.*

Then Josh, drunk in the kitchen the other night,

rambling about his wife. *You know she wouldn't even go to the funeral? Has she told you that?*

Whose funeral? I'd asked. *Her father's—Alex's?*

No, he'd replied . . .

He had talked about it like it was some awful thing, but why would that be—unless it was someone else's funeral that she absolutely should have gone to. Say, her mother's . . .

And finally I remember Olivia herself, talking about Elsa like she was a stranger.

Are you and your mother close now? I had asked.

Not exactly . . . She's dead.

But what might have split them apart long before that?

It crosses my mind again, as it did through the night, that I could alert the authorities. Surely this photo is enough to get them interested. I can hand all I know on to other people and step back to my own life. But the first thing to do is to leave here, so I can think everything through and stop just *reacting*. I just need to go.

Downstairs, I hear Olivia before I see her. "I don't care if Sabrina's upset, Josh. She's got to respect my house if she's staying under my roof."

I pause in the hallway to the kitchen, waiting for Josh to answer, but he doesn't. So Sabrina's in her bad books—it hardly matters now, but I can't say I'm not pleased.

"Morning," I say brightly, from the kitchen doorway.

Even if I hadn't heard Olivia, it would be obvious

I'd walked in on something from the way they are facing off. Josh breaks first, turning to lean on the counter, his head down.

"Well, I think I'm going to set off soon," I say.

"You're going?" says Olivia.

"I thought with everything that's going on you wouldn't want to do a session today," I say bluntly. "We can pick it up again over the phone. I'll e-mail over the sample chapters later."

Something in her face flickers. "Nicky . . . let me think, we can still have a session. Let's say early afternoon, we've guests coming later."

"Are you serious—after all this?" says Josh, turning to look at her.

"Everyone is coming," she says calmly. "They're not on these forums. And they're always telling me how little they know about what I do."

Josh doesn't say anything.

"Well, it's tricky," I say. "It's a long drive, and the traffic will be bad as it's Friday . . ."

Now that I have a plan, I don't really want to change it.

Olivia looks thoughtful. "You're right. You should stay for dinner."

I look at her, puzzled, and she continues: "You'd be very welcome. And now we're one short. You'd be doing us a favor. Wouldn't she, Josh?"

His manners kick in after a beat. "Yes, of course." He walks out, clearly still angry.

So they're missing a guest. It could be anyone, but I would bet money that Sabrina's husband, Leo, is the no-show again, after I was drafted in to cover him in their tennis match. It doesn't take a genius to work out there's something going on with their marriage: he does not seem keen to be reconciled with his wife.

"But I haven't brought anything to wear to a dinner party." I say, as a last-ditch excuse. I am guessing the dress code will not be jeans and a sweater.

Olivia looks amused. "You've seen my wardrobe. And then we can wrap up the sessions, finish the week with everything done, like we planned."

She brushes invisible crumbs off the counter into her hand and tips them into the sink. "I've a few things to be getting on with. I told people to start coming from seven." She turns back to me. "So, can we meet at say, four?"

"Four it is, then."

"And Nicky?"

I turn round, already at the door.

"I'm going to talk about it. It's out there now. I'm going to talk about what happened to my family."

I go back upstairs, a little bewildered at the change in plans. But it makes sense, to hear what she has to say. It was what I wanted, wasn't it?

And the panic of the night is receding rapidly. The way Olivia and Josh were bickering just then, it was so normal. If you'd seen someone snooping in your own house, wouldn't you just call them out? And now Olivia is opening up to me, too.

I can picture it now: what must have happened. Sabrina hearing me going past her door last night, following me downstairs. The woman must be cracking up—like her relationship. If she says anything to Olivia about what I was doing in the cellar, I will have explain it away. But maybe I needn't have felt *quite* so scared . . .

I spot a missed call and voice mail on my phone screen, interrupting my thoughts. Joey.

Chapter 37

He doesn't bother to introduce himself on the voice mail, launching straight in.

"OK, it was just something I got interested in when I was twelve, thirteen, how fires began. So I started a few in the garden, but that got old, so I went off into the countryside. I ended up setting a whole field on fire, and no one knew it was me, until I told some of the kids at school. I suppose I thought it might impress them . . . then the police turned up at my door."

He carries on: "I haven't done anything like *that* for a long time. They said, actually, photography might be a very good hobby for me, that was how I got into it. Gran just worries what people might think. So can we meet?"

I click delete, then stand there for a second. I'm not angry with Joey, not anymore. But he has given me an idea.

"Joey's been very upset," Marie Crompton says, setting a cup of tea in front of me.

She looked surprised to see me at her door. Her grandson was out, she told me—but she let me in when I said it was her I was hoping to talk to. Just a quick word.

"I'm sure he is upset," I say now. "But Marie, I've been a little upset with you, for suggesting that Sam Gibbons was dead. When he was very much alive and kicking."

She looks away. "I just thought it was best not to stir things up. Joey can get very single-minded, and I didn't want him to get caught up in that . . . that horrible fire, of all things. But I am sorry if it caused you any trouble."

"I appreciate that. And now I understand why you didn't want to talk about the Vanes, the other day. But can I ask you about them, without Joey here?"

"I suppose . . ."

I don't see the point of being anything other than direct now. "I know that Olivia and her mother weren't close. And something someone mentioned to me . . . am I right that she didn't even go to Elsa's funeral?"

She nods, thoughtful.

"Do you know why?"

She purses her lips. "I can guess. Grief does funny things to people. But it was indecent, how Elsa behaved after the fire. Taking little Alex and waltzing off without Olivia. Packed her off to her grandmother, didn't she?"

"Her grandmother?"

"Old Mrs. Vane, in London. Who was a cold fish, from what I've heard of her, though I shouldn't speak ill of the dead. So Olivia could go to a posh new school down there, they said. But it wasn't right."

"What was she like—Elsa?"

No one has really given me a sense of how they saw her, the way that they have with golden, charming Alex. There's a blank where she should be.

"Well, it's hard to say." She sniffs. "Her ladyship didn't get involved with anything in the village; even when everyone's children were at the primary school together. Preferred to waft around up there in her big house."

"So she kept herself to herself."

"Well, I wouldn't like to . . . but no. Let's just say, she wasn't a woman's woman." She raises her eyebrows meaningfully.

It takes me a second to interpret. "You mean—she liked men a bit too much?"

"So they said. Gave that poor husband of hers quite the runaround. But she liked money more, and he had enough of that."

"Who she's supposed to have—would you know?"

"Oh no, it wouldn't have been around here. They'd go off to London, there'd be parties, vacations, I suppose. . . . Then, after the fire, she just took off." She shakes her head. "So there was talk. But I didn't agree with that, either, for all her faults."

"Because she was seen driving away, hours before it happened. So it was nothing to do with her, really," I say, slowly.

"Well, quite." Marie is surprised by the suggestion that it could have been anything but that. "Of course not."

"Of course not. Marie, this shortbread is amazing. What *do* you do to get it like that?"

We chat until I've finished my tea, then I thank her, meaning it, and she shows me out.

"And will you tell Joey you're not annoyed?" she asks, hesitant. "He doesn't have a lot of friends out here."

"I will." Feeling awkward, I pick up a photo on the hall table: Joey at primary school, one lick of sandy hair sticking up. "He was very sweet."

"He still is," she says, her face brightening. "Now, that was taken when he was, ooh, six or seven . . ." I admire it dutifully. Grandparents love to show off their grandchildren, don't they? And something nudges at me, some memory . . . What it is?

As she opens the front door, I feel a pang of sympathy—for Marie, as well as Joey.

"Thanks again. And Marie?" I add impulsively. "When you see Joey, would you tell him"—I don't want to alarm her—"tell him, it's turning out to be a good week after all. Very productive. And I'll stop by tomorrow morning to say bye, on my way back to London."

Sitting in my car, I wait a second before setting off again. Because I've just remembered what Joey's photo reminded me of.

I was in Pete Gregory's front room, trying to look at the photos on the mantelpiece behind him. His grandkids, I thought then, a family man.

But I didn't really get to look properly, because he stood in my way, didn't he, blocking my gaze. So I only got a fleeting impression.

Young smiling faces. Freckles. Red curls.

And now I have one more place to go.

Chapter 38

"We're not open yet." Paul Bryant is outside his pub, moving a big metal canister, when I park up at the Bleeding Wolf.

"I know." I follow him in anyway. "I just hoped you might help me with something," I say, as he goes behind the bar. "Something that confused me a little."

"Go on."

"Did anyone else see Elsa's car passing through the village the day of the fire?"

"Anyone else? I don't know." He's not as friendly as the last time.

"OK. And when did you see the car?" I ask.

"I told you, didn't I? Around midday, I couldn't be exact."

"You did. But just one more thing, if you don't mind—a lot of cars go past here. Why did you remember hers, in particular?"

"I . . ." He closes his mouth then opens it again. "I've always had a good memory for cars."

"That makes sense." I glance behind me, checking something. "So what kind of car do I have?"

"What?"

"Humor me," I say pleasantly. "You saw me drive up. So what kind of car do I have?"

From where we are, I know he can't see it through the windows.

He is silent.

"Never mind the model, then. What color is it? That's easy."

"I'm not playing games—"

"It's a Fiat. Lemon. But I'd have given you yellow." He won't meet my eyes. "So why did you remember her car, that day? Because it was so late? Because Elsa Vane was driving so fast? Or because you had already seen the flames from the house?"

He laughs, but I hear the infinitesimal silence before he does.

"And when exactly did you see her—a while after midnight? It must have been about then," I continue thoughtfully. "When she was leaving the scene."

He shakes his head now. "You've lost the plot."

"Is your daughter here today?"

He looks at me, warily.

"You know, Emily's very lucky to get her coloring from your side of the family."

It's true: they're so striking, those freckles and red curls—and that's what finally connected her in my mind to those photos at Pete Gregory's.

The children in them are her sisters and brothers and cousins, I'm pretty sure. Maybe I'd have spotted her among them, if he hadn't stopped me from looking more closely.

"So what exactly is he to you, the policeman?" I say

now. "You don't share a surname. He's not your dad. Your mum's brother?" I watch his face closely. "That's right, isn't it: he's your Uncle Pete. Which you were careful not to mention before."

What had he said the other day? . . . *when I told, uh, a police officer what I'd seen, he said it was useful. It could help them confirm that the family were absent. Thank God.*

But I bet I know who that policeman was. His uncle, Pete Gregory.

Paul is just standing there, listening to me. I don't think he knows what to do.

"So did Elsa actually pay Pete off, to cover it up? But," I say, remembering, "you said money was tight. So, did your parents get the money? Did you get a nice treat—"

"No!" he says. He leans forward on his arms. "I'm telling you to leave," he says, his voice full of controlled anger. "Right now. And don't come back."

"Fine. I'm going."

It doesn't matter if he is furious. His reaction lets me know I was on the right track with the rest. Of course he would have gone straight to his uncle, the policeman, with what he saw. I don't know exactly what inducement Pete Gregory got from Elsa to cover it up. But he is something of an intimidating man, even now. I can see why his nephew, then still a child, would have done what he was told.

And if young Paul Bryant was told to lie about what he saw that night . . . *when* he saw Elsa's car racing out of Annersley village . . . turning a red flag into an alibi . . .

That changes everything.

* * *

It is like a line of dominoes, I think, as I drive back to the house. Knock one over, then they all start to fall.

I couldn't check earlier, with Josh and Olivia in there, but now the kitchen and living room are empty. And there, round the corner, is the painting that I admired before, tucked away behind the bookshelf in the living room.

It is beautiful, this scene of the silver lake and the willow tree, but now I know that is not what drew me to it—what nagged at me.

"*It's getting a bit wild down there,*" said Josh. "*Cav needs to do something about it.*"

He's right. I have been down there in the garden myself: seen the tree, huge and vast, sweeping over the water.

But that's not what I see on the canvas in front of me. I didn't realize before, what was wrong: the painted willow is young and green, only a few meters tall. It must have been painted years, decades, ago.

Which now makes me wonder. How did this painting survive the fire?

I saw the devastation in Joey's pictures, saw what few sad items were saved in the box in the cellar. The antiques specialist, Rafferton, confirmed it to my face: oil paints burn.

And yet this canvas doesn't have a scratch on it; the colors are still bright and fresh.

There could be an explanation. Maybe it wasn't in the house at the time of the fire; maybe it was painted by a guest with an arty bent, and given to the family afterward, as a sad memento. I remember what Olivia said about it: "*Sentimental value only.*"

There is no signature on the painting itself to tell me where it came from. No date, either, but there is something I want to check . . .

Because maybe it *was* in the house. And maybe, I think now, as I lift the painting off its hook, someone moved it to keep it safe that night, before the flames could seize it. Someone took it off the wall, and jammed it in the back of a car, maybe . . .

Carefully I turn the painting over. The brown paper on the back of the frame is peeling, but there is some writing in pencil in the top right-hand corner. The painter has dated her work, in elegant looping writing.

June 1989. Years before the fire.

And somehow I know, even before I decipher the signature below, what it will say. Because who would want to save this painting from a burning house? Who left and never came back? And whose daughter turned her back on her forever?

Elsa Vane.

I take some time upstairs to let it all sink in. Feeling the need to do something routine, sensible, I have been packing my things, folding clothes, ready for my departure tomorrow. Soon the thought no longer feels so foreign.

Elsa did it.

Beautiful, mysterious Elsa.

How did Olivia put it? *Artistic temperament. Great highs and lows.*

Volatile, you could say.

I've tried to picture it: an act done in the white heat of passion, surely. There must have been an argument— a confrontation—before she went too far, reached for the gun on the wall—and it went off. Maybe she didn't even know it was loaded, was making another dramatic gesture. I hope.

Then she covered her tracks and left. Not when everyone *thought* she'd set off from the house, but hours later, when the fire she'd begun was taking hold. So that little Paul Bryant saw and remembered the car as it raced past in the dark.

Elsa did it. No wonder Elsa stayed away, all those years. I wonder if she ever told anyone.

But Olivia *must* know, she would have been with her mother that day. That night. She was thirteen, by my calculation, not a young child. And that would explain so much—why they were estranged, why they never reconciled—maybe she even witnessed the shooting . . .

I feel almost tender to Olivia. No wonder she is so cold and controlled, having hidden this secret all these years.

Can I prove it? No, not all that I am putting together in my mind. And there is so much I don't know. Yet the words run through my head, a talisman to hold on to:

Elsa did it.

I shiver. They may be dead now, Alex and Elsa both,

but the horror of it all is as sharp as a knife, cutting through the years.

Yet I feel a satisfaction, too: I know what I set out to know. At last, things are making sense for me.

And now it's time and I am ready. Ready for my final session with Olivia.

Chapter 39

I should be going down for the dinner party. It is time to celebrate the end of the week, with drinks and good food and an evening of strangers, which will be a blessed relief.

Instead I am sitting here on my bed in a wet towel, not doing anything. It will stay with me for a long time, that hour that has just passed.

I hadn't known quite what question to ask first.

We were in the living room off the kitchen, as usual. Annie was looking after Bea, upstairs; Josh had gone out to pick up some more wine. Olivia started talking, with me still fumbling to switch on my digital recorder.

It's next to me now, a small black shape on the bed-side table. And my head is full of her story, the images her words conjured up in my mind.

The quiet night. The roar from within the burning house. The knock on the door at a cottage, far away. And running through it all, the soft trickle of Olivia's voice . . .

Afterward I opened my laptop. I felt compelled to start writing, while it was all still fresh in my mind.

I was falling back on what I do, as a ghostwriter: it is my way of understanding, processing things. I have not written much so far, and I know I can't tell the whole truth, laying out all that I know.

But, at last, I have made a proper start to her story. No wonder I couldn't get to grips with it before, when I was missing this—the foundation stone of who she is.

Now I glance over it again, on the laptop screen. As usual, it is not her words, not exactly, but I think I have captured their essence. The story just flowed out of her, like a dam had been broken. There were tears, a shocking amount.

In fact, I reflect now, it was almost as if she had just been waiting for the chance to tell her story. For some people it can be like that: an unburdening.

But I really must get going. I haven't worn makeup all week, but it's a party, isn't it? And I want to blend in with her crowd . . .

As I stand up, I press play again to listen to the session as I move around the room. I hang the black dress Olivia loaned me in the bathroom, so the steam from my shower can get out the creases.

Her voice on the tape is measured, her composure intact—for the first few minutes.

"The main thing I want people to know is that they can get through hard times—tragedy, even. If I can, they can, too. Does that sound about right?"

I had nodded. Then she started to tell me what happened.

"It had been a long, hot summer. No rain . . ."

I begin to put on foundation, letting the story wash over me, one ear alert to any gaps I must fill in later. I don't think there are many.

"*We hadn't been away until then—perhaps because the weather had been so beautiful. But before the summer break was over, Mummy had arranged a little vacation for us, a cottage getaway.*"

"And your father planned to join you later?" I prompt.

"*Well,*" she replies, her voice heavier. "*Daddy was going to come, and then he wasn't, not until later—he had work to do—I don't remember exactly.*"

I set down my makeup brush for a second, feeling uncomfortable.

"*. . . we played on the beach, swam, ate ice creams. It was like any other family vacation. Nothing really stands out to me, no . . .*"

I can picture what's coming: her whole face crumpling up like a little girl's.

"*. . . the policemen came to the cottage in the night. I crept out on to the landing. I couldn't hear what they were saying. I just remember seeing Mummy at the table, tears running down her face . . .*"

Olivia's own eyes had been glassy with tears, but she held it together a bit longer.

"*. . . we couldn't stay here afterward. The house was in such a state. My mother didn't want to anyway, she didn't cope so well . . .*"

But it's funny how different a voice can sound, shorn of any accompanying gestures. She's more clipped and decisive on the tape than I remember.

And I'm gentler, more tentative—I hardly pushed

her that hard, I reassure myself, as I dust on blusher. Of course there was no way I could bring up everything I know about Elsa . . .

"*. . . afterward, I was spending a lot of time at my grandmother's, my father's mother, in London. No, she's not with us today . . .*"

Really, it's hard to understand the reaction I provoked, that flood of tears I know is coming.

"*In the end it made sense that I went to school down there—made a fresh start. My mother was still young and beautiful. She started over, too . . .*"

But I did my job. I got behind the perfect facade.

She couldn't tell me the full story of that night. Yet everything she said fitted with what I've discovered, like a jigsaw puzzle coming together.

"*Grief can—well, it doesn't always bring people together . . .*"

Of course it couldn't bring her and Elsa together, in their circumstances.

My voice sounds on the tape again, cautious: "*Of course. And perhaps you could just talk a little more about your father—Alexander, or was it Alex?*"

"*Alex. But to me, he was just Daddy.*" I pause to listen, mascara wand in one hand. "*What can I say? He was the family's golden boy, even as a grown man, everybody loved him.*"

She is starting to cry in earnest now. "*And if he hadn't stayed behind at the house*"—she draws in an ugly shuddering breath—"*if he hadn't been there the night of the fire . . .*"

She can't spell it out, but I know: it could have gone so differently for them all. I still can't say she is easy to warm to. But it's not nice to see the polish crack.

"I think about it even now, you know? If only," she says, *"If only."*

I pause, mascara wand in one hand. Because something feels different, listening back without the person in front of me . . . what is it?

"I'm sorry." She is struggling to get the words out between sobs. *"I'm not used to talking about it."*

It takes me a second to put my finger on it.

Despite the tears I know were pouring down her cheeks—her chest heaving—her delivery remains steady and even. She is always poised, even in her grief.

"Look." I sound worried. What had I unleashed? *"We've covered a lot today. Let's leave it there."*

"Thank you. I would appreciate that."

Of course we ended it there. On the recording there are light footsteps, then other noises: I went into the kitchen and turned on the tap, got her a glass of water.

"Why don't I give you a moment, unless you'd like company . . ."

"Would you mind? I just want to collect myself. Thanks."

I hear my footsteps petering out as I pass into the hallway from the kitchen, then the recording goes quiet.

My makeup is done now, so I go into the bathroom and pull down my dress, the hanger swinging noisily on the shower rod. I wriggle into it, hurrying now. I have my Nicky necklace on, as always, but I remember to slip on some gold hoops.

In the bathroom mirror I check my reflection—that red lipstick is too much for tonight—and wipe it off, still thinking about what Olivia left unsaid: she didn't just lose a father that night. She lost a whole family.

And yet I can't help it: I feel lighter, close to happy even, for the first time since I've arrived at this house. Because it's over now, I've done what I came here to do, I've got her to open up, to trust me—and as I slip on my shoes and pull open my door, already I can feel the tension lifting, ready to relax and drink and smile and forget the week that's passed, for an evening.

My part in her story is nearly done.

Chapter 40

Olivia is checking something in the oven and stands up as I walk in, her cheeks pink. "You look nice." She sounds surprised, and I wonder if I've made too much effort.

"Can I give you a hand with anything?"

"I'm OK, thanks," says Olivia, looking around. "Josh was just getting another bottle up, he said . . . everyone's in the dining room, let me take you through."

I follow her through to the dark-papered dining room, the French windows showing a pale pink sky above the terrace. An older man in a salmon-colored shirt is concentrating on mixing a drink in the corner, not bothering to look up as I am introduced as "Nicky, from London," to "Harry and Lucy, they've just had a little boy."

Harry is tall, baby-faced with a receding hairline; Lucy limply pretty in a floral dress. I'm sure Olivia posted the same one, shot on a hot August day, a few weeks ago; it doesn't translate as well into the evening. Olivia hands me a glass of straw-colored champagne as Lucy launches into a story about the traffic on the way there.

". . . we thought it had to be a cow on the loose to have a traffic jam on a Friday night, but no—they'd put in a temporary traffic light for the road construction!"

The punchline falls flat, but Olivia smiles. She starts asking Lucy about the baby, and I tune out.

I feel a little shell-shocked to be back in the everyday world. And they are different from the people I know at home. They don't seem Olivia's type, either, somehow . . . I wonder how much she has in common with them.

But as Josh sweeps in with another bottle of champagne, I change my mind—he's right at home, backslapping with Salmon Shirt.

"Leo, mate! You made it, how brown are you, been at the Mantan have we . . ."

So Leo turned up after all. The long table is set for seven, so I suspect someone has already laid an extra place for me, avoiding awkwardness. But where's his wife? I haven't seen Sabrina all day, I like to be prepared.

I glance back at Lucy, who is still talking—". . . yes, he is sleeping through."—and get a cold look. She knows I wasn't paying attention.

Oh well. As I knock back the dregs of my champagne, a woman sweeps in in a cloud of cigarette fumes and heady perfume. It takes me a second to place her, then I recognize Sabrina, done up to the nines in heavy eye makeup and looking slinky, if overdressed, in a silver dress. She makes a beeline for Olivia—"Liv darling! Leo left the front door ajar for me. I know how you feel about smoking," she adds pointedly—before dispensing double kisses to everyone, including me.

There is the usual confusion as Olivia calls for us all to sit down, Josh assuming helplessness, until eventually we are seated with Olivia at the head of the table, Leo to her right, then Lucy, and Josh. Harry is on Olivia's left, Sabrina on his other side. I am wary of being stuck on the end by Sabrina, but she doesn't give me a second glance.

For a while I just listen. Soon Leo is holding forth about a bachelorette party he and Sabrina hosted at their farm. They run some sort of vacation getaway there, and he is careful to give the impression it is all a hilarious joke, a not-so-serious second career.

". . . whole tent collapsed in the rain, Sab had to let them all sleep in the barn . . ."

Harry laughs a bit too loudly. He has already made it clear that Lucy is driving. I can sense Josh is waiting to break in with his next story, vying to top Leo's.

It feels practiced somehow, this group of friends falling into a familiar groove. But it's a relief, too, after the intensity of this week, as my glass is refilled again and again. I don't have do anything but laugh and eat. Olivia has been refusing offers of help as she heads in and out of the kitchen, and the food is delicious.

After the main course, the conversation breaks up

into tête-à-têtes: next to me, Sabrina has turned her back to focus on Harry on her other side. I spoon up my chocolate pudding and let the noise flow over me. I start thinking of the route I can take in the morning . . .

"What are you two talking about?" says Lucy from across the table, directing her question to her husband and Sabrina.

"Oh—just our trip to Antibes, did you know Sab lived there for a bit?" says Harry. Then he turns back to Sabrina to continue their hushed conversation.

Lucy looks annoyed. On her side of the table, Josh and Leo have pushed their chairs back to talk about cricket; while Olivia has gone out again.

". . . what's sauce for the goose is sauce for the gander," I hear Sabrina say darkly.

"Well," says Harry. "You know I'm a big fan of Leo's. Hope you two can work it out."

I catch Lucy's eye—we are both being ignored—and regret it instantly.

"And you, Nicky, tell me about yourself," she says in a loud voice. "You're working on Olivia's book, I hear?"

Oh great. She's using me to show how social and unbothered she can be.

"That's right. I'm a ghostwriter . . ."

Before I can launch into my usual explanation, she interrupts with questions: how fast can I type, to keep up with Olivia; how good a speller am I; and how many pages will the book be?

I answer as best I can: quite quickly, but it's not dictation, actually; pretty good at spelling; and it really depends . . .

But she's not finished drawing me out. "And do you have children, Nicky?"

"No, I don't."

"Oh." Lucy tilts her head at me. "I suppose at least that means you have lots of time to write . . ." she says, doubtfully.

"Actually, yes," I say. "I like my freedom. I set my own hours, I'm in control—"

"But don't you want to write a book of your own?"

"Well, maybe I am doing," I say, needled. I've drunk too much. "I mean, I will."

"Oh?" Lucy raises her voice: "Did you hear that Olivia? Nicky is writing her own book, too."

Olivia, who has come back in with coffee, smiles politely. "I'm sure it will be great."

"When yours is done, I mean." I don't want to sound unprofessional.

"Well, of course," she says. "It must be hard to write your own story when you're trying to tell someone else's."

"That's right," I say, feeling a flash of rapport with her, for once. No one has asked a single question about her work, I noticed.

"Now," says Olivia to the table, "would anyone like more pudding with coffee?"

But Lucy, having been locked out of the other conversations, isn't about to let this one go.

"Isn't it a bit strange, Olivia," she says earnestly, "to have someone write a book all about you?"

"I suppose." I don't think she is going to say any more, but then Olivia adds, thoughtfully: "It's not exactly what I expected."

"Oh," says Lucy, pleased to get a reaction. "Don't you like it?"

"It's not that, really." I wonder if Olivia is drunk, too—more likely, she knows that none of them will remember. "It's just . . . different. After all," Olivia directs this at me, "you know everything about me. And I know nothing about you."

I don't know what to say to that. "Not everything," I reply eventually.

"What's that?" Sabrina has caught the end of our exchange. "Not everything, does she, Sticky?"

She laughs, looking around the table for attention, so doesn't notice the expression on Olivia's face. It is so quick I could almost think I imagined it, as Olivia tips her head down to pour the coffee.

But I am chilled, still seeing the hostility in Olivia's eyes.

With sudden clarity, I want nothing more than to go back to my own life, tough and messy as it can be. I don't like this world. Her world. I want to go home.

Leo gets up then to open the French windows, heading out to smoke, and everyone starts to scatter, the way people do when the evening gets on.

I get up, too, trying not to wobble on my heels.

Upstairs, I look a little wild-eyed in the bathroom mirror.

"Keep it together," I tell myself. "You're nearly there." Downstairs, the nearest bathroom was occupied, so I headed up to my room.

I touch up my makeup, reluctant to go back down, but eventually I move toward the bedroom door.

"Hello?"

I stop on the threshold, before I hear the whisper again.

"Hello? Can you hear me?"

Chapter 41

"*H*ello? *Yes, I can hear you now.*"
For a second, fuddled by wine, I think my phone is on speaker and a caller is talking.

"*No, I'm so glad you caught me.*"

Then I realize: it's just Olivia's voice on my recorder. I reach for it on my bedside table—

"*Yes, that would be great for a conference call.*"

It does this if I forget to switch it off: just keeps playing the recording on a loop. Some digital setting I don't know how to correct, but it drains the battery.

"*Actually,*" she says briskly, "*could your team make 3 p.m.?*"

There is another brief pause as I look for the off button: the recorder has only captured her side of her phone conversation.

"*Perfect. Thanks so much. Bye.*"

Although—when exactly was this? I don't remember her taking this call when I was there.

On the tape, there is silence for a few seconds, then footsteps, then I hear my own voice, tentative.

"*Hey, I don't want to intrude—I just wanted to check you were really OK . . .*"

"*Thank you. I just needed a moment.*" Olivia's voice is full of sadness again, mournful.

And now I know when this was.

I had wandered downstairs to check on her after, what, twenty minutes? She was exactly where I had left her after our final session, tear-stained on the sofa.

"*Really,*" she sniffs on the tape, "*I'm fine.*"

Against the big cushions, she had looked very small.

"*Well,*" I say, awkwardly. "*I appreciate you sharing your story with me.*"

Did the recorder somehow splice two different recordings together? Because it's like two different sessions, that phone call just then and her now . . .

"*It's just a lot, you know?*" She gives a little sob.

And suddenly I understand: I had gone out of the room, and before I returned Olivia had taken a work phone call, quickly. Why not?

On the tape, she is still talking to me: "*Do you think you have enough, on this part of my life?*"

There is a silence—I was nodding.

So she had got it together, I tell myself now, what else was she going to do? Cry down the phone to a client?

"*Good,*" she is saying, giving a delicate little sniff. "*I do think I've given you all I can.*"

The only question is, why did she start to cry again?

There is a comforting murmur from me. "*Absolutely. We can stop there.*"

But I know why. Olivia wasn't crying because she

was upset, not really. She was crying so that I'd stop pushing—so that I'd leave her alone.

She didn't open up. She seemed to say so much, get overwhelmed, but really . . . she was fobbing me off. And I bought it.

Because I have never questioned whether she loved her father. That she grieved. That she was sad that Alexander Vane was dead.

Until now.

I go back down the stairs, feeling off balance in every way.

It's the alcohol making me feel so fluttery and anxious, I tell myself. Because I have got it right, I have it all wrapped up. I just need to shuffle my view of things a little, to make this bit of information fit with the rest.

But how exactly? I wish I hadn't drunk so much. My head feels so muddled.

Downstairs, the dining room is echoing with chatter— too noisy for thought—so I push through the long glass doors, my movement making security lights click on.

On the terrace, Sabrina blinks in the bright light, swaying slightly. It's hard to see her as a threat right now.

"Mind if I steal one of those cigarettes?" I don't smoke anymore, not really, but I want to steady myself.

"Sure." She offers me her pack.

"Thanks." The air is cool out here, the trees dark shapes all around us.

"That one of hers?" Sabrina points at my dress: black and simple but with that indefinable something— cut? finish?—that shows its quality.

"Yes, she loaned it to me."

"Thought so. You look like a cut-price clone. No offense."

"None taken," I say, but my inhibitions are gone, and I rise to the bait. "You know, I don't think anyone expected Leo to come tonight, I hope that means everything is OK between you again," I finish insincerely.

But the jab sails over Sabrina's head: she must be very drunk. "Leo? He loves a party. No, I told Olivia *I'd* have to think about it, when I went home yesterday. I'd had quite enough of her and her rules. Bloody rude, if you ask me."

Oh. So that means Sabrina didn't stay here last night, after all . . . that feels important, too, but I can't think why right now.

"So you've known Olivia a long time?" I want to drown out this feeling, like everything is shifting around me. "How's that, then?"

"School, mostly," she says. She names a day school in London that I'm supposed to be impressed by. "But our parents were friends before that, from living up here. Though we'd moved away from Annersley by the time of the—you know."

I nod, acknowledging the fire.

She pulls out a lighter. "But I came back eventually. Like Sticky."

I lean toward the flame to light my cigarette, inhaling the bitter smoke. "Why 'Sticky'?" I realize I've never had a chance to talk to Sabrina with her guard down.

She seems to consider for a second. But she is drunker than I am.

"You know how it is with nicknames." She leans closer to me, so that I can smell the wine on her hot breath. "Sticky Fingers. Sticky stuck." She sniggers.

I don't want this cigarette after all, I am already feeling nauseous. "Sticky Fingers?"

Sabrina pulls back from me, theatrically. "Oh, so she didn't mention that . . . Not the sort of thing you want to put in a book, I suppose."

"You mean, Olivia was—stealing things?"

Sabrina, distracted already, is scrabbling in her little jeweled bag. "Hm?"

I glance through the window behind us, but Olivia is talking to Lucy.

"What you said," I say more quietly. "She was stealing?"

Sabrina starts clicking the lighter again. "Stupid thing," she says, a new cigarette clamped between her teeth.

I try again. "I can't imagine Olivia ever doing anything like that. She just would never—"

It's a childish tactic, but it gets her attention.

"Oh yes, everyone at school loved Little Miss Tragedy," says Sabrina bitterly. She takes the cigarette out of her mouth, her lipstick gleaming wetly on the paper. "But they didn't know, did they, that she was a thief."

"A thief?"

She raises her eyebrows, happy to be sharing the gossip. "And that's why," she jabs a long finger in the air, for emphasis, "her parents sent her away."

*   *   *

I must still look confused, because Sabrina spells it out for me. "She was pinching money," she says, then rubs her thumb and two fingers together.

"No . . ." I frown, then almost smile, amused. She's embarrassing herself, she's so patently jealous of Olivia. "No, she went to her grandmother's because of the fire, that's why she started at school down there."

Sabrina shrugs. "That's what everyone thought. But I knew she was going to be starting at my school, even before the fire. Her parents had spoken to my mine about it. They thought somewhere more insthtitut . . ." she gives up on the word, "*stricter* would help. Because it did so much for *moi*," she says ironically, then hiccups.

"But why would Olivia need to steal money?"

She rolls her eyes. "Course she didn't *need* to." She takes a deep drag of her cigarette. "My mother said they blamed the boyfriend, thought he was a bad influence. The Vanes never loved the prospect of Olivia ending up with a pub landlord for a father-in-law, however remote. Sending her away would solve that little problem, too."

At my expression, she straightens up.

"Of course, I didn't say anything to anyone when she did start," she continues, reading my look of shock as disapproval. "It was all very sad. 'Sticky' was just my little joke . . . Look, this is strictly entre nous, yes?" She gestures between us with her cigarette.

"Absolutely," I nod. I try to rearrange my face to look more normal.

"OK!" someone cries inside, and I look to see Josh

is standing, getting people to their feet. "Everyone out. It's a bit early in the year, but who cares. Let's go!"

And now everyone is already pushing back their chairs, Lucy exclaiming: "Oh how fun . . ." and heading out through the French windows to join us on the terrace.

I linger near the house—I want to digest what I have just learned, as the night air sobers me up—but then a hand in the small of my back gives me a shove, harder than necessary. Lurching forward on my heels, I turn to see Josh's unapologetic grin, showing gleaming white teeth.

"Can't miss this," he says.

Chapter 42

As we are herded to the edge of the terrace, everyone is shouting and whooping around me, drunk and excited—and not only drunk, I realize, placing the manic energy and remembering how everyone had disappeared together earlier.

The night is taking on a surreal air, the garden lit up like a stage by the security lights, Lucy shrieking with laughter. In front of us, Josh and Leo are kneeling on the flat stretch of lawn, fiddling with something on the ground.

"Get a move on, boys!" bellows Sabrina.

One thing is clear to me now: this woman is not so much protective of Olivia as protective of her position by her side—and deeply envious, too, some toxic old dynamic dating back to their schooldays. She's a mess.

And yet . . . I shiver, though I am not cold.

That money that went missing, that Alex's business associate first told me about: Vane had thought it might be someone who'd worked for him.

Then the old policeman had confirmed that, yes, there been some unpleasantness with one of the staff.

But that was all resolved, after the money turned up again.

Or was it? What if the problem went away, not because it was all a misunderstanding, but because they found out it was *Olivia* who was stealing?

That would make sense, too. The family would want to deal with something like that privately. And so she was being sent away, to a strict new school, like Sabrina said.

The idea puts a whole different light on the end of that summer, that happy family . . .

The group parts for a second, and I am looking at Olivia, standing at the front. She isn't flushed with wine or disheveled like the rest of us. She is still composed, her face expressionless, her golden hair gleaming under the security lights. The whole evening has been perfectly executed, another triumph.

How might she have felt, to be caught being less than perfect, and punished for it? She would have been furious.

"The pheasants will think we're firing guns," says Sabrina, next to me. "Bloody stupid birds," she adds mildly.

I'm trying not to listen, not to lose this train of thought; the fresh air is starting to help me. What else did Sabrina say just now, about some boyfriend, and his landlord dad?

Because Olivia said she didn't have any boyfriends before Josh, she was very sure—and yet there *was* this boyfriend, who Olivia never mentioned at all.

And I find myself thinking about someone else who grew up round here and is, yes, about the same age as

Olivia. Paul Bryant, who took over the Bleeding Wolf from his parents.

Paul, who lied about when he saw Elsa's car driving away from the fire—because his uncle, the policeman, was paid off, I had thought. But what if it wasn't Elsa who Paul wanted to protect? What if it was his girl-friend—Olivia?

The night air is taking effect, clearing my mind.

And now my focus is not on Elsa, I can think of someone other than her who might have wanted to save that painting from the fire. "*Liv likes it*," Josh had told me.

Panic is starting to rise in me, and something I don't want to name—I need to get out of here. I start to squeeze my way past Sabrina and Lucy, but everyone is clustered around me.

"Oh, you can't go," says Lucy, grabbing my arm. "You'll miss it all!"

And now the mood is changing, everyone hushing, as Josh and Leo scrabble up the steps toward us, shout-ing: "Back, get back!"

With an electric wail, the first firework soars up over our heads, then explodes.

For a moment it feels like daylight again, as if some-one in the sky has flicked on a huge switch. The flash illuminates the wide terrace, the smooth sweep of lawn, and the trees all around.

Then a shower of green sparks arches across the sky, like a vast umbrella opening up. I feel the noise through my whole body.

"Leo ordered them from China," says Sabrina. "Good, aren't they?"

"Wow," breathes Lucy, "but aren't they a bit close to the house, it's been so dry . . ."

I am shaking. I've never liked fireworks. That is why my whole body is trembling, like I am afraid. Not because something else has just clicked into place in my mind.

That *Sabrina* was the one they thought wouldn't turn up tonight, not Leo. Because, she said to me just now, she had flounced off home yesterday after being told off by Olivia for smoking. So I got that wrong. Which wouldn't matter, only . . .

That means Sabrina wasn't sleeping here last night. That whoever followed me down into the cellar in the night to scare me, it can't have been her, like I thought.

I shake my head, as if to dislodge the thought. Everyone else is still having a good time. Ahead of us, Josh has gone back down the lawn again, stomping something into the ground; next to me, Sabrina is chatting idly with Lucy about that weekend they have planned, as we wait for the next explosion.

But then if that thing in the cellar—and the pin and the tile, too, I suppose—if they were not Sabrina's spiteful jealous tricks, what were they?

"And what about you, Lucy, are you going to come out with us next time"—Sabrina's loud voice cuts into my thoughts, her tone baiting—"or are you still too nervous?"

"Actually," Lucy is defiant. "I've been practicing. Olivia took me to the range."

"Oh, did she," says Sabrina, and takes a step over to Harry, rebuffed.

Down on the grass, Josh is holding a light to the thing on the ground, and then it registers with me, what Lucy meant . . .

"Olivia shoots?" I hear myself say.

Because I asked her. When I was angling to find out about her dad . . .

"*God no . . . I never tried anything like that.*" That's what she'd told me.

"But of course," Lucy says, then jumps and claps as Josh jogs back up.

"Get ready for a big one!" he shouts.

As the firework goes up with an electric scream, I take a tiny step backward.

"Oops, careful," Lucy gives me a gentle shove.

"Sorry," I manage to get out. "It startled me." I lift my head to watch the sparks drift slowly down, painting our upturned faces pink and green . . .

But it wasn't the firework that made me stumble.

It's almost funny, how you can try to close your eyes to an unpleasant truth, push it away, until you're forced to confront it and your whole world teeters on its axis.

I knew what happened, didn't I? I had it all worked out . . . Elsa killed Alex and then they fled. Unless . . .

What if . . . what if Olivia wasn't the one staying away from Elsa?

What if Elsa stayed away from *Olivia*?

And now I force myself to be still. I stand there with my face upturned to the night, barely seeing the lights and colours, as my mind races over what I know.

That Olivia was blamed for stealing money, about to

be sent away. That young Paul Bryant might have had a reason to protect not Elsa, but Olivia. That Olivia faked those tears about her father, on my tape.

That she didn't want to tell me she can shoot.

And I can't help it, I glance over at Olivia, following my thoughts, but that is another mistake. Because she is already looking directly at me, her features lit up by the firework above—really looking at me, almost expectantly. Like maybe she is waiting for me to realize something. Because maybe she heard what Lucy just said.

I tear my gaze away. "I need to go to bed," I say to no one in particular, and none of them tries to stop me this time. They are distracted by the fireworks as I head inside, trying not to hurry.

It is cold in the dining room now, the chill of the night spilling through the open doors. I am still stunned as I move through the house, turning to check that no one is following me, and yet I feel as if I am seeing everything clearly for the first time.

All the strange things that have happened to me here—not Sabrina. Not spiteful tricks. Somebody else. Something else.

Warnings, maybe, as I looked where I shouldn't. Or punishments . . .

I am half-running up the stairs now, racing to get inside my room. At the top of the staircase, the dim hallway flushes red—no one has pulled the curtains shut—but the screams are quieter up here, the thick glass muffling the sounds.

I understand it now: what she has done to this house. Not only a restoration. But an act of reparation, atonement . . . re-creating what was destroyed . . .

And as I wrench open the door to my room and slam it shut, pressing myself against the wood, the fear I have been keeping at bay overtakes me, hot and wild and overwhelming, making my hands tremble, making me sink down to the floor.

Because now I am telling myself a different story. Not one that belongs to the past, like I thought, but one that is living and breathing and dangerous.

A confrontation that got out of hand, yes. A mother who covered it up, that still holds. But I know now, what I missed: *Olivia's hands on the gun.*

I can see it now. Others will see it, too—they must. Won't they? They must.

I just have to make it through the night.

PART 2
OLIVIA

Chapter 43

There are two sides to every story. Everyone knows that.

I'm not going to rehash what's behind us. As I told her, I don't like to live in the past. What's done is done.

And honestly, when she arrived on my doorstep, I didn't think much of her at all.

Slight, nothing clothes, hair that could do with some highlights, a face bare of makeup, not even mascara. Could be pretty if she made an effort, though you're not supposed to say that.

I saw her reading the contents of my house and clocking Josh, though.

And afterward, once she was gone?

I was worried, yes. Increasingly anxious—even fearful, you might say—as time passed. That was true, if not quite in the way they interpreted it.

But my first instinct when she disappeared, before people started to panic?

Pure, overwhelming relief. *Thank fuck that's over.*

* * *

But I am getting ahead of myself. By now, of course, I have gone over in detail what happened that Saturday, the day after the dinner party. It wasn't until later on that the alarm was raised—but I'll get to that.

So I had the morning to myself—the calm before the storm, let's say.

Admittedly, when I woke up I was not feeling too hot. But I got up, grabbed the glass from my bedside table, and held it under the cold tap in my bathroom. I drank it down, twice. Then I rushed to the toilet, crouched down, and started retching. Josh wasn't there to hear, at least; his side of the bed was empty.

Afterward I pulled on my running gear and went downstairs. Annie was already there, trying to get out what looked like a wine stain on the living-room rug, while Bea watched cartoons, sucking her thumb on the sofa.

"Don't worry about all that, Annie. In fact, that rug might have to be totally chucked away." I toed it with one socked foot.

She looked up. "Off for a run already? Why don't I make you a nice cup of tea?"

"No, thanks," I said. "This is just what I need."

"Exercise is the perfect cure after a heavy night!" I once wrote, back when I used to do more blogging. There is never an excuse for letting things slide.

But it was more punishment than pleasure as I started to run. I had to stop behind the tennis court, leaning against the fence to take a break out of sight of the house. I could smell the cut grass and feel the warmth from the compost heap as I bent forward and emptied my stomach again.

* * *

Back in the kitchen I took a can of Diet Coke from the fridge and looked behind me. "Morning," I said to Josh, as he walked in. "Annie's already tidying up."

"I know." Josh came over and dropped a kiss on my head, his hands on my shoulders. "You're an angel, Annie."

I put the cold can back, hesitating, and pulled out a carton of coconut water. That would be better for my stomach.

"How are you feeling?" I said, shutting the door and turning round. "You were up early."

"Mm," he shrugged. "Bit of a sore head. I could do with a run, like you."

"But you've already showered." His hair was still damp.

"I felt rough." He rubbed the back of his neck. "Thought it might freshen me up."

I smiled. "Poor old you. Annie," I said, turning to the figure in the corner. "When you've a moment, would you mind taking a cup of tea up to Nicky, see if she wants to join us?"

As Annie busied herself with the kettle, I laid the table for breakfast. I always like to help her where I can: I like Annie to think well of me.

"It's a little rude though," I added. "Staying in bed all morning."

When Annie returned to the kitchen, she was still holding the cup of tea.

I looked up. "She's still asleep then?" I shook my head.

"No," said Annie. "She's not there. She's gone."

I can picture the two of us, Josh and I, sitting there at the table among the breakfast things, framed in that instant: before everything changed.

I spoke first, my voice steady. "What do you mean, she's gone?"

"She's not there," says Annie. "But all her things are still there."

"Well, she must have just gone out then."

"Her car's here, too, I saw through the window." She sounded a little worried. But she is such a worrier, Annie.

"She must have just gone out for a run then, like me," I said, and refilled my coffee cup. I could feel Josh's eyes on me. I didn't look up.

And so the day progressed, its mundanity taking on a grim inevitability in retrospect. *So that was the last time*, you think afterward, *that was the very last time that we would do this or that, before everything changed.* Of course *then*, it looked like just another day.

At about eleven in the morning I was in the hall, Annie helping me to get Bea's shoes on so we could go out, when Josh came down the stairs.

"Maybe we should give her a call? Nicky," he added, as he shrugged on his jacket, like I might not realize who he was talking about. "If we're both going out. Say good-bye?"

He wants everyone to like him. It was one of the things that appealed to me about him, when we first met. Right then it just irritated me.

"I suppose so," I said. "I've got her number in my e-mail. I'll find it in a bit."

But I didn't. After Josh left—he was already late for golf, he said—I went to say good-bye to Cav, collecting branches into a pile in the garden: Nicky might come back, could he tell her we had gone out?

Then I dropped Annie in the village, thanking her for all her hard work, telling her to have a good night off—she was spending it with a friend in the village, more of a break for her that staying in the house. After that, I drove out to the show farm half an hour away, so Bea could see the baby animals. She always enjoys that.

It was sometime in the afternoon, not long after I had got back, when it happened. The three of us, Josh, me and Bea, were in the kitchen. I was making Bea's tea: cutting up chunks of cucumber for her into batons, the way she likes.

"Hold on," Josh said, frowning. "Can you hear that? Ringing."

We both listened for a second, as the unfamiliar ringtone sounded through the house. It was coming from upstairs, of course.

Chapter 44

Later, I couldn't really explain why we both went up, him taking big steps up the stairs, me following with a protesting Bea in my arms.

I suppose you know, I told them, don't you, when some detail is not right: some part of you knows what it might mean. After all, I pointed out, her car was in the driveway.

As we pushed open the door to her room, the phone was still ringing, vibrating on the side table.

Josh picked it up. "Joey," he read aloud, before putting it to his ear. "Hello?

He listened for a moment then held the phone away from his head. "He's hung up already."

"Well, call him back," I said.

"I can't," he said, fiddling with it. "It's locked now, you need a code to do that." He proffered the phone so I could see the screen: there were four missed calls from Joey. "Look, anyway. I've got to go out. Can't you deal with this?"

I couldn't believe his lightning-fast switch of focus. "You're going out? Now?"

"I need to go check on the site this evening. One of the boys called before, said they'd driven past and seen someone dodgy looking around . . ."

"You're going to look at your property project," I repeated. "But it's Saturday night—can't someone else go?"

"Who? Anyway,"—his mind was already onto the next thing—"I don't have time for this."

I turned to look at him as he brushed past me. "But what should we do about Nicky?"

"Mummy cross again," said Bea conversationally, and rested her head against my shoulder.

He stopped in the doorway, hands braced against the frame.

"Report it, if you like," he said, heavily. "Ten to one she's just embarrassed, gone out—dealing with a hangover somewhere. She was pretty gone last night."

"You all were," I said sourly. "But without her phone?" I add.

"If you're that worried, call that police number—101. Report it. And I'll drop by the pub on the way back, see if she's ended up there." His voice carried down the corridor, as he left me and Bea in there. "It'll be fine."

After that I took Bea back downstairs to finish teatime; then I was busy with bath and bed. It was still light in the evenings, making her want to stay up and play. When I came out of her room, I felt a wave of tiredness. I stopped in the hallway near the top of the stairs and looked out through the window, over the low roof. I'd have to replace that missing tile, I remembered, looking at the space it had left.

I had things to do, of course, but I stayed there a moment more. The wind was growing stronger, lifting the branches of the trees all around the house, and for a second I felt quite alone, surrounded by all that green.

But that was stupid, I was never afraid in the house: I was not the sort of the person to be scared of shadows. To say the least.

And I was already turning to go down the stairs, to tidy up, when I pivoted on my heel and walked the short distance into Nicky's room at the end of the corridor.

It was dim, and I flicked on the overhead light, making the sky through the open curtains appear suddenly darker.

I don't know why exactly I decided to do it. I suppose you could just say I just like things to be neat. Already it looked empty, abandoned, even with all her stuff in there. And it was such a mess that it bothered me. You cannot have an ordered life without ordered surroundings. As I had told Nicky in one of our sessions.

So I wiped down the toothpaste she'd left in the basin in her bathroom, and hung her dress—*my* dress, puddled on the floor—on a hanger. Then after I straightened up the bedspread, I went over to her suitcase, clothes spilling over the sides.

That was where I found them, the sheaf of papers and photos.

I wish I could have felt more surprised.

* * *

There was no need to panic.

I simply took them down through the house and the kitchen, out to the garden, where Cav had been burning leaves. The embers in the bonfire bin were still warm, and it didn't take long to stir them up into flames again.

The floor plan went first, then the big color printouts showing my burned-out home. I recognized them from that horrid website Marie Crompton's boy had set up. I didn't get involved of course, but Annie had let it be known that he needed to take them straight down. Marie had been very embarrassed; she couldn't apologize enough.

I thought that business was all done with. But it is hard to escape the grip of the past. I of all people should know that.

Last of all into the fire went my family photo, the edges turning black. I knew where Nicky must have found that; she must have been all over the house, to get into that box. But as I watched the flames take the four smiling faces, I stopped seeing them. A moment from the night before—it felt like an age ago by then—kept replaying in my mind.

We were all outside watching the fireworks.

I thought the day had gone OK. I'd had that final session with her, made all the right noises. She had seemed to buy it all.

Then I had looked at her, and she had looked at me.

It was then that I saw it, before she wiped her expression clean and turned to go back inside the house, like she had to get away from us. From me.

That was why I couldn't feel sorry, and why—

despite the dangers that I knew must lie ahead—I couldn't help but cling to my first instinct: to feel relief that she was gone. Call it a survival instinct, maybe.

Because I had read what was written on her face under the bright flashes of the explosions above. And I understood what that dawning realization meant.

She knew too much about me.

Still. There are two sides to every story, everyone knows that.

But what matters, in the end, is who gets to tell it.

Chapter 45

By the time I was back in the house, I was yawning—exhaustion slamming into me after the stress of the week—but strangely peaceful. There was nothing else for me to do, right then. Josh was gone for the evening, Bea was in bed, and Annie was away for the night. I fell asleep on the sofa in the living room, something I never do.

When I woke, the room was dark and my throat was dry. For a moment, staring at the unfamiliar shadows on the wall, I did not know where I was. Then I heard it again, what had woken me: someone knocking, from the back door.

Josh. He must have assumed I'd put the chain on the front. Sometimes I did, pissed off that he wasn't home yet. At least he hadn't rung the bell and disturbed Bea.

I swung myself out of the soft sofa and wandered through the dark kitchen into the utility room. Still foggy with sleep, I registered the tall familiar figure through the frosted glass of the door, as I twisted the key and—

"Nicky?" said the stranger.

With a jolt of alarm, I took him in as the security light clicked on: a teenager in a navy parka, his bike propped behind him against one of my huge—and expensive—urns.

"No," I replied. I smoothed my hair behind my ears. "I'm Olivia."

"Oh, sorry," he said blinking at me owlishly. "I thought she might be in . . . Uh, the gates were open, I couldn't find a doorbell round the front."

The kick of adrenaline was already subsiding as I took in his gangly build, his diffidence.

"Can I help you?" I said briskly.

"Uh, yeah. I'm looking for Nicky?" His voice was a question, asking permission.

"And you are?" A friend from London? I'd have to play this right.

"A friend—but I don't know where she is."

"Well, you and me both." I was pleased with the mix of exasperation, tinged with concern, that I could hear in my voice.

"You mean—she's not here?"

"I'm afraid I don't know where she is."

"But her car's here."

"And hopefully she'll rouse herself to come and get it soon."

"You mean she's . . . gone?" Finally he got it. Was he stupid?

He just stood there, his arms by his side. He looked odd—stunned, though nothing I'd said was that shocking.

And then the last drifts of sleep vanished and I realized I'd seen him before: cycling that bike around the village. Not a stranger from London, some friend or contact who'd come to see Nicky; but a local. The Crompton boy, and older than he looked—back from college now, Annie had told me.

"We were supposed to meet today," he said slowly, as I remembered his name: Joe. Sometimes Joey. The same name that we had seen on Nicky's phone. This was who'd been calling her earlier. "But she didn't turn up."

I could feel my heart start to pulse in my chest. What had Nicky told him about me? What did he know? But I held his gaze evenly.

"Look, I'm afraid I really don't know where she's got to today. But I'll certainly let her know you were looking for her. Now, it's late," I said, starting to close the door slowly, "but when she turns up, as I'm sure she will"—now he'd back off, slope away to his stupid bicycle—"I will of course ask her to call you back."

He stuck a foot in the door, stopping it from closing.

"Call me back? But I didn't say I'd been calling her."

Anger flooded through me: but I refused to act as if this situation were in any way alarming, even as I kept the pressure up against the door.

"So you know she's left her phone, too," he said. "Her stuff's still here? And you haven't called the police, have you?"

He sounded bewildered, like he couldn't quite believe it, as if doing so would confirm something for him. I was doing this all wrong, and maybe I should have blustered through regardless.

But as I sensed the pressure lessen against the door in his shock, I gave a sharp hard shove to catch him off guard. His foot slipped away and I slammed the door shut, twisting the key in the lock.

I couldn't hear anything; I was expecting to hear the rattle of the door handle or shouting through it. But I didn't; he stayed there, spotlit behind the frosted glass, and said something muffled by the wood between us. I backed away, still watching from the darkness as the figure started to move, and heard the jangle of gears as he got on his bicycle.

Then I turned and ran through the kitchen and the hall, right up to the window at the turn of the stairs—wanting, animal-like, to get to higher, safer ground—and watched through the glass as the figure on the bike rolled onto the gravel, standing on the pedals to build up traction. And then a turn of the driveway took him out of sight.

I leaned against the wall, suddenly breathless. Of all the people, Joey Crompton.

He'd been inside this house when it was still a wreck; exposed it all on that website, with the floor plan and everything, for everyone to see. And still he was sniffing around, years later, far too interested in what happened here—a threat, even now.

Because his voice had been muffled, through the door, but I heard it all the same, what he said. He didn't sound angry, so much as horrified. That was the worst thing of all.

What have you done to her?

Chapter 46

I am good at compartmentalizing, I always have been. I do what needs to be done, and I don't worry about the things that are out of my control. Face each problem as it presents itself.

So I did what I always did: I got on with things. And I called the police first thing on Sunday morning. I could have done it the night before perhaps, but the timing felt reasonable—Nicky had her own key, we weren't her keepers, it was a very safe area. . . . Really, though, I needed time to gather myself after Joe Crompton's visit.

Josh had come home late the night before; I pretended I was asleep when I heard him crashing around. He showered before he got into bed though; as if that wouldn't wake me. I knew what that meant, where he had probably been—but I would have to think about that later, I told myself as I padded downstairs with my phone.

I went through the kitchen doors onto the terrace, warmed by the morning sun. 101? No—999. Show them I was taking it seriously.

* * *

The operator, a woman, kept me on the phone for a long time as she took all sorts of details: when I'd last seen Nicky; what she looked like (middling height, brown hair, I couldn't remember her eye color). No, no distinguishing marks. No, I had no reason to think she was in immediate danger. Yes, she had a car—but it was still here. I could hear the pause at the end of the phone. Perhaps I should have called them earlier.

A lot of things, I couldn't answer: her address, who her nearest contacts might be—and any inquiries that had been made to establish her whereabouts.

"Well," I said vaguely, "I don't really know who to contact."

This time the disapproval down the phone was palpable.

But I knew how to handle this, how to explain away my lack of urgency.

"Do you think I should be, well, concerned? I do hope nothing—I mean, she seemed very sensible." I trailed off doubtfully, my eyes on the horizon, letting myself take in the serenity of the lawn and the trees and the water at the bottom of the garden. "But I don't really know much about her . . ."

Yes, all I had to do was hide behind my money and vagueness and the assumption you'd expect from a woman like me: that nothing really could go wrong in a place like this; nothing really bad could happen.

Of course, I knew different.

They would send a patrol car over, they told me.

* * *

Soon, I heard the sounds that signaled Bea had woken up, so I went and brought her down and did breakfast, letting her eat in front of her favorite cartoon: I could not face a battle with a toddler right then.

When Josh appeared, rumpled with sleep, I said he had to look after her while I showered and threw on clothes myself, then went to my study at the top of the house.

Because I could not stop at calling the police. That was just the first step, to keep them from looking too closely at me.

This morning's phone call had demonstrated—if it wasn't obvious—that they would want to know Nicky's address, the names of her family and friends, any boyfriends.

I didn't have any of those details. I couldn't even say for certain that she had those people in her life, not really. She was a stranger to me. But what would a normal person do in a situation like this? She would want to help.

As my laptop powered up, I felt a surge of frustration at what I was having to do. How had I let this happen? I pushed my anger away: no point in reacting, not now.

I had to find out all I could about Nicky Wilson.

But it was harder than I expected, digging into someone's life. I googled Nicky Wilson. There were a lot of them. I went on Facebook, hoping to narrow it down, but there were countless Nicky Wilsons from London, and I gave up on that. She didn't seem to be on Instagram. Eventually I found some old articles with her byline, but they were news stories from grim court cases that had nothing of her in them.

And then I remembered something. Nicky had been speaking to her agent earlier in the week. I had interrupted when she was on the phone, when I knocked on her door to apologize for my reaction to her questions.

I felt a leap of satisfaction at the idea it gave me: I would get hold of her agent's details, so I could pass them to the police. Then I would call her agent, too, to check in with her. I would ask her if she had heard from Nicky.

That would be the most helpful—and natural—thing to do. I just had to track her down.

I had already seen Nicky's professional profile on her agency's website, of course; I had checked all that out, after I was approached about the book idea. I wasn't sure about it, at first, but the money was tempting. It would require a minimum amount of work from me for what I knew could be substantial returns. So I looked into her.

I had read the bit on the site about her time as a journalist and the *Sunday Times* best sellers she had written, albeit under other people's names. I understood she couldn't advertise openly the titles she had ghostwritten, but the literary agency's name was familiar. And I had browsed through their other clients; some of them were household names. But now I couldn't remember what the agency was called.

I propped my head on one hand. I wasn't sure, actually, that I'd spoken with anyone there—it was Nicky, wasn't it, who had approached me with the idea of doing a book? It was a while ago, but now I came to think of it . . . Yes, it *was* Nicky who initiated it all. Not her agent or any other go-between; it was her e-mail, via my website, that had first raised the prospect of us working on a ghostwritten book.

I had replied as "my PA Julia," as I always did with business propositions. I didn't like assistants and managers and other people trying to run me. I could do it myself. But it could be handy to have that extra buffer.

After that, we had gone back and forth over e-mail for a while, her setting out her credentials, explaining why a book was the logical next step for my brand . . . until there was a break in my schedule, and "Julia" finally invited her up.

Nicky, in a funny way, must have been the same as me: working alone. Still, the agency must have drawn up the contract, mustn't they? That NDA, the nondisclosure agreement that Nicky signed and sent over ages ago . . .

Bingo. I sat up and pulled the contract up on the screen from the folder where I filed them all: agreements for sponsored posts and the rest. I scanned it again, noting the initials of the agency set out in reassuringly ornate lettering. This was the one.

The switchboard number on the agency's website just rang out. But eventually, trawling through the site led me to the cell-phone number of an agent's assistant who made clear, through his exaggerated politeness, just quite how affronted he was to be contacted on a Sunday.

I could be just as icily polite, however. He didn't soften when I said who was calling, but finally agreed to give me the number for a Barbara Macmillan, Nicky's agent, after I told him it was an emergency.

It went through to voice mail, so I left a message: "Hello, this is Olivia Hayes, have you heard from Nicky—Nicky Wilson? I'm trying to reach her. We don't quite know where she has gone. Perhaps you could give me a call when you get this."

Worried, but not too worried. Responsible. I gave my cell number then hung up.

Then I sat there for a second, not moving. The light through the study window was tinted green by the boughs of the shifting trees outside; I could hear the rustle of wind through their limbs. Everything was beautiful and serene except me. I was still riled by the assistant's attitude, and more than that, oddly unsettled, in a way I hadn't been so far.

I frowned. I was being ridiculous. So one bitchy assistant didn't seem to recognize my name. That didn't mean anything. There was no reason everyone who worked at the agency would know about me or the book—

The study door swung open. I smiled as I saw who it was: Bea, wearing the remains of the lunch Josh must have given her. She smiled back at me, happy and excited about what she had to tell me. "Mummy. They here, Mummy. Police!"

Chapter 47

I found them in the kitchen, with Josh. I had got Bea settled down for her nap as quickly as I could—once I'd explained that they had no police dog with them, she was much less interested.

As I looked at them at my table, real police officers in their dark uniforms, I felt a wave of unreality wash over me: I couldn't quite believe they were here. They introduced themselves as PC Coben and PC Berry, who looked even younger than his colleague.

I hadn't known they would come so soon, and I said as much to them.

"We take all missing persons seriously," said Berry.

They were polite, formal. Josh did most of the talking, as they took us through all I had expected: why we were worried, when we had seen Nicky last, why she was here.

She had left the party early, we told them, going up to her room at about midnight, as we finished watching the fireworks. The rest of us had gone into the living room and drunk Irish coffees that our friend Leo made.

Nicky had seemed a bit tipsy, yes. Everyone had been drinking. No, not out of control. But definitely, well, drunk.

And how was her mood? That was Coben, the older one, with a long mournful face. That question seemed directed at me. Women were supposed to be more in touch with emotions, after all.

I thought for a second. The others might have noted her abrupt departure, too.

"I don't really know, she seemed a little withdrawn. But that was how she was. Is."

"And do you have any ideas as to what could have happened?"

I felt myself shrug, then regretted the gesture: too casual. Josh didn't say anything.

"No, I mean, I have no idea." And I repeated again what I had told them already: "We just woke up and she'd gone. Only all her stuff was here, we realized later. But, really, I'm sure she's fine," I added.

"I see you have a lake out there," said PC Coben.

"It's more of a pond," I said.

"A pond then. Did you see her anywhere near it on Friday night, Mrs. Hayes?"

"Near the water? No, there would be no reason for her to go near there. No, I definitely didn't."

"We might have to check that," he said, more to his colleague than to me.

"Check the pond?" said Josh.

"Well, yes," said Coben. He didn't need to spell out why.

* * *

I showed them up to the guest room Nicky had stayed in. They made it look very small, in their boots and uniforms. I saw them take in the suitcase on the floor. They put her phone, still on the side table, in a neat little plastic bag,

"What about a handbag?" That was Berry, stocky, with a very pink neck: sunburn from the long summer.

"I don't know . . ." I gestured to the room. "I think she had one—a tote bag." It wasn't there now.

Coben was still looking around. "And her computer?"

"A computer?"

"She didn't bring a computer? You said she was a writer."

"She did . . ." I said slowly. "A laptop. I haven't seen it. I mean, I haven't properly looked . . ."

"Anything else electronic? Did she record your conversations?"

You're sharp, I thought. "Uh, yes. A little black thing . . ." I looked around vaguely.

They didn't find that, either.

They had us show them the rest of the house, after that.

I was reminded, as I led them through my home, of the tour I had given Nicky, just days before. We took them all over, although I explained that she wouldn't have had any reason to go up to the attic floor, or down into the cellar.

They pulled open cupboards and wardrobe doors

without asking—as if she might just be curled up inside, fast asleep—and trod heavily past Bea's door, left ajar as she napped.

Eventually it was done, and we led them back into the kitchen. I didn't offer them a seat again, in case it would encourage them to linger, but they didn't go quite yet.

They wrote down the names of everyone who was at dinner on Friday and their contact details. I had Nicky's e-mail and cell-phone number ready to give them, culled from my inbox; I didn't have anything for her family or friends.

She hadn't mentioned anyone by name. I didn't know her home address. But there would be a photo of her on her agent's website. I remembered seeing it.

Then they wanted us to tell them all about Nicky's movements over the week, who else she had spoken to, where she had planned to go when she left.

Josh took over: she did go into the village a bit; who she had spoken to, we didn't know. But she was going to drive back to London, her apartment was there; in fact, she had mentioned an ex-boyfriend, come to think of it . . .

I felt myself relax a little. Once, when Josh and I had just started going out, we were pulled over in the BMW he roared around in then. He had been speeding, and I watched as he employed just the right amount of respectful chumminess to get away without a ticket. I had been impressed by him, how he had handled the situation.

Surely, I thought, they would go soon. Maybe it was a slow Sunday, I should have called on a Saturday when they would be rushed off their feet . . .

"And where were you on Friday night, Mrs. Hayes?" said Coben. "After you last saw Nicky."

The question seemed to come out of nowhere, and for a moment I couldn't speak.

"In bed, of course," said Josh. I felt my husband shift a tiny bit closer to my side. "Where else would she be?" He gave a little laugh—not rude exactly, but just to make clear what he thought of the question, the situation. "We both went up once everyone had left, but I imagine it was about two, two thirty."

Then, under their prompting, he explained patiently how the evening had ended.

"Leo drove off first, I think, he was blocking Harry's car in, and then Harry followed. Oh, but his wife Lucy was driving their car. And then it was just Olivia and me. Of course we were with each other all night."

"Is that right, Mrs. Hayes?" said Coben.

"That's right," I said, finding my voice. "We were with each other all night."

"One of you could have woken up," he said, his tone neutral.

"We could," Josh replied, just as easily. "But Liv isn't a deep sleeper, so if I had got up she would have heard me. And vice versa."

I nodded.

Coben kept going a bit longer. "And what time did you say your housekeeper took the tea up yesterday morning?"

"We didn't," I said. "But about nine."

"And Nicky had left by then, you believe."

"Well," Josh said thoughtfully. "We couldn't be to-tally sure. But I think before seven."

"Seven? And how would you know that?"

"Well, that's when our daughter, Bea, tends to be up," he said smoothly. "I got up with her, to give Olivia a break. And our housekeeper, Annie, was also up and about. Weekends are her time off, usually, but she was helping with the party aftermath. So one of us would have heard Nicky leave, surely."

"So she left the house sometime between midnight and seven. You believe."

"That's right." Josh smiled blandly. "I assume you are planning to speak to Annie?"

"Yes, we will. Thanks."

Josh was trying to put them on the back foot, I could tell. But he kept making the right concerned-sounding noises for a few minutes more, politely signaling that we were prepared to assist in any way we could, at the same time sorry we couldn't be more use, we had no idea where Nicky Wilson could be . . .

"So, is there anything else we can help you with?" Josh said finally, putting his arm around me. "This is very distressing, you must understand, for my wife. For us both."

"We appreciate that," said Coben glibly. "We appreciate you putting yourselves out." Something dry in his voice sounded like a rebuke.

To my relief, they left after that. Josh and I showed them out together, taking their numbers, giving them ours, promising we would be in touch if we thought of anything else; it was fine, really, routine, but in those last moments, at we stood at the front door, I could barely speak, my chest tight, I just needed them to go, now.

As I shut the door behind them, I felt my husband's arm drop from my waist.

"Josh," I said, and then didn't know what to say next.

"There was no need to complicate things," he said, his face cold even in the dimness of the entranceway. Then he turned and walked away from me.

Because, as he and I both knew, we weren't with each other all Friday night.

Chapter 48

I was still staring after him when my phone rang. I'd left it on the hall table after I'd come downstairs.

I snatched it up: I didn't know the number. *Face each problem as it presents itself.* "Hello?"

"Hello? It's Barbara Macmillan." The voice was full, theatrical.

It took me a second to place her, my head still full of the police visit.

"Barbara, of course. Hi." Nicky's agent. I sounded hoarse, and swallowed. "Thanks for calling me—I'm trying to get hold of Nicky Wilson."

This was what I had to do—keep doing. The right thing.

"Nicky Wilson," she repeated.

"Yes, would you have another number for her, maybe? I've just got her cell phone."

"Goodness, no, I don't think I do. Sorry." She sounded slightly confused.

"You are her agent?" I asked sharply. "She's on your books?"

"Nicky? Oh yes." I breathed out. "And what was

your name, sorry? It's a bit noisy here, I'm just in a café."

"Olivia. Olivia Hayes." I waited a beat, to see if that landed. "I'm an influencer." I had always hated that word. Right then I didn't care.

"Ah yes," she said slowly. "You know, I have been trying to get hold of Nicky myself. I had a new project in mind for her, really quite a good one—do you know the Coupon Queen?—but she hasn't got back to me about it."

I felt myself go very still.

"I presume she's been getting on with some of her own writing, she said she had something in mind. So, anyway—flat white please, oat milk—you're Olivia Hayes? *That* Olivia Hayes?" She had recognized my name now. "I'm so sorry, engaging brain now! I'd love to talk to you about a book, if you're thinking of one."

"No, no," I interrupted, my voice hollow. "My mistake. Got my wires crossed."

"I follow you on Instagram myself, actually." She was sounding a lot warmer. "With your sort of following, that really could be very interesting—"

"Really," I said. "I must let you go." Maybe I should have told her about Nicky going missing, and the police, but I couldn't; I needed to get off the phone.

"Well"—she sounded reluctant—"why don't I give you a call tomorrow, and you've got my number . . ."

"Thanks so much," I said firmly. "So sorry to disturb you on the weekend."

Then I hung up and stood still for a second, staring straight ahead.

* * *

Don't panic, I told myself, don't panic.

Because I was absolutely sure that Nicky's agent had no idea that Nicky was supposed to be writing a book about me, or that her agency's details were being used on the contract that Nicky had given me.

But so what? So Nicky hadn't mentioned it to her. She wouldn't be the first writer to moonlight, or to not keep her agent totally in the loop.

She was legit, I told myself, I am not an idiot. I read the small print, I do my checks.

And that contract was watertight, recognizing that the copyright was all mine, that it was my story, that she couldn't do a thing without my consent. The risk was all hers.

I wasn't even committed to producing a book. I could pull out at any time. That was why I had agreed to it in the first place.

Although I suppose if her agent didn't know about it, no one had spoken to any publishers yet, either . . .

Really, it was a big investment of Nicky's time, without a guarantee she would have anything to show for it. Almost as if it was designed to put me at my ease.

Well, that didn't matter now. It's OK, I told myself. People do it all the time, don't they, talk up their contacts, their prospects, to make things happen? So maybe Nicky blagged her way into my life, that's not the worst thing a person could do . . .

I didn't want to think about that.

Instead I thought back to what had made me call her agent in the first place: the afternoon I had knocked on Nicky's door, left ajar, and heard them on the phone.

"*. . . do you think publishers will still go for it, if she doesn't seem to want to talk about anything personal?*"

I had knocked again, catching her next comment— "*OK, I won't do anything for the mo—hold on one sec*"—before she opened the door to me, still on the phone.

"*Let me call you back, Barbara . . . I was just on the phone to my agent,*" she told me then.

I already knew she wanted me to open up, to get a good story; that call made it even more clear that it could be crucial to the book's success, piling on the pressure.

That all stood, even if I had been mistaken about one thing: they couldn't have been talking about *my* book, like I'd thought. Because Barbara didn't know anything about me.

Bea woke up after that, so I was busy until her bedtime. Josh had gone out somewhere; for a drink, to the site, I hadn't seen him to get his latest excuse. But I wasn't going to force a confrontation. That was not how we operated. I made sure of that, keeping things polite, civil. As if that could make us polite, civil people at heart.

Later, I went through my usual Sunday night routine, going to my office to check traffic to my site and social feeds. It was doing well, given that it had not had my undivided attention. I tried not to think about what exactly was keeping the engagement so high, that post on the forums a few days earlier . . .

And so the evening progressed, me keeping busy,

my mind occupied, until I felt it was late enough that I would go to sleep quickly, without dwelling on anything.

So of course, it was only as I was dropping off that the truth presented itself to me, in all its simplicity. That if Nicky wanted to cut her agent out of her latest project, but convince me of her bona fides, even as she piled on the pressure for me to give her a juicy story, turning the screw, there was an easy way . . .

There was no one at the other end of that phone call at all.

Chapter 49

The police came back the next day, half a dozen of them in their dark blue uniforms, tripping back into my beautiful house in their ugly shoes. Maybe I could ask them to take them off, I thought, hilarity bubbling up. I was starting to feel very odd.

Annie let them in, tight-lipped as they followed her into the kitchen. She had started work early that morning, punctual as ever. As Mondays went, it wasn't a good start to her week—or mine. I recognized two of the officers from last time and wondered why they hadn't asked me in advance. They were here to search again, they said.

Josh offered to accompany them around this time. I wasn't about to insist I did. That would look like I was worried. So I left them to it, heading up to my study, Annie following with Bea. They had said the rest of us had to be in the same room—"Standard procedure," according to the officer supervising us from a seat in the corner.

He said this new search was standard, too, "in case someone's fallen or got stuck somewhere." With his open freckled face, he looked like someone's dad; but when I asked how long his colleagues might take, or why there were so many of them here, he couldn't—or wouldn't—say.

So I stopped asking questions and from the study window at the top of the house watched the small dark figures fanning out across the yard. Later, I would discover they had taken away Nicky's little lemon car on a low-loader trailer, despite it being on private property, behind our gate. Even now, I find that faintly ridiculous.

When Bea started fretting, bored of the small room, the officer said it was OK if she and Annie played with her toys on the attic landing, so long as the study door stayed open. I wasn't sure the invitation extended to me.

In the background I could hear the noises from the rest of the house: doors opening, cupboards slamming, the officers searching the premises, methodically.

So, I got down to work, as Annie kept Bea entertained. It would not help anything to abandon my routine; the last week had been disruptive enough already.

I had photos to finish editing from the last shoot and a sponsored blog post to sort out after the client had sent me the wrong links, then I checked the comments under the Instagram photos that had gone up over the weekend.

Among the usual messages, there were some expressions of sympathy in relation to my childhood tragedy, heartfelt messages of congratulations at the life I had created for myself (#phoenixfromtheashes was the tag on one of the more lurid ones).

I read them through carefully. They were OK, so far. Of course, I couldn't articulate to Josh, or anyone, why I feared the exposure of my past. He couldn't understand it. He thought it was all to do with me having to appear together, perfect. He was wrong.

I checked the comments one last time. People were definitely not yet aware a woman was missing from my house, but perhaps the police would not need to publicize my involvement . . . perhaps it need never get out.

And then I focused on the next jobs at hand, putting everything else in a separate compartment of my mind, as I have done with so many other things. I let myself be soothed by the succession of tasks: sometimes challenging, but always, eventually, solvable. Work has always been a refuge for me, and I could almost pretend things were back to normal, that Annie would soon be by with a cup of tea.

When I heard someone coming up the stairs, it took a second to register the hushed conversation on the landing, before another uniformed figure filled the study doorway. "Mrs. Hayes, could you come with me," she said. It wasn't a question.

I followed downstairs, running through my head as to what they might need; the key to the garage? I hadn't had a chance to let Cav know they might be looking around, I hoped he had not been difficult or obstructive in any way; he could be quite grumpy.

But it wasn't that. There were two new people with my husband in the main hall, all three looking up at me as I went down the main stairs.

I took the newcomers in: she had neat brown hair and too-pink lipstick; he the bulky arms of a gym-goer under his gray suit. They were not uniformed, but somehow matching: something in their expressions, the way they stood together. They were a team.

Under Josh's worried gaze they introduced themselves to me as DC Kate Barnett and DS Neil Moran. Detectives.

The four of us sat in the living room off the kitchen, on the L-shaped sofa. The officers were on one leg of the sofa; Josh next to me on mine; an arrangement that now felt incongruously pally.

For a moment there was a silence, before I filled it: had they heard from Nicky, had they got in touch with anyone who had? Friends, family?

They hadn't heard from her, no. There had been no sign of her at her London apartment. They were making the appropriate inquiries. They didn't offer any more.

"Did you try her ex?"

They had. He had still been on the electoral register for her current address.

"And he can't think of anywhere she might go," said the man, Moran. "In fact, no one in Nicky's life has heard from her. And everyone we speak to says it's out of character for her to just pick up and go. They are getting very concerned."

His tone was even, but his words seemed to hang in the air, almost accusatory.

"What about her agent, Barbara something?" I jumped in. Oh so helpful. "I've found her number actually, if that would be any use . . ."

"Olivia," said the woman then—Barnett. "May I call you Olivia? A young man called Joe Crompton has also been in touch with us. He's very worried about what could have happened to Nicky."

"Oh?" I was expecting this, in a way; but I couldn't think of what else to say. "Of course, call me Olivia."

"He says he was supposed to see her on Saturday."

I shook my head. "Nicky hadn't said anything about that to me." That was true, technically.

Barnett continued: "And he says that he's never known her to do this before; that it's out of character for her to go AWOL."

"Out of character?" I couldn't just let that pass. "He's known her a week, if that."

They couldn't even get the basic facts right. I wasn't surprised. I knew how useless the police could be.

"Actually—" started Moran; but his partner carried on as if neither of us had spoken.

"Now, Joe Crompton says Nicky left a message with his grandmother on Friday, to say she'd be round to say bye to him the following day. And he says that if she wasn't going to turn up on Saturday morning, she would have let him know; that she's reliable." There was no mistaking who was in charge here. Not such a team after all.

"Yes, I suppose so," I said in response, registering that Nicky must have gone to Marie Crompton's when she went out on Friday. "Nicky did seem reliable," I added then, sensing more was expected from me. "That's why I was happy to work with her."

But Barnett didn't want to talk about working together: she stayed on topic.

"Joe Crompton also says that he knows you, too. Is that right?"

"We live in the same village," I said, "we know *of* each other, it's not quite the same thing . . ."

"Until he came to your house on . . ." she pulled out a notepad and flicked to a page. "On Saturday night, telling you that she hadn't turned up to meet him." I knew she had no need to check that.

"That's right," I said after a pause. Next to me I felt Josh shift a little on the sofa.

I'd known Joe Crompton would contact the police—that was what had prompted me to call them myself. But I hadn't mentioned his visit to the officers who arrived yesterday, or to my husband. My instinct is not to volunteer information.

"Joe says the two of you had a bit of a run-in over some photos he took a while back," she continued, sounding casual, light almost, but her eyes never left my face.

"Well, I don't think I'd say that," I gave a small laugh, "It just seemed a little . . . bad taste at the time. I don't think I was directly in touch with him over that," I added. "I believe it was my housekeeper, Annie Robson, who handled it."

She ignored that. "And he says Nicky Wilson was very interested in what had happened in this house when you lived here before. Would you agree, Olivia?"

"I don't think I would, particularly," I said. "Of course we touched on my past, in our sessions."

I could feel Josh turn his head a little, to look at me. I stayed composed: I did not get flustered, or blush, or cry. Perhaps that was a mistake, too.

"We talked about it a little," I said evenly. "I didn't want to go into detail."

"Are you quite . . . protective over your past, Olivia?" asked the woman, Barnett.

I shook my head. "No more than most people would be, given the circumstances. I'm a fairly private person, I suppose, but I share a lot of my life online. For my work."

"OK," she nodded.

I could feel it coming, perhaps with less fanfare than I expected, after all these years. The question I think I had always been waiting to hear from the police.

"Is there anything you haven't told us, Olivia? Anything we ought to know?"

Chapter 50

"Look," I said, calculating quickly. I had to head them off. "There is something you should know about Nicky Wilson." I sighed heavily, like I was troubled to share it. "She did *seem* reliable, steady. But how can I put it? I'm not sure that was the full story."

Of course I wouldn't tell them everything. But I could tell them some of what I knew about her, so that if they were thinking—well, anything I didn't want them to think—I could get ahead of the momentum that this whole affair was taking on.

Because I could feel that it was. Sometimes that is how it is: things fall apart, and even if you can see what is happening, you can't do anything to stop it, not really.

"You see," I said, "when I spoke to Nicky's agent, she didn't know anything about her being here to write a book. Which seems odd, to say the least."

I waited for them to react. Yet they didn't seem to care, or even to be surprised.

"And did that make you angry, Olivia?" said Barnett.

"No," I said. She was beginning to annoy me. "That's not what I'm saying. I didn't know that while Nicky was here. But don't you think," I added, my voice soft, concerned, "that gives some indication to what we are dealing with here. That this woman might be a little . . . unpredictable? Unstable?"

"Was that your impression of her?" she replied.

"I really wouldn't know," I said, exasperated. "But surely you should look into it. In case she's, I don't know, a bit obsessive—even disturbed? That might explain . . ."

"Might explain what?"

"Well. Why she might have—done something stupid. A vulnerable woman like that."

Moran spoke then. "Why do you think something bad has happened to her, Olivia?"

I couldn't answer.

"No, that's understandable," said Barnett kindly, as if I'd spoken. "No, I can understand that, Olivia. Given the trauma in your past."

I looked at her, alarmed as to where she might be going.

"Although," she continued in the same sympathetic tone, "Joe Crompton thinks there might be a bit more to that story. And so did Nicky Wilson."

She paused then, thoughtfully, as if deciding how to phrase this.

"He thinks that, maybe, before she disappeared, Nicky had found something out about the fire that wasn't widely known. What would you say to that, Olivia?"

Part of me couldn't believe this was happening; that she was actually asking me this. Suddenly, I laughed: a harsh sound, without humor. "You cannot be serious. That is ancient history."

But they just waited, watching me. Even Josh didn't try to bluster through this for me.

"It was all investigated at the time, you can check that." I sounded flustered, upset—wrong. All of a sudden, I had to get out of there, I couldn't bear it any longer . . .

I stood up.

"I'm sorry, I don't mean to be rude. But I really have no idea where Nicky Wilson could have gone, or why. I don't think there's anything else I can help you with. And I need to look after my daughter. Could we leave this for now?"

My question hung in the air. Then . . .

"That's fine," Moran said lightly. He got up slowly from the sofa, as if he had all the time in the world.

"Well," said Josh, attempting some of his former heartiness, "do let us know if there's any other way we can help." It rang hollow. "Let me show you out—"

"No, no," said Barnett, already heading toward the open French windows in the kitchen, "we can go out this way."

At least it was over now, I told myself, as I followed them across the terrace, but my heart was starting to pound as it started to sink in, what had just happened, how much of a mess . . .

Barnett paused at the top of the steps to hand us each a card with her number on it—"if you think of anything else, don't hesitate"—and glanced back at the house. "You really have a beautiful home," she said pleasantly, as if everything was fine. "Georgian, is it?"

"That's right," I said shortly. She shot me a look, almost amused; I just wanted them to leave, and she knew it.

But Josh took the social cue, relieved. "The front is, but the rest of it," he said cheerfully, "is quite a hodge-podge, they never really stopped building in those days."

Stop talking, I willed him; this is not small talk, she wants you on her side.

"But, of course," said Barnett, "the more, er, recent renovation must have been an enormous job. How did you manage it all?"

Of course he lapped it up. Thank goodness Moran seemed ready to go, shifting on his feet, looking around abstractedly—then he froze.

I followed the direction of his gaze.

Something small glinted in the late afternoon sunlight, picked out against the dry dark soil of the flower bed where the lawn meets the bricks supporting the terrace. It was sheer bad luck really: another inch to the left or right, and it would have been hidden by Cav's shrubbery.

The policeman darted down the terrace steps, quick despite his bulk, and knelt down, snapping on a glove. I saw it in his hand as he walked back up, the blue latex taut over his palm as, wordlessly, he showed Barnett what he'd found:

Nicky, the necklace read, in gold writing, on that tacky gold chain.

"Do you recognize this?" said Barnett, looking from me to Josh.

I replied quickly. "I do, yes. That's Nicky's." No point lying about that. "It must have fallen off when we were all out here the other night," I added.

"It hasn't been undone at the clasp," said Moran. "The chain's broken."

"It doesn't look to be very good quality," I said, and regretted it immediately.

There was a silence, as Moran decanted the chain into a little plastic bag and pocketed it.

Barnett looked back at us, the pleasantries over, her expression utterly serious. "If you can think of anything else you'd like to tell us, anything at all, it might be an idea to tell us now, rather than later. Do you understand what I am saying?"

I smiled brightly—too brightly. "Of course we will. I'm sorry, but I think I can hear my daughter calling. Good-bye."

And then I turned round to walk into the house, refusing to look back, passing between the French windows and through the kitchen until I reached the main hall. Finally out of sight, I put out a hand to steady myself on the banister, feeling the sweat on my back sticking my T-shirt to my skin.

I had felt relieved Nicky was gone. I had thought I was safe.

I was wrong.

Chapter 51

I needed to talk to Josh. But I couldn't go back out there, not until I was sure they had left. I waited inside the house, longer than I expected, until I heard car engines starting up and the gravel crunching outside; it sounded like they were all going, at last. It was getting dark now—despite the deceptive warmth of the day, it was September, not high summer—and they had been here for hours.

When I checked out of the window in the hall, to make absolutely sure, I saw Josh's black Porsche was gone, too. That shocked me, though maybe it shouldn't have.

So instead of talking to my husband about what we were going to do next, I went to relieve Annie and get Bea into bed.

Annie didn't take much persuading: she was not in a good mood. "That Nicky," she said, unprompted, as she left. "No better than she should be, if you ask me."

I looked after her, surprised. It was unlike her to be so uncharitable, but she seemed to have taken the police presence as a personal affront—maybe she was looking for someone to blame. She bustled away, up to the attic floor, to check that the officers hadn't left anything of hers out of place.

Bea was out of sorts, too, perhaps picking up on the tension in the house. After she had finally agreed to have her story and the light off, I crept out of her bedroom and pulled the door closed.

I had so much to think about in the wake of that police visit, next steps to plan; but there was something I had to consider first. Something I had been resolutely trying not to think about, until I was ready.

Now I slumped against the landing wall and let myself remember what the woman detective, Barnett, had said about Joe Crompton: "*. . . he's never known her to do this before; that it's out of character for her to go AWOL.*"

In response, I'd said Joe Crompton had known Nicky for a week, if that. The other detective had started to say something then, but Barnett had talked over him.

At the time, I'd read it as her steamrolling him; and yet that didn't quite sit with my first impression of them, or—come to think of it—any impression I had of them. Yes, she had talked more, but that was the only time that she'd cut him off.

"*Actually . . .*" he had started to say, about to . . . what? Because there was only one answer I could think of, that had been batting at the edges of my mind all evening.

He was about to correct my mistake.

Because I had assumed that Nicky had made contact with Joe Crompton while she was here; that the police got that detail wrong.

But what if *I* was wrong: what if she had got in touch with him long before that? Then all she'd have to do was, say, send a text to nail down a meeting when she arrived in Annersley.

No, I told myself, and I shook my head to clear the thought. That would mean she was already looking into my past well before she arrived. That the whole thing was so much more orchestrated than I ever considered. *No.*

But *Yes*, whispered a cold voice in my brain, of course it was all planned from the start. She lied about having her agent involved, didn't she? Don't you think she could have manipulated you in other ways, too?

Suddenly feeling exhausted, I slid down the wall, landing comfortably on the carpeted floor. It was quite all right, I told myself, really it was; it was just a lot to take in.

Because I was remembering something else, from right back at the start, when Nicky Wilson first came to stay. She had missed the e-mail about accommodation, she said, and then Josh—affable, stupid Josh, who loves to be liked—had stepped up and offered her our home.

I knew that she been sent a very detailed attachment explaining the places to stay. After all, I had sent it to her, as my assistant "Julia."

So, I was annoyed, although I swallowed it. It was just down to her ineptitude, part of the package along with her messy hair and lateness and diffidence and general air of helplessness.

But now everything was starting to be in cast in a different light . . .

What if she wanted to be here, inside the house?

That was enough, in itself, to contemplate for a moment, to try to take in, as I sat there and breathed, slow and steady, just like I learned in yoga . . .

Sabrina. Did she do something to get rid of Sabrina?

I lifted my head, focusing on this new thought.

Because hadn't Sabrina insisted that she had not been smoking in her room, when I brought it up? She swore blind that she hadn't, before she flounced off in a huff. Any sort of naked flame in my house was a non-negotiable. She knew that, which made me all the more irritated—but maybe I let that cloud my judgment.

I knew Sabrina could be rude, territorial. She had been like that since school, envious of me, but equally jealous of anyone getting too close. She was rude to Nicky . . .

Nicky, who had "noticed" the smell of cigarette smoke coming from Sabrina's room.

Suddenly I saw how it could have unfolded: all Nicky would have had to do was nip into the guest room where Sabrina was staying, a few doors down from her own, and light one of the Camels she always left lying around. Then she told Annie, who went in, found that half-smoked stub floating in the toilet, and told me.

It all fit.

But if that was the case, I thought, feeling my breath come a little faster, tighter, that would make Nicky Wilson a very different person from the woman she seemed to be that first day. Far more determined. Ruthless even, willing to do whatever it took . . .

"No," I said aloud then. "She wouldn't . . ." even as I was clambering up, running over to the door to the back stairs. I took them two at a time.

Chapter 52

As I told Nicky, I don't check the forums. What I did-
n't tell her is that they used to fill me with dread
when I first started out online. What would I see? What
might people see in me? So I stopped looking, long
ago.

On the attic floor, the door to Annie's room was
closed; she goes to bed early. I was quiet in my dim
study, as I fired up the browser on my laptop, clicking
until I had found that thread about me.

When I reached the right page, I read the comment
again, the one that had kicked it all off: "This is her,
right? So this is why we never hear about her background. Guess who her dad is? Or should I say *was* . . ."

And there was the marriage announcement, that
Josh's bloody mother had placed in the newspaper
after I had expressly said I didn't want it, brushing
aside my concerns with that indomitable certainty that
This Was How It Was Done—tying me to my past for
anyone to find . . . and then someone had.

It was a bad night, when I first saw the thread. It

brought up a lot of things—bad things. Afterward, I had pushed it all to the back of my mind. That was what I always did.

This time I didn't. This time I was not so focused on the post itself, or any of those that followed it. Instead I looked at the username of the person who had started off the thread: FUNMUMMY99. I clicked on it, to open up the user's profile.

There was nothing alarming, at a glance. No streams of bile about me, no horrifying details spilled about my life in other posts. Nothing about any other unfortunate influencer who had found herself in the user's sights, either.

Nothing at all.

This was this user's only post. She had never posted on the site before or after. She had just opened an account to drop a bombshell, then disappeared.

It could be just a coincidence, of course.

But I knew not to believe in coincidences. I pulled up Twitter, and found the message that someone had tagged me in, alerting me to the existence of the thread—that the genie was out of the bottle:

@TheOliviaHayes so sry to hear about your dad that is so sad babe can't believe it x

This was from another nonsense name: Tuttifrutti86, with no photo attached.

I clicked through to the profile and felt coldness move down my spine. I read the words again.

Sorry, that page doesn't exist!

The account had been deleted.

I am not one to waste tears. "No use crying over spilt milk," Annie would say. But I knew. Nicky had done this to me. She had started that discussion in the forum.

I should have realized from the timing: it was so recent, relatively, that the post had gone up. For someone to have found out about my past and shared it online, just before she arrived? Then for a follower to alert me to it the very week Nicky was here, asking me questions that I wouldn't answer?

I knew how hard it was to just stumble across that information: I had checked, more than once. And I knew I had not been giving Nicky what she wanted; I wasn't opening up.

And so she had laid my past bare in front of strangers to pore over. To try to pressure me into talking, into telling her my story.

OK. So maybe Nicky Wilson was far cleverer, more manipulative, than I had given her credit for. Not such a, well, *victim*, after all.

I had to face the facts. It was crystal clear, however you looked at it. This woman had planned it all for months: setting herself up to get some lurid tug-at-the-heartstrings tell-all, cashing in on my profile. She must have thought she could persuade me in the end—just think of the book sales.

She couldn't have imagined, as she prepared to come here, what the real story was. For a second I pictured her, hunched in front of a computer in some dingy apartment: going through the old newspaper stories, finding out everything she could about me . . .

I couldn't believe I had let her get so far, could feel the sick dread swelling in me even as I tried to stay calm: she was in my house, she stayed under my roof, she met my child; *the police even asked me about the fire* . . .

But she couldn't hurt me. Not *now*.

Could she?

It was hard to breathe; I needed air. I went to the window; Annie had pulled the blinds half down, practiced in all the cozy touches that make even a house like this a home.

The wooden frame was cracked open to the still night, but not a breeze stirred the room. And standing there, I was suddenly very aware of the silence around me.

It works that way sometimes; in an instant you wake in the night and tune in to the far-off drone of hotel machinery, an electric buzz from a strange TV, the high-pitched whine of a mosquito, and know that even if, until then, you were able to ignore the noise quite comfortably, sleep is lost now.

And in the same way, standing at the top of my house, looking into the blackness of the late summer night in the country, I now heard it, all around me: the vast quiet pressing in; the nothingness rising up to meet me. It was implacable, immutable, and yet all too familiar . . . *no one is coming to help.*

Violently I yanked on the cord to pull up the blinds and threw the window wide open, leaning precariously into the night. I took in a deep heaving breath, and another and another.

Afterward, I went back to the chair at my desk and sat there, until the sickness had subsided a little, the sweat cooling on the back of my neck.

Looking up, my mind almost blank, I saw the flowers in front of me, a vase on the edge of my desk holding lilies, large, white, and scentless. They had been sent to me by a PR person looking for coverage of her brand.

I had often sat in that chair, admiring the latest arrangement in my vase, the frilly china and soft blossoms offering the perfect counterpoint to the solidity of my aged wooden desk.

You wouldn't have known, from the gentle harmony of the room, that I had thought so very hard about it all, how to draw together the color scheme, how best to display its small but elegant proportions, how to perfectly showcase my taste and judgment and authority, without ever buckling under the weight of tradition, without ever being crushed by the history of this house.

And yet I had managed all that, I had lived with all that, making a success of my life, doing what I was supposed to, making the correct choices. I had got every tiny detail right, down to that delicate vase in front of me. I had searched for a very long time to find one that fitted with my memories.

I leaned over and picked the vase up in both hands, balancing it for a moment, feeling its weight, the water moving inside.

Then I pictured what would happen next, just as I did with my tennis serve: how I would throw with all the force of my upper body, in a practiced overhead shot against the shut door, watch it smash dead center, water dripping down the cream paint, broken china and long-stemmed flowers scattered over the rug . . .

I put the vase down, carefully, nudged it an inch so it was back in its place.

I was in control. I had to stay in control. I was always in control.

Or was I? Who was writing my story, even now?

I don't know how long I would have stayed there, frozen.

But then I heard it, breaking the silence of the night. I lifted my head and listened, as the noise came again.

Downstairs, floors below me, somebody was beating down the door.

Chapter 53

As I ran down from the top to the bottom of the house, I had visions of Joe Crompton returned, angrier than before, shouting things at me. *What have you done to her? What are you hiding?* But then the noises resolved themselves, echoing up the narrow back stairs—not knocks on a door, but heavy thuds.

As I opened the door onto the ground-floor corridor, I saw the overhead lights were on in the kitchen, the cellar door open, and knew what the sounds were. Someone was down below, crashing things around.

I went into the family room and glanced out of the window at the driveway to confirm what I thought: Josh's car was back.

At least the police had been quiet, methodical. He was moving heavy items about, and roughly, from the sound of it. Already, I knew what he'd be looking for: what I had left down there. I thought he might have forgotten I'd even put it there, in all the chaos of moving in, years ago. I had told him I would deal with it later, when I had more time, but I never wanted to.

I walked back into the kitchen, trying to compose myself for what lay ahead, and heard him breathing heavily with the effort as he carried it up the cellar stairs. There was another crash as he dumped it down on the floor, carelessly. All that dirt and pain.

He looked up, unsurprised to see me. He has always needed an audience, Josh.

"So," he said, his tone challenging. "Aren't you going to open it now?"

The box was already open anyway: the masking tape had been torn off. Had the police already been through it? Or no, that would have been Nicky, when she found that old family photo.

He directed a kick at it, enough to make it jump a little way along the floor.

"Josh," I said, a warning note in my voice.

But he did it again, almost experimentally, like a child who has just been told not do something.

"Why not, Olivia?" he demanded. "What've you been hiding in here all these years?"

I kept my expression neutral. *I will not react.*

And so I stood there as he kicked the box with more force, and then began to put his full strength into it, as he stamped down, again and again, with grim determination. He was silent and I was, too, listening to his small grunts of exertion and the stamp, stamp, stamp, of his foot on the cardboard, sweat starting to bead on his forehead.

I waited, not saying anything, as he kicked right through the cardboard, one side collapsing open. He coughed a little at the dust that had come up and paused to wipe his eyes, so I could see what was inside before he did; what I'd left down there, unwilling to unpack. But instead my mind was showing me things I never let myself touch on: about my family; what happened here; what I covered up . . .

"Olivia," said Josh, and I looked up to meet his gaze, his face showing genuine shock.

Because there was nothing in there. Nothing worth keeping, just those few smoke-worn objects.

"Jesus . . . you kept all this crap. But why?"

He was right: it was rubbish. It didn't matter to me now. But what he'd done was another betrayal.

He wiped his brow with his shirt sleeve, and I could feel his angry energy evaporating into confusion as I walked to the kitchen door.

"I'll get Annie to tidy that tomorrow," I said. "Unless you're going to."

I kept my tone the right side of scathing, wanting to tip him into self-consciousness. He was always quick to temper, I knew, but it would go quickly, too, if I didn't react. And I never did.

As I reached the door I thought: if I've handled this right we can leave this here, another thing we won't talk about when he's calmer . . .

"You've got to be kidding me," he spat out.

I stopped. I'd played it wrong. He was embarrassed now. He had gone too far and needed a confrontation to match the drama of the moment he had staged.

I turned round.

"Our house is crawling with police, a woman's missing, and you've nothing else to add," he said. "Don't you think you owe me an explanation?"

I kept my face blank, a little disdainful. "Of course,

Josh, I'm happy to talk about what's going on. Fire away."

I could tell by the pause before he spoke that my reaction had left him a little unsure. "For starters, after our dinner party—did you really just sleep through the night? Because how can I know if you did . . ."

"And I could say the same of you, if you really want to go there," I said coolly. "But I was in bed, just where I was supposed to be. And let's just remember, I didn't ask you to lie to the police about that night." Fight fire with fire. "That was your decision."

I could see him think about that for a moment.

"All right," he said. "So where is Nicky? *Do* you know where she's gone?"

I shook my head, my stomach clenching—but better this chilly civility than screaming, surely. "No, I don't."

"OK." He took a deep breath. "Do you know why the police are so interested? Because I don't have to be a detective myself, to work out what they're thinking: that she hasn't just gone off somewhere of her own accord."

"I don't know what they're thinking," I said, still calm. "But there is nothing to worry about."

"Oh? And you aren't a bit worried by what she might have been finding out?" He was watching my face closely.

"It's all very sad, of course it is—for her friends and family; but why would I worry?"

He shook his head, as if he couldn't believe me, or the situation. "You know, I think we should give this whole thing a rest now, Olivia."

"Fine by me." I was careful not to show the relief I was feeling, how rattled I was. "I am more than happy to draw a line under this whole conversation . . ."

But he shook his head again. "No, I mean us. Our marriage."

Chapter 54

"It hasn't been working for me for a while now," said Josh, his expression determined.

"Oh, it hasn't been working for *you*?" I heard myself say, with heavy irony. I sat down heavily on one of the kitchen chairs behind me.

"I need more, Olivia. I deserve more."

"You're really going to do this now?"

But he did. And as he kept talking, after that, it struck me that it was like he was repeating a script he'd pulled from somewhere, but I didn't know my part.

Soon I was barely listening. Because I had tried so hard, for so long, to keep us together, trying to make us feel like we looked from the outside, the perfect couple. Even after Bea, when I thought we might get closer, he disappeared further away, jealous again of my split attention, needing shoring up—I had been so calm, so reasonable, so controlled, careful never to touch the things that were wrong between us, never to voice them out loud, as if doing so would break the spell.

Instead, he had.

As I tried to absorb the shock, my attention closed in on what he was saying now: ". . . should never have let you bring me up here."

"Me? You couldn't wait to get up here!" I don't know why that got me in particular; him rewriting our history. "You couldn't wait to jack in your job, and be the big man up at the big house."

He looked briefly shocked by my unusual bluntness, and some part of me found it almost comical. But he recovered quickly.

"Well, work isn't everything," he said, his neck flushing red. "Better that than be obsessed by it; you've made it your whole life, put *our* whole life all over the Internet. That's what you wanted."

"Yes, it *was*," I said, the emphasis heavy on the "was." And maybe when I started all that I was making a point: look how perfect my life, my house, my family is—was. "But I'd have stepped away years ago if I could, and you know that."

"And if you hadn't let that woman come here to write a book about you," he said stiffly, ignoring what I'd said, "we wouldn't be in this situation now."

"I let her? I didn't even want to do a book!"

And with that—after a day of dealing with the police, with Annie, with Bea; after a whole week of Nicky poking around the place—I felt my anger, long tamped down, start to slide out of my control.

"But while you played property developer, someone had to pay for all this," I stood up, gesturing around at the beautiful house. "Someone's had to keep our family together."

"And a great job you're doing of it," he said, "police all over the place, people talking."

"I've held up my side of the bargain, Josh, you can't say that I haven't."

But he raised his voice over mine, throwing words to wound: "Are you even thinking of our daughter, what all this will do to her?"

I took a furious intake of breath.

And then both of us went for it in a way we never had before, in a way I'd never let happen—the stress and anger exploding between us—as the immediate disaster facing us was overtaken by all the long-buried hurts of our marriage:

"You know I've been the perfect wife, perfect mother—"

"I can't do it anymore, it's exhausting, you're exhausting—"

"One of us had to be the grown-up, one of us had to carry this house, our life—"

"It's not normal, for someone to be so cold—"

"I've tried so hard, you know I've done the best I could—"

"You're messed up, you'll mess Bea up, too—"

"*You knew who I was when you married me.*"

My words hung in the air between us; too late I realized my mistake.

"Did I?" he said slowly. I met his eyes, expecting to see sadness, grief maybe, but his look was crafty. "Did I know who you were?"

I was silent, panic rising in me; I'd pushed things too far.

"You think I don't know, Olivia," he said, his tone

controlled again, and that frightened me more than before, "but I do. I know a lot."

"Josh," I said—my voice sounded hoarse, "I don't . . ."

Of course I hadn't told him what really happened the night of the fire: I was not an idiot.

"At first I thought it was your way of coping, that you wouldn't talk about it," he said. "Even when you wouldn't go to your own mother's funeral. You just said something bad happened that night."

But things were different at the beginning. I trusted him.

"And now I know other things, too. I know that you were in trouble before the fire, that your parents wanted to send you away."

It's hard to hide who you are from someone, however much you try.

"You've been talking to Sabrina," I said hollowly. I'd never worked out how much she knew, but it was enough to want to keep her on my side. "She's never really liked me," I said, my only defense, and it was true—but it was like a red rag to a bull.

"Don't blame her," he said, raising his voice again. "Tell me, Olivia. What really happened the night of the fire? And what has it to do with Nicky going missing? Because I don't think it's a coincidence, any of it."

"Josh," I said, desperately. "You can't really believe . . ."

"I know you. I know how you operate."

The silence stretched between us. I didn't know what to say. Then, from behind me in the hall, I heard the slow tread down the back stairs that Annie insists on using.

"Annie's coming," I said quietly, not daring to show my relief at the reprieve. We behaved in front of other people, it was one of the unbroken rules of our marriage.

But as I turned on my heel and walked down the corridor to the main hall, I heard his voice, raised deliberately to follow me, my husband not caring who heard.

"Tell me the truth, Olivia! What have you done?"

Chapter 55

The next morning, I got Bea ready and went out. Josh had slept in a guest room overnight . . . or, at least, I thought he had. Still, that was the best thing, I decided: give him time to cool off, like always.

It was Tuesday, and I had work piling up. But instead I buckled a mildly protesting Bea into her car seat and drove to the supermarket, the big one in Mansford.

I took my time in the aisles, picking up a few things. We looked around the shops for a bit. Then Bea and I sat in the window of our favorite café, where they gave her a babyccino—all froth—that she decided made her "a big girl."

I started to feel a bit better for the break, for the interlude of normality.

But eventually I had to go home again. And, as I drove up the driveway to the house, I leaned forward over the wheel, craning to see in the brightness. My pulse started to quicken.

Josh's car was in front of the house, along with a police car and an unmarked one, dark and sleek. I hesitated, then parked awkwardly on the side of the driveway, so I didn't have to drive past the house windows. My car was big and hard to maneuver around so many other vehicles. If anyone asked.

Then I didn't go straight inside—instead, I took Bea by the hand, skirting the far edge of the driveway, so you wouldn't see us if you happened to glance out from within.

"Let's go round the back way shall we, Bea? We'll check on the blackberries, see if there are any for you to pick." This had been our routine for the last few weeks, although of course things were not exactly routine anymore.

We were rounding the side of the house when I stopped. They had driven a police van right across the lawn and down to the edge of the lake, leaving dusty brown tracks on the thirsty grass.

And there were people at the bottom of the garden: half a dozen figures by the water's edge, a couple of them in black diving kits. The water was deeper than it looked, and cold. So they were already searching the lake—for a body—*oh God*—

"They been swimming, Mummy," Bea piped up. It brought me back to myself.

I started to walk on, her hand in mine. "Never mind that, let's go and look at Cav's garden."

In the walled garden by the kitchen door, Cav grew runner beans and berries and other good things. Josh had been on at me to tell him to stop taking them for himself, too. To my relief, Cav was there, kneeling among the beds.

"Would you mind keeping an eye on Bea just for a second, I need to . . ." I trailed off.

I need to see what is waiting for me in my house.

He straightened up and nodded at me. "No bother. I'll keep an eye on her."

I smiled, reflexively. *I should never have left Josh alone. What are they saying to him?*

No one was in the kitchen. But as I walked into the main hall I stopped. I could hear voices, low and urgent, coming from the front sitting room. I never used it.

I listened for a second, before I placed who was speaking: the man, Moran?

The door was almost closed, cracked open just an inch or two. I went to it carefully, soundless in my expensively scuffed sneakers.

I could see the back of someone's head: yes, there was Moran, sitting on a sofa, and there was Barnett's brown ponytail next to him. And opposite, standing by the mantelpiece, was Josh.

"But I've told you everything I know." He sounded upset. "My wife will be back soon."

"As you've said"—that was Moran—"and we're keen to speak to her also, when the moment is right. But you need to understand that this is a very serious situation."

I shifted a little closer and Josh's face came into view. It was tense and pale. He looked angry, no—

scared. This was getting too close for him; he wasn't used to things going wrong.

"I don't know anything about where that bloody gun is. This is harassment, you know."

They didn't seem very bothered about that.

"Let me mention a few things to you," said Moran, steel entering his voice. "Aiding and abetting. Assisting an offender. Concealing an offense. Preventing a lawful burial. Do you know what those charges mean, Josh?"

"Charges!" Josh sounded horrified. "Good God, I . . ." He broke off, running a hand through his hair.

Barnett spoke now, more sympathetic, conciliatory: "I know how hard it must be for you, Josh. But if you know something, you need to tell us now. You can't protect anybody. However much you'd like to."

My husband looked down into the empty hearth, and I felt a sick heat in the pit of my stomach, sweat at the back of my neck. He just needed to stick to what he had already told them, stick to his story.

"You've got to do the right thing," I heard Barnett say soothingly. "For your own sake."

"I'm sorry," His face was grave as he turned back to them, and for a moment I had hope—*I can't help you any further*, I finished for him—"but I'm afraid I've not been entirely forthcoming."

He was going to do it, I knew then, he was going to tell them.

Josh took a deep breath—my husband has always had a sense of theater—and said, "I can't lie: I've got to be accountable. Got to face up to what I've done."

The room was utterly still: the two heads frozen as both detectives waited for him to speak.

"I don't know where Olivia was the night Nicky disappeared," he said slowly. "Because I wasn't with her."

For a second I think Moran heard it as something else: a confession.

"Are you saying . . ."

But no.

"I was with someone else," Josh said. "All night."

Barnett got it first. "Are you saying you were cheating on your wife?"

My husband gave a cough. "Well—yes. I'm afraid I am."

He looked as if he were apologetic, but I could read the relief in his stance. He had relaxed now he was actually doing this: he could see his way out.

"It's very awkward, but this person will be able to vouch for me. I was with Sabrina Alderson—you'll recall that she was one of our guests that night. Her husband Leo wanted to leave before she did, and so we offered her one of the guest rooms, as we often do, and I, er, joined her in there."

I knew this already, of course. He has never been very subtle about his activities.

Even if I hadn't still been awake when he left our bed that night, the early morning shower he had taken, breaking his usual weekend routine, would have given him away the next day.

I remembered how the party had ended that evening: Leo and Sabrina standing out by their car, her hushed angry whisper reaching us as we said our good-byes to Harry and Lucy: ". . . so much to drink, Leo." Like she could talk.

His response, carelessly loud, carried through the night: "Stay then. I'm going." And then he had got in the car and driven away, gravel spurting up from the wheels.

Well, of course Sabrina had to stay, Harry and Lucy were going in quite the other direction, Josh said. And so he set her up in a spare bedroom down the hall from us, and I felt the mattress shift and roll as soon as he thought I was asleep.

She had gone by the time I went downstairs the next morning: he must have given her a lift. Perhaps even Josh couldn't face his wife and mistress and daughter sitting around the breakfast table together when he had a hangover.

"And is this the first time that you and this woman have . . ." That was Moran.

"No. No, I'm afraid not. Things being what they are between my wife and I . . . we have tried to do our best, for our daughter. But our marriage has its problems."

"And she will say the same, will she? This Sabrina."

"Yes . . . I rather think she will." He sounded so mild, so gentle—so reasonable.

Things were worse than I had realized, then, if Josh was so sure she would vouch for him that night. Inside the room, he was still talking: "And as Sabrina is still living in the family home herself, for the moment, I trust you'll be suitably discreet . . ."

Barnett tipped her head to one side in a questioning

gesture I could read as clearly as she had spoken: *Really?* Tiptoeing round the niceties of his shagging was not her priority. I liked her a little more for that.

But now his wrongdoing would give him an alibi and put all of their focus on me. Josh didn't need to spell it out, but he did anyway. "So of course, the unfortunate thing is . . . I cannot say what my wife was doing that night, after all."

Chapter 56

Despair surged up in me, my eyes prickling. I moved away from the door quietly and went through the house, out to the kitchen garden. Bea was examining a worm that Cav had turned up, curling pink and exposed against the brown soil.

I walked over to the arch of the wall to compose myself, not wanting her to see me upset. Down at the bottom of the lawn, it looked like the diving team was finished for the day, putting equipment away in their van. Thank God.

I turned my back on them to watch Bea, my throat still burning as I fought back regret. I should never have let Sabrina under my roof, whining about her issues with Leo—as if I didn't know why her marriage was really in trouble.

Not that my own was in a better state. Josh taking up with the nanny was bad enough; I'd turned a blind eye to that for as long as I could, not wanting to disrupt things for Bea.

Sabrina was trickier still: I'd known her for a long

time. I didn't want a rift. So I told myself, let him get bored, let it burn itself out. Just keep it all together. Don't crack—even when she turned up at the house last Tuesday, interrupting that quiet meal, supposedly wanting "our" support and advice.

But it was worse than I could have imagined, having her stay. When Leo failed to turn up for tennis the next day, of course I knew why—and couldn't hide my frustration from anyone.

Then, when the information about my past leaked online, I made the mistake of telling Josh. Reading it on my phone, I hadn't thought of a lie quickly enough to explain my shocked expression. His anger surprised me—he was sick of the drama, he said; Sabrina was surely stirring the pot: *Poor you, having to deal with Liv's baggage.*

When he wanted to cancel our dinner party, coming up with some excuse about the chatter online, I knew he was worried people would be talking about him and Sabrina—especially if she was a no-show, after I'd told her off about the cigarette.

I didn't see why I should cancel; Nicky could take her place. When Sabrina turned up after all, I ended up seating the two of them together—I didn't want Sabrina anywhere near Josh, if I could help it. But that was another mistake; she was so drunk. What could she have told Nicky? I'd never been sure exactly what she knew . . .

I shook my head. There was no point doing this to myself, not right now.

"Bea," I called. "Time to go in. Cav's got to get on. Thanks for looking after her," I added.

He nodded, as she trotted over. "Found treasure,"

she said confidentially, then bent down with a huff to pick something off her shoe.

"Did you, Bea," I said absently. "Just like Peppa." The little pig's treasure hunt was her favorite episode.

"No," she said firmly. She put a hand on my jeans and pulled. "Found treasure."

And then I finally paid attention to where she was looking, and turned round.

There was no sense of urgency in the scene before me, no one rushing or running about, no one in the water, from what I could see.

But something about the way they were standing, the lines of their bodies not quite relaxed, held me there on the grass, still under the vast white sky.

And then I saw what was on the ground, what they had dredged up from the water.

Eventually I found my voice. "No, Bea, that's not treasure."

It didn't look like anything to be afraid of: no telltale bundle of clothes and something else lying by the rushes. It was just a small dark shape flat against a yellow tarpaulin. It was covered in mud, although in one spot the dirt had come off, perhaps where a diver had handled it. But I saw the dull gleam, and I knew what had surfaced from the lake, what could bring my house of cards tumbling down completely.

They hadn't found what—*who*—they were looking for.

But they had found the gun.

* * *

There was nothing to do right then but take Bea back inside.

I kept up a stream of loud chatter to announce my approach through the house: ". . . time for tea Bea, fish sticks I think, are you hungry yet—everything OK?"

That was to Josh, already in the hall with Moran and Barnett. My husband's guilt was written all over his face—I had to bite back an impulse to ask him what was wrong, calling him out. But they all acted as if this was a routine visit; as if the detectives had just been checking in. We both saw them out.

The rest of the day passed in its usual fashion. Josh kept looking at his phone and going to make calls— Sabrina? The police? I didn't know—then he went out again later, saying he had a few things to do. He didn't bother to make anything up.

At one point I went up to my study. I phoned the guy who normally helped me with my contracts and asked for a recommendation. He gave me a name of a firm in Chester, the nearest city to us. I knew I needed a lawyer now, that it was just a matter of time after the detectives' talk with Josh—and them finding that thing in the lake.

Then I went through the motions of Bea's teatime, bath time, bedtime. Everything was beginning to feel dangerously muffled, somehow removed from me, as if I were underwater. And yet I knew everything was moving far too fast. I had to stop it. I asked Annie to listen out for Bea, in case she woke up, and went out.

As I walked up the dark cottage path, I wondered how to play it. I hadn't seen him for years, only from a distance since I had been back. Of course we hadn't talked. But I had nowhere else to turn now, except to the person who had helped me long ago.

He opened the front door, light spilling into the night. Behind him I could hear the buzz of the television. There was a faint smell of cooking in the air, onions sizzling.

And I could see from his expression, as he recognized me, that it was a mistake to just turn up.

"You shouldn't have come here," he said, immediately.

"I'm sorry, but please let me explain—I just need your advice. I'm in trouble."

He stepped deftly in front of the door, pulling it to behind him. "I can't help you."

"I know what you did for us, all those years ago . . ."

He just shook his head, then, his mouth closed. He is a tough man, I thought, his job has made him so.

". . . and I've always been grateful, Mr. Gregory, to your nephew, too . . ." I could hear the ugly pleading tone in my voice.

From inside the house, a woman's voice called: "Pete, love? The film's about to start. Who's that there?"

We were silent, my eyes searching his face: I could see the distaste written across it, and something else, too. That was when I knew he would not help me: he was afraid.

"You need to go," he said, his voice low but emphatic. "Now."

I knew how risky it could be to press him. I didn't wait for him to tell me again.

*   *   *

Back home, I went to my bedroom and sat on the bed, feeling the house vast and silent around me. I switched on the TV on the wall. When Josh came back, I heard him disappear to a guest room again.

I couldn't sleep. I went up to my office: I had time to arrange some loose ends, but there didn't really seem to be anything much worth doing, when it came to it. Eventually, I closed my laptop and went in to see Bea as she lay sleeping in her painted jungle.

"I never meant for any of this to happen," I whispered to her. I touched one soft, hot cheek. "All I wanted was to forget what had happened. I don't know how I can make it all right again now. But maybe one day you will be able to understand."

Chapter 57

I was ready and dressed, when they arrived the next day: the gruesome twosome, Moran and Barnett, with two uniformed officers behind them. As if I was going to kick off, make a fuss. I stood back from the door and let them all into the hall, waiting. In a way, I had been waiting for this to happen for a very long time.

"We've got a warrant to search the address. Section eight PACE warrant," said Moran. "I'm arresting you on suspicion of the murder of Nicola Wilson."

I sat down on the stairs behind me. For some reason I still felt the shock of it, now that it was finally happening.

"And of disposing of her body in a manner likely to obstruct the coroner," he continued.

So they thought I'd hidden Nicky's body somewhere.

"You do not have to say anything, but it may harm your defense if you do not mention when questioned something you later rely on in court. Anything you do say may be given in evidence. Do you understand that?"

"Yes," I said, finally. "But I didn't do it."

"We can speak to you at the station," he said. "These officers will transport you there."

I saw Annie at the top of the stairs. "Tell Josh I have been arrested," I said then. "Look after Bea." I couldn't say good-bye to her.

At the police station in Mansford, I had to give my fingerprints. Someone swabbed my skin and my mouth, for DNA, collected scrapings from under my fingernails, and plucked a sample of my hair. They took away my clothes and gave me a too-big gray tracksuit and sneakers to wear.

I was polite, and they were, too. There was no point making things more unpleasant than they had to be. They had done it all before, and for some reason that scared me more than if they were all riled up, shouting and swearing like on TV.

I told them I wanted a lawyer, one from a firm recommended to me, and they said they would contact them. "I need to make arrangements for my daughter," I said then, and they were quite reasonable about letting me make that call also.

Not to Josh, but to Lucy. I asked her to please go and pick up Bea from my house, could she and Harry look after her for the night. Maybe for the next couple of days . . . I couldn't go into why just now. Lucy was confused, then alarmed, but agreed.

I didn't want Bea in the house while things unfolded, and Josh was never great at handling her alone at the best of times. I couldn't leave it all to Annie.

Then, after the suddenness of it all, everything moved slowly again. I was put in a cell, small and boxy and with an undertone of vomit that the smell of disinfectant couldn't mask. I was alone, for which I was grateful, but I had nothing to do now—they'd taken my phone and handbag. So I waited, trying to stay calm. Trying not to think about things that couldn't help me.

It felt like hours before an officer showed me into the little room where my lawyer was. Nadia Malik, she said her name was: tall and glossy despite her gray suit, but surprisingly young-looking.

"The first thing you need to know is that with something of this seriousness, it's standard procedure to arrest before they question you," she told me briskly. "It doesn't mean they have enough to actually charge you. OK?"

I nodded. But I couldn't say I was reassured as she started to explain what the police wanted to talk to me about. "There was minimal disclosure," she said, more to herself than me, as she opened her notebook. She only had the barest details.

Yet it still seemed like a lot, as she read out the outline of the case they'd given her, starting with the potential evidence of a crime. The fact that Nicola Wilson hadn't used her phone—had left it behind, in fact—or her bank cards. That she had not been heard from by friends or contacts since Friday night—it was now Wednesday, she reminded me unnecessarily. The unknown whereabouts of Nicola's laptop and voice recorder. The discovery of her necklace, possibly torn off in an altercation.

And then she moved on to their suspicions relating to me, in particular.

The circumstances of the fire that had occurred at the house some years ago. And the gun found on my property, which might have a bearing on a potential historic crime.

Her eyes flickered from her notes to my face at that: I didn't react.

Signs of disturbance in a second cellar, she continued . . .

I wondered if that was where they thought I had put the body, at some stage.

"I do know Nicky was in there," I offered. "They might find, I don't know, her hair or something, but that doesn't mean anything. She went down there of her own volition."

She didn't react. And, she said then, the police had an account from my husband. "I gather," she added, raising her eyebrows slightly, "that your alibi for the night Nicky disappeared has been withdrawn."

"Yes. But they haven't found a body." I clung to that fact.

My lawyer seemed less moved than I'd have hoped. "That's true. But if the evidence is sufficient, they can prosecute in the absence of a body. And of course they'll be in your house now, looking for trace amounts of blood, any signs of violence."

I pictured officers in white plastic suits, dogs sniffing around the place . . .

She closed her notepad with a snap and steepled her fingers.

"Now, Olivia," she said. "It's difficult for me to assess the strength of the case at this point. When the police interview you, it will be recorded and could be used in any trial. So, my advice to you is to make no comment, and in due course we can assess all the evidence they have. Do you understand what I'm saying?"

Don't commit us to something we can't take back, she was telling me. *Get your story straight later.*

I nodded, pushing down my panic. "OK."

When my lawyer was sure I knew what to say—nothing—she went to tell an officer that we were ready. We were moved to another stuffy room where Barnett and Moran were waiting for us at a small Formica table. A battered-looking camera was fixed in the corner of the room. They checked that I knew it was recording, announced who was present, our names, my details. I was reminded, incongruously, of Nicky, just days ago in my living room, getting our names for the tape in that first session.

"Olivia," said Moran. "I'll caution you that you do not need to say anything, but anything you do say . . ." and he ran over those familiar words again.

They checked I knew what the caution meant; reminded me I could break to speak to my lawyer separately, at any point, if I wished. And then we began.

Chapter 58

"So, Olivia," said Moran. "We're here to talk about the disappearance of Nicky Wilson. And the offense we are investigating is murder."

Nadia interrupted then, to tell them that she had advised me, her client, to say "no comment," before starting to read from a sheet of paper she had prepared. "My client wishes to exercise her right not to answer any questions but has asked me to read out this statement . . ."

As we'd agreed, it denied the offense, repeated what I'd already told them—I had been asleep in my bed all that night, I did not know what had happened to Nicky Wilson—before concluding: "My client will now answer no comment to any further questions."

They didn't react; Nadia had said that people facing a murder charge almost never gave an account under questioning at this stage.

"Now, Olivia, no decisions have yet been made as to whether you will be charged," said Moran evenly. "Of course, as you know, we have not found a body yet."

"So if you do have any idea where Nicky is, now is your chance to tell us," said Barnett, picking up the baton smoothly. "We need to understand your role in all this. We need you to give us your side of the story, Olivia."

They had started using my name a lot. I didn't take that as a good sign.

Then Moran began.

"Do you know where Nicky Wilson is now?"

"Can you tell us what happened to Nicky?"

"You are one of the last people to see her, if not the last. Did you speak to Nicky after your party?"

"Did you have an argument about what she was writing about you?"

No comment, I said, no comment. I kept my expression polite but interested, meeting their eyes when they spoke to me. I just had to get through this, I told myself.

"I'm suggesting to you," said Moran then, measured as ever, "that Nicky left her car at your house because she had died, she had been killed, in your house. Is that right? You tell me."

So that really was where they were going. I looked from him to Barnett, taking in their serious expressions, and felt my lawyer move in the seat beside me, reminding me:

No comment.

I thought they might stop soon, if I didn't say anything. But then Barnett started to ask about Josh.

"Your husband told us he has been very concerned about your behavior recently. Is that fair, Olivia?"

No comment. The trick, I'd always found, is to just let the words wash over you; don't react and they can't hurt you.

"Josh says you've been arguing a lot recently—and you've had a lot to argue about, haven't you?"

No comment. And Nadia had said this could be helpful, I reminded myself, we could find out their line of thinking. Still, it was harder than I could have imagined to hear these things said out loud.

"We recovered a shotgun from your lake this week. An old-fashioned one, but potentially lethal. Do you know anything about how it might have got there, Olivia?"

No comment. I'd stopped looking at who was talking and fixed my gaze on the table, my head inclined to signal I was still listening.

"You're a good shot, we hear. Would you know how to handle a gun like that, I wonder?"

Focus on other things. Josh must have spoken to them again yesterday, if they had all this. When he went out, he must have come here and given a statement, I decided.

"Would you say you have a temper, Olivia? Your husband says you're wound very tight, at times."

Josh, I reflected, was someone who would always take the easiest route: he had thought saying we were together that night was the quickest way to make any unpleasantness go away.

"Now, you told your husband, years ago, that something bad happened that night of the fire, the night your father died. Isn't that right, Olivia?"

I didn't want to think about that night.

"It was bad enough, I am sure, that your family suffered such a tragedy. But was that all you meant by that, Olivia?"

But then Josh got scared and talked too much; and now they were putting it together with other things.

"I'm suggesting to you, Olivia, that something else happened that night. Is that right?" asked Barnett, in far too chummy a tone.

I wondered what she'd say if I asked her, which night do you mean, then or now? And I looked up at her, an impulse I couldn't stop.

She looked back at me. "Did anything else happen that night, Olivia. Something bad?"

Nadia spoke then, her tone reproving: "I don't need to remind you that putting the same question to my client could be seen as intimidation."

There was a pause in the room.

"No comment," I said again.

I was glad when, after that, they moved on. They asked me everything from when I had last seen Nicky's laptop, to when I had last been down in the cellar. And they kept circling back to the party, asking me how I had felt, seeing Josh and his mistress in the same room. It must have been very upsetting for me, they said. They were trying to push me into reacting, unsure whether I already knew about the affair.

It was not, in any possible sense of the word, enjoyable. But I was starting to suspect something, taking in my lawyer's slightly more relaxed demeanor—she had stopped making notes—and Moran's faint air of frustration. The police could not quite connect the dots. Crucially, they seemed to have no coherent theory to explain the night of the fire, despite their questions about the gun found in the lake.

They were dogged, I will give them that. In the end, I broke first, for the most practical of reasons. I requested a toilet break.

Afterward, I wasn't taken back to the interview room; there was some sort of delay, and I was put in my cell again, for what felt like ages. It was another warm day and I could still smell the ready meal they'd given me for lunch earlier. I was feeling a little sick by the time they hauled me out again to see my lawyer.

"Keep doing what you're doing—don't give them anything," Nadia told me. "But I reckon they'll wrap up soon. They're just keeping us waiting now because they can. I'm going to go and give them a nudge."

"OK." I nodded at her, letting myself feel a modicum of relief, as she swung open the door of the room we were in. That was the only reason I happened to glance past her and see it: a door down the corridor closing on the backs of two people. It was a uniformed officer with someone else, in another regulation gray tracksuit, but there was something familiar about that tall gangling figure . . .

I frowned, trying to place him, then I did. Joe Crompton.

I sat up in my seat. I knew he'd been talking to them already. But what was he doing here? Hadn't he told them everything he knew, days ago?

Only prisoners were interviewed in this block,

Nadia said. So he had been arrested, too? That was a good thing, surely—it wasn't only me they were looking at.

But I couldn't mull it over much longer, because Nadia came to collect me. Barnett and Moran were right behind her, looking more refreshed by the break than I felt.

But it was nearly over. I knew what to expect now, and I could do it, I told myself, as we all filed into the interview room and sat down. Moran started the camera again, reminded me the caution was still in effect. I was trying to concentrate, but I kept seeing the Crompton boy. Now the detective was pulling something out of a beige folder to place on the table: a few sheets of paper stapled together, covered in small black type.

"I'm showing you a printed document," he said for the benefit of the recording. "We believe Nicky e-mailed this shortly before she went missing. Have you read it before?"

There was a sudden noise in my ears; I shook my head to clear it, and swallowed. "I don't know . . ."

"As I said, my client will not be commenting," Nadia said sharply.

"Do you recognize this, Olivia?" said Moran, as if she hadn't spoken.

In front of me, the type blurred on the page—I couldn't seem to focus.

"It was e-mailed to Joe Crompton in the early hours of Saturday. 3:13 a.m., to be exact."

And then the words resolved again in front of me, in all their hideous clarity. The first were in capitals:

OLIVIA HAYES
MY STORY

"You should have disclosed this," I heard my lawyer say, irritated.

"New evidence," said Barnett, her tone chirpy. "It went to his junk mail. He didn't see it until yesterday. And we became aware of it today."

"It's what Nicky was working on before she disappeared," Moran said, as if he was helping me to understand. "Your book, Olivia."

Chapter 59

*I wanted to write this book to let my fans into my
life. I'm someone who believes that if you put
your mind to something, you can achieve it. And
I want every woman to take charge of her life
and*

That was how the text began, as Barnett read it
aloud, her voice clear and agonizingly slow. She had to
for the recording, they said.

But then Nicky had stopped, and started again:

*I loved growing up here, all the space to run
about in. Swimming in the lake, playing hide-
and-seek in the meadow. That's what I like to remember.*

Did I tell her that, too? I must have . . . No wonder
Nicky hadn't had anything to show me yet: she had
clearly been struggling to even make a start.

*I'm not perfect. But perfect gives you some-
thing to aim for*

"That wasn't—" I stopped myself. I'd said that jok-
ingly; it felt different when read by the detective in her
flat, neutral tone.

"I believe my client's signaling that she wants to
speak to me privately," said Nadia.

"No, it's fine—keep going."

I kept listening, recognizing other phrases as my
own, from my interviews with Nicky, until Barnett
reached the end of the page and turned it over.

On the next, I could see the scrappy attempts finally
turned into something more coherent. So Nicky *had*
started writing properly . . .

*One terrible night would mark the threshold
between before and after, when our happy family
became shattered by tragedy. I know now that it
took six fire crews to contain the flames.*

I tried to keep my face calm as she read on, but the
weight on me started to lift.

*At first, the police just wanted to get in touch to
tell us what had happened to our house. It was
only later on that it became a missing persons
search—and we learned that my father had died
there.*

*In the weeks that followed, I went to live with
my grandmother in London, to whom I owe so
much. She is no longer with us today. My school
was also wonderful: a second family for me.*

*The main thing I want you to know is that you
can get through hard times—tragedy, even. If I
can, you can, too. You can overcome adversity.
You can rely on yourself. You can endure, like me.*

That is the woman I am.

Barnett looked up then, signaling she had reached
the end of the page.

I felt weak with relief. It was fine. Better than fine.
Because, after everything, this wasn't so far off what I
had thought Nicky was here to write in the first place,
after all. She must have written this last chunk after our
final session, but before—

"Do you recognize that, Olivia?" said Barnett.

"I'd advise you not to answer that," said Nadia.

"It's OK," I said. "I'm guessing they will be able to
check the e-mail is Nicky's."

"Oh?" Barnett smiled at me, like she was pleased
with me for being sensible. "So you agree this is what
you told Nicky? These are your words?"

"Well," I said drily. "I don't love what she's done
with it—it gets a bit maudlin with this last bit. But yes,
it's basically what I said."

I was having to stop myself from smiling. This was
not a disaster for me, no, not at all: she really had captured the essence of what I intended to say.

The detective nodded. "OK. There's just a bit more
overleaf I'd like to read to you."

I sighed, like I was already a little bored of the whole exercise, as she turned the page again. Under the table, I was kicking one foot, ready to get out of there.

I could see there was just another small chunk of text left. At first, as the detective began to read aloud once more, I thought it simply repeated the previous page; that Nicky had mistakenly cut and pasted those few paragraphs again.

And then my heart started to pound in my chest.

One terrible night would mark the threshold between before and after, when our happy family became shattered by tragedy. I know now that it took six fire crews to contain the flames.

At first, the police just wanted to get in touch to tell us what had happened to our house. It was only later on that it became a missing persons search—and we learned that my father had died there.

That's one version. Here's another.

I could give you reasons for what happened. He said I was a thief. He said I kept bad company. He was going to send me away to my grandmother's.

I argued with him. I was so angry. I lost my temper.

And then there was nothing else to be done. Why ruin all our lives? The fire hid everything.

Afterward, when they had stopped watching, my mother never spoke to me again. She lost a husband. I lost a family.

I have lived with my secret for a long time. But now it is time to tell my story.

Because I took the gun down from the wall. I shot him. I did it.

That is the woman I am.

The room was very quiet as she finished reading. Everyone's eyes were on me. Finally, I found my voice.

"That isn't right." I made an effort to control my volume. "Nicky's made that up."

Moran nodded. "OK." He didn't seem surprised. "That's got to be quite a shock to you, then. Given that she was your ghostwriter, here to write your story."

"Yes, but I didn't tell her that—it isn't true. She's put words in my mouth."

I had to make them understand, but my thoughts were a tangle. Nicky must have written these last few paragraphs after dinner, after I saw her looking at me as the fireworks went off, and I knew then that she was dangerous . . .

"It's certainly quite a tale. Have you any idea why Nicky might have written that, Olivia?" said Barnett. "What could have been going through her head?"

"I don't know—I . . ."

Nadia began: "I'd advise—"

"But Nicky's made it all up," I spoke over her, desperate to convince them. "She's a fantasist." I forced out a laugh, but my heart was pounding. "It's really disturbing, the way her mind works."

"OK," said Barnett reasonably, "but just so we understand this right, the other quotes, before that final page—all those *are* accurate?"

"No—I mean, I—no. I don't remember saying all of that." The lie rang hollow in my ears. I saw Moran glance swiftly at his colleague and forced myself to continue.

"I mean, this woman seems to think she's cracked some mystery," I sat back, trying to look more relaxed. "But it's laughable, it really is. She was—she is, I mean—clearly disturbed. And that's who you should be focusing on, now that she's missing. Not me."

"Absolutely, we're focused on Nicky," said Barnett. "So can you tell us anything else, Olivia, anything at all, that might help us find out what's happened to her?"

"I told you, I don't know anything." At that my frustration spilled out. "Why do you keep asking me? I don't even know her. Ask her friends, her family!"

"We've spoken to her friends. And yes, you did tell us that you don't know. And yet, Olivia, you've never seemed to wonder where she is. Is there any reason for that?"

"Of course not," I said, suddenly seeing the scale of my mistake there: what my lack of curiosity could signal to them. "I've just had a lot going on—my marriage . . ."

"Because it seems to us, Olivia, that Nicky was very afraid that night she disappeared: that she wrote down what was on her mind, and sent it to the one person who would understand—who would believe her. In case anything happened to her."

There was a beat. "No. No comment," I added, finally remembering what I was supposed to say. I looked to the side and caught my lawyer's expression: she looked stunned at how quickly this had just unraveled. This was a catastrophe.

She collected herself. "If you have any further offenses you wish to put to my client, we need to stop this interview right now, and you need to provide full disclosure. So I can properly advise her."

Moran put up a palm. "She's not being held accused of anything other than what we've already explained. We're only trying to understand what's happened to Nicky."

"Olivia," said Barnett slowly, ignoring their exchange, "you need to tell us the truth now. Did Nicky discover something bad about you—is that why she had to disappear?"

"No comment," I said. I felt like I was in a nightmare.

"Did you kill Nicky deliberately, so she couldn't tell anyone? Or was it a mistake, did you just lose control?

"Is that what happened, Olivia, after you'd all been drinking at that party, things got out of hand? You killed her and you have been covering up ever since?

"If that's what's happened, if it was an accident, a row that just got out of hand, you need to let us know, Olivia. Do you understand? You need to tell us what happened."

She leaned toward me: "Because Josh is very worried, Olivia. Your husband thinks you might have done something very bad, a long time ago. And that you tried to stop Nicky from finding out what. He always feared you'd let your past catch up with you."

It was too much: I could feel the emotion build in my throat, a telltale burning.

"No comment," I forced out once more.

There was a long pause, then Barnett spoke again.

"I've no further questions for you. I'm going to ask my colleague now . . ." Moran shook his head, anticipating her, his eyes still on me. "Is there anything you wish to add, Olivia, before I conclude this interview?"

"No."

"Right then." She checked the clock on the wall. "This interview concludes at . . .'

Chapter 60

They let me go after that, having left me a few more hours in my cell. It was a breathing space, that was all: I was released under investigation. An officer gave me my handbag back, without my phone; Nadia said she would give me a lift home.

"They can't have found what they wanted in your house today," she told me. She looked as tired as I felt.

Our journey back to Annersley was not reassuring. It seemed that after raising his concerns about Nicky's disappearance, Joe Crompton had been very cooperative with officers—until he realized they were regarding *him* with some interest: this oddball new friend of Nicky's . . .

He panicked, and shut down. But, when they arrested him—on suspicion of kidnapping, putting on the pressure, said Nadia—he started to talk again. That's when he revealed what he had found in his junk folder. If they had handled him better, they would have had their hands on the document sooner, she reflected. Still, they didn't have enough to arrest me over anything else . . . anything historic. *Yet* I finished silently.

"Don't say any more, to anyone," she added, as she dropped me off. "Don't do anything stupid. Get some sleep. We'll speak tomorrow. We've a lot to talk about."

At least I was home, I could regroup, *think* . . .

But as the security lights switched on, spotlighting me as I walked up to the smooth white facade of my house, it felt less a refuge than a trap. I wasn't safe here, either. If news of my arrest wasn't yet out, it would be soon. People would be talking about me. Josh . . . Sabrina . . . she wouldn't keep this secret. It would mean reporters arriving, like the last time.

The place was silent when I let myself in. On the kitchen table was a hurried note in Annie's rounded hand: she didn't know when the police would allow her back in, she said, so she was staying at her friend's in the village. She'd be back in the morning to see what was happening. It was too late to use the house phone to call her, I decided, or Lucy to check on Bea. I wasn't going to try to track down Josh.

Instead, I looked around the house, uneasy at the thought of people going through it while I wasn't there; anonymous figures in white suits and hairnets, moving slowly through the rooms . . .

Everything seemed fine, but things were subtly different, untidy: heavy chairs and beds returned to their places a few inches off; an odd dirtiness to the surfaces which confused me until I realized they'd been dusted with fingerprint powder. My computer was missing from my study, which was what prompted me to check out of the window and confirm what, in my daze, I had failed to register as I had arrived: my car was gone, too. This search had been far more thorough than before.

For some reason, I ended up in Nicky's guest room last, maybe reluctant to go back in there. It had already been emptied of her suitcase, but I went into the en suite bathroom, and switched the light on. It was as if she'd never been there, either.

I looked in the mirror at my reflection, colorless with weariness against the gray of my cheap tracksuit. They hadn't given me my own clothes back.

How had it all gone so wrong? I should have realized the danger I was in far earlier, should have guessed days ago when the police didn't do the big media appeal for a missing person, trying to shake out an answer from strangers. They didn't need to: they already had a main suspect in their sights. . . .

But I should have realized before that. That very first interview, when Nicky realized that I didn't give my real age—I should have called an end to it all, there and then. Or I should have been nicer to her, kept her on my side. Even that tennis match—I couldn't lash out at Sabrina, so I let my frustrations out on Nicky. And I should have brushed off her question about shooting, not given in to a panicked impulse and lied . . .

There was no point to doing this. I just had to decide to take the next, necessary step. Like I always did.

Staring ahead unseeing, I considered what I knew. What about the gun? After all these years in the water, what would they find if they tested it? Surely nothing. And any other evidence from that night was long since destroyed in the fire.

And the stuff from today—the document Nicky sent to Joe? I had not attempted to backtrack and deny it came from her, although perhaps a better lawyer might suggest that . . . Yes, that was worth considering.

Still, I couldn't just focus on the detail: I needed to change tack. What did that detective say, about me not knowing what had happened to Nicky? ". . . *you've never seemed to wonder where she is. Is there any reason for that?*" I hadn't been reacting in quite the right way.

Well, it wasn't a crime not to care. You could go crazy wondering why one person's life went one way, and someone else's another. You had to face things as they were. But I needed to act more like everyone else, as if it was an enormous shock that bad things happened, and spend time wondering why. Be more like Nicky, in a funny way. Because she was always curious. Just take her conviction there was a mystery here that she needed to solve, even when everyone else had settled it in their minds long ago . . .

Focus. What I needed now was to give them a satisfying reason for her disappearance, something solid, and nothing to do with me at all. What could I tell them? Where could she have plausibly gone? What else could have been going on with her?

Nothing came to mind. I wasn't really used to considering other people's inner motivations, wants. Selfish, some might say. Tunnel vision, I called it. And I was so tired. I examined my reflection, letting myself be distracted. I needed a Botox top-up.

The thought occurred to me, idly, that Nicky would have looked in this mirror, too. What did she see? She was somehow hard to picture. Ungroomed, badly dressed, her whole presentation just . . . nondescript. Could be pretty if she made an effort, I had thought. What would other people make of her?

A memory rose to the surface: opening the back door to Joe Crompton in the darkness on Saturday night. "Nicky!" he said, relieved, taking me for her in the dark, before he'd realized his mistake.

It wasn't the most flattering comparison. I turned my head in the mirror, unsmiling, looking at the familiar slopes and angles of my face dispassionately. Yes, I suppose, in the dark, give or take twenty pounds, I could see why you might think . . .

I froze, seeing alarm in my eyes. I had just remembered something else, as clear as if I could see our reflections before me now: Nicky next to me in my dressing room mirror, our hair pulled back, faces side by side, before she ducked away . . .

It was creepy really, like she didn't want me looking too closely. But don't think about that now, think about something to tell the police. Who was she?

Another person entirely. The thought repeated in my mind. And then it was somehow hard to formulate another, the mirror memory dislodging something in my brain, and now all I could see was Nicky, my mind intent on showing me images from the week, like skimming through an Instagram feed.

Nicky on that first night she turned up, disheveled and apologetic. Nicky heading into the library before me on the house tour, making my anger spike—too at home, I'd thought. Nicky in Bea's room that same day, exclaiming at the jungle mural—like she knew that wasn't how it should look in there, I thought now. Nicky twisting her hair around a finger, betraying her nerves—and now touching a chord of memory . . .

"No," I said, "No . . ." I breathed, even as I felt my mind start to fragment; more snippets of the last few days rushing back, swirling together.

Nicky losing her temper in my car, going too far: "*But you do realize, Olivia, you can't just erase the past* . . ." "*Olivia*," my husband's voice sounded in my mind. "*What have you done?*" And then me to the police: "*Ask her friends, her family!*" "*We've spoken to her friends.*" But what about her family? Hadn't they found anyone?

It couldn't be, it couldn't . . . but as my pulse started to thunder in my ears and dark spots danced before my eyes, I thought again of Nicky's absolute conviction that there was a story here, something to be discovered, how she was so sure . . .

Then all I could see was my family as we once were, captured in that photo that I burned in the ashes. There was my father, my mother; he handsome, she beautiful. There was me standing between them, blond and neat. And last of all, before the flames dissolved our whole family, looking up at me, with those messy brown curls, small and plump and adoring, was little Alex . . .

Suddenly I bent over, my stomach cramping painfully, as the full weight of realization hit me, like a car slamming into a wall in slow motion. Who was she?

She was Nicky and she wasn't.

She had come out of the past, a ghost made flesh again.

Nicky—for Nicola, I remembered now.

And a Wilson. Because Elsa remarried, I did hear that.
But once she was a Vane, like me.

"Alex Vane. Alexandra Nicola Vane."

As if saying it aloud was what finally made me understand, as I forced the words past the sob in my throat.

Could it be?

Yes.

"It was her. It was Lexy. My sister."

Chapter 61

I don't know how long I was there, curled on the bathroom floor. I couldn't think, I couldn't move, could barely breathe, my mind wiped clean of thought by the tidal wave overwhelming me: grief, sorrow, anger, guilt, and a pain too raw to touch.

After a while I realized I could hear someone whimpering, and knew it was me. When that passed, I lay there a while longer, my body shaking so hard that my teeth chattered; my ears filled with the sound of my raw tearing breaths.

I had tried so hard, for so many years, to keep the walls up around me, and now they were all falling down. It was what I'd always dreaded: total emotional breakdown.

When I sat up finally, the tears still drying on my cheeks, I took a long shuddering breath. Then I got to my feet slowly, feeling dizzy.

At the sink, I filled a glass with water and drank it

down, then washed my face and dried my hands, noticing they still trembled a little.

The bathroom around me was just as it had been: the tiles bright and white, the towels fluffy, the tub gleaming. And yet if someone had told me I had never been in there before I might have believed them.

Everything looked different now; the familiar strange again—now I knew who had been here.

My sister, Alexandra. Our father had hoped for a boy; when another girl arrived he must have decided it was time to pass his name on, anyway. But it was a big name for such a little girl, and so she was Alex to everyone. But Lexy, to me.

I had so many questions . . .

Just as she had, of course. I knew now that that was what must have drawn her to this house. To me.

I wondered how much she had even remembered. Very little, it seemed, from the fact of her coming here at all. She had been so young at the time of the fire, just seven to my thirteen. I hadn't seen her since we left Annersley, she going with our mother, I to my new school in London and my grandmother's.

Until she had come back, to find the answers she was looking for.

To blame me. To punish me. Even now.

Eventually I walked through the house, down the stairs. I unlocked the front door and went out into the night.

I felt a little calmer, on the surface at least, as I headed to the garage. I had decided some things, over the last few hours. I left the garage doors open, moths fluttering in from the night to dance around the light-bulb overhead, and started to root through the junk stored at the back.

I didn't have my cell phone, or my computer. The police had even taken the iPad that controlled the home entertainment system. But I needed to do something, and I didn't want to wait until the daytime.

Finally I found it, covered in dust: my old university laptop. Either the police didn't go through these boxes or decided the thing was too ancient to bother with.

Back in the kitchen, I plugged it in and fetched the scrap of paper where I keep the Wi-Fi password for guests. The computer took a while to flicker and whir back to life, as I thought over the course of action I had settled on.

Because one thing was clear to me: I couldn't tell them. I couldn't tell the police who Nicky really was.

Even if they believed me, it would raise more questions than answers. It would make her disappearance look even stranger. And it could only make the incriminating things she wrote appear more credible. They wouldn't believe any story I could offer them now.

No, there was nothing that I could say about who she was that couldn't endanger me further, entrenching what they thought: that I had reason to want to get rid of her.

So let them ask me as many more questions as they liked, about what had happened here—I was not going to help them. It wouldn't help me.

And I couldn't talk to the only person I wanted to talk to. I couldn't undo what had happened, or what I had done.

Still. There are two sides to every story, everyone knows that.

It took me a while to find it on my blog, the picture that I wanted to repost: the one that started my whole career off, the photo of my house. I'm not good with words, I never have been. So I kept my final message short.

This is a strange post to be writing.
You might be learning a lot of things about me that you don't like.
Things that might surprise you about my life—about my past.
You might be wondering what the truth is.
The truth can be hard to face. Maybe we want to lock it away in a box, hide it in the darkness, and forget. But eventually, maybe we have to look inside.
And the truth is, despite what my life may seem—it's not perfect. I'm not perfect. I've done a lot of things wrong.
But please believe me, that I am sorry.
I am so sorry.

Always your
Livvy

I checked it over, wondering how it would be read by my followers—by anyone and everyone who might see it. Then I pressed "publish" and waited for the sky to lighten.

*   *   *

They didn't hang around this time. When Thursday morning arrived, the police picked me up, took me to the station, and charged me straight away.

Of course, I should never have taken the painting with me, all those years ago. But it had been so long since the night of the fire, it didn't really occur to me what story it could still tell.

Some bright spark had turned it over during that last house search and read the date and inscription on the back. Later, they realized it shouldn't have survived the blaze without a mark.

It was the last piece of evidence they needed to build a solid case against me, amid what they termed a complete disruption to Nicky's usual patterns, her inactive social media accounts, her failure to access any banking services, the fact that no one she would normally have been in touch with had heard from her at all. So my lawyer said it was already out of my hands: my final Instagram post was just the final straw.

In the end though, I suppose it's the same whichever way you look at it—Josh was right, when he told the police what he feared might happen.

My past has caught up with me.

Chapter 62

And so this is where I am now: under a regulation blanket on a vinyl-cushioned bench. I have been here at the police station since yesterday morning, when they charged me. That makes today Friday, by my reckoning.

I have slept—a little. I have not showered. To fill the rest of the hours in my cell, I have let myself relive the events of the last fortnight, from the moment Nicky arrived at my door to the moment I knew who she really was. I have thought it all through, from start to finish. I needed to: to finally make it real.

Now though, they have brought me a hot breakfast in a tinfoil tray, and I know it must be time to face the day ahead. To distract myself, I try to imagine it as an Instagram post: how to dress for a court appearance? Follow my formula: floral collared dress; low-heeled pumps. Leave all your big-label bags at home, pick something stealthily expensive, so as not to alienate the courtroom . . .

As it is, I am back in another gray tracksuit. Still,

now that the worst has happened, it is a relief—almost. I've just got to get through today.

And I do. I watch what unfolds, as if it is happening to someone else; that is the only way I can do it.

The magistrates' court in Mansford is an ornate red-brick building, which reminds me vaguely of my old school. Inside, I am put in another cell, in the basement, as I wait for my turn in front of the judge. My lawyer, Nadia, speaks to me through the door, telling me what to expect. She hadn't been able to get us a room to talk in.

I will not be first up, she says, I will have to wait for them to get through dozens of other cases. There is an air of suppressed excitement about her, despite her solemnity. This is a big thing for her.

But finally, it is my turn, and I am led up a narrow spiral staircase that leads directly into the courtroom from the cells. The Victorians designed these places to intimidate, I reflect; the courtroom feels taller than it is wide, all dark wooden paneling fencing everyone off from each other. And it is full of people, their faces turned toward me.

Nadia had expected interest, and explained who would be where, to prepare me: the lawyers ranged on the benches at the front; seats for the press at the side; more for members of the public at the back of the court—anyone who feels like it can wander in to watch, she told me—and the district judge, a gray man in a gray suit, overlooking us all. Off to one side is the small wooden box of the dock holding me.

I am not handcuffed. I sit down on the chair, automatically, but the custody officer who has led me in jerks her head: get up.

A tall man in glasses, sitting under the district judge on his high bench, addresses me now. The court clerk, I tell myself, checking him off. It's helping me to pretend that I am just an observer, not intimately involved.

"Can you give the court your full name, please."

I do, then confirm my address. My voice doesn't wobble, I am relieved to note.

"Please sit down."

I don't have to enter a plea today. Today's hearing will be just a matter of minutes, Nadia assured me—or maybe warned me. On a charge of this seriousness, my case must be sent straight to the crown court.

She is sitting at the end of the bench nearest me, more people in suits clustered behind her—fellow lawyers waiting for their clients' cases to come up after mine. I am just one of many to pass through the courtroom this Friday afternoon.

On a bench farther away from me is the prosecution, a tall woman with brown curly hair, who now stands to address the judge.

"Sir," she says, her voice carrying and clear. "This is an allegation of murder. The district judge will know that the procedure should be to send the defendant for trial at Chester Crown Court. There needs to be a bail review, so we would suggest that the next hearing be on Monday at the crown court."

I feel panic mounting. I look around, trying to focus on details to calm myself. On the bench behind the prosecution lawyer, I see Barnett and Moran whisper-

ing to each other; sitting next to them is a big red-faced
man in a suit. I would guess, by the way he surveys the
courtroom, that he is the detectives' boss.

The press bench is full of pale-faced skinny reporters in suits and dresses with notebooks and pens
and one woman in a blocky purple suit and immaculate
bob that tells me she's ready for her TV close-up.

I am glad I didn't have to brave the pack outside.
There are no cameras allowed in court, but I glimpsed
the photographers through the window of the police
van as it rounded the front of the court: a dozen men
with big black lenses swinging round to zoom in. I was
taken in through the back.

And there is Josh, sitting in the public gallery, wearing a white shirt without a tie, staring straight ahead.

I wonder if he had to run the gauntlet of the photographers outside. He will have loved that: head down,
jaw square, the careworn yet dashing husband. For
now.

I can't imagine any divorce court would favor someone serving a life sentence. He could move Sabrina in.
Who could even object, thinking of that poor man and
his poor motherless daughter?

And maybe even that would be for the best, too.
Perhaps it is only right.

But then I see Sabrina, and anger flashes through
me. She is in the row behind him, eyes downcast, wearing a demure collared dress I've never seen her in before. Give me strength.

My lawyer stands up now, and I turn my head to
look at her: "Sir, this court has no power to take a plea.
But I would like to record that the defendant is indicat-
ing that she will plead"—the tiniest pause—"not guilty."

There is rustling from the press bench, as they digest it: I deny the crime.

"Silence!" The district judge raises his voice over the murmurs, then addresses me rapidly: "I have no power to make a decision on bail in your case. You will be remanded in custody and sent for trial at Chester Crown Court, your next appearance will be at the crown court on Monday at 9:30 a.m., or such other time as the crown court directs."

He looks down at his list, his mind on the next case already. "All right, take her down."

And now the custody officer is guiding me through the door at the back of the dock, down the steep stairs to the cells below.

Grief hits me from nowhere, surprising me, as my eyes fill with tears.

Bea . . . don't think about Bea. This is nearly over . . .

"Silence!" says the district judge again, but the noise only seems to get louder. I look back, but my view is partly blocked by the doorframe.

"Quiet in the courtroom!" says the judge again, over the hubbub, and this din can't just be about my not-guilty plea, can it? Because the hum at the back of the room is getting louder. On the press bench heads are turning to see something to their left.

I am craning to see, too, and the officer doesn't try to force me down the stairs, sensing something is happening.

And now everyone in the courtroom is turning round to see what it is, the whispers swelling louder into chatter, and I hear the wooden benches creaking as people start to stand. "What is it?"—a woman's voice rises above the noise of the crowd—and I glance across at my lawyer and see Nadia mouth something very unprofessional.

"Silence!" says the district judge, red-faced at the challenge to his authority. "I say, I will have quiet in my courtroom!"

"But look!" says the woman—it is Purple Suit, pointing at something. Then someone takes a few steps forward into the courtroom, and at last I see, too.

Hands clasped, chin up, she is there, living and breathing, and I can't quite believe it, what is happening in front of us all.

"It's her!" says Purple Suit, her voice carrying. "It's Nicky Wilson. She's alive!"

Chapter 63

The courtroom is in an uproar. Someone has their phone out to capture it all, and the court usher is striding over to argue: "No photos, sir—sir!"

And there she is amid the chaos, standing in the center of the courtroom so everyone can see her, a small, worried-looking figure.

Then the court quietens, as if everyone is taking a collective breath, and she speaks.

"There has been the most terrible mistake."

No one knows what to do, I think. But courtrooms are places where the unexpected happens: there is procedure for everything.

The judge looks down behind the prosecution lawyer, directly at Barnett and a white-faced Moran. "You over there, are you the officers in the case?"

Barnett glances at her colleague, sees his pallor, and stands. "We are, sir."

"Is this true? Is this Miss Wilson—the murder *victim*?"

"I believe it is, sir." She looks straight ahead.

"You believe?" the judge asks, his voice dripping with incredulity.

"It is, sir."

Another bubble of chatter rises from the press bench. The detectives' boss, sitting next to Moran, looks furious.

The judge turns to the prosecutor: "Well, Miss Fincham?"

"Would you rise for half an hour, sir?" She wants a break to collect herself, and I don't blame her.

"Well, the victim of this murder is standing in my court very much alive." He sounds as if it is a personal affront. "What *do* you need to think about, Miss Fincham?"

With so many journalists watching, the judge is not about to make himself a ready target for tomorrow's headlines: *Murder victim walks into court. The bunglers in blue!*

The prosecutor looks down at the papers in front of her, as if they hold the answer, while everyone waits.

"Surely, Miss Fincham," the judge continues, "you are now about to offer no evidence against this woman— who, as far as I can see, is being held in custody for a murder that, as is patently clear, did not take place?"

I hold my breath: Nadia told me what that phrase means. To offer no evidence signals they are about to drop their prosecution . . .

Miss Fincham lifts her head. "Yes, sir. I offer no evidence against Mrs. Hayes."

But I can't think anymore, because the judge is turning to address me.

"No evidence is to be offered against you on the allegations that you face here, Mrs. Hayes." He nods at me, almost friendly, as the courtroom waits. "Mrs. Hayes," he pronounces every next word, deliberately, "You. Are. Free. To. Go."

There is another explosion of noise, everyone talking and shouting. I hold on to the wooden dock, to steady myself.

"Silence! I will have silence in my court!" The judge is roaring to be heard. "Siiii-lence!"

Then the doors bang as the first person breaks from the press bench, running to relay it to the team outside, if they didn't catch her on the way in; racing to be the first to put the news out on the airwaves.

The judge stands, giving up on trying to keep control. "Clear the courtroom!"

Mrs. Hayes, you are free to go.

I don't wait to be told twice. The dock is not closed off from the rest of the court. I simply walk out from behind the wooden barrier down a couple of steps, all my focus on the person in front of me.

She looks so different. She is in just jeans and a sweater, her hair pulled back. But her shoulders are back, spine straight. She looks me in the eye as I touch her navy sleeve, just to make sure. I wonder if I am in shock, I feel so calm.

"Hi Livvy." She says it softly.

"So you do remember."

Because that's who my final post was for, of course. It was the only way I could think of reaching her, if she was out there. To tell her what I would have told her if I could. I'd signed it with the name she'd used to call me. Lexy and Livvy, we once were.

She nods. "When I found out the truth about the fire—your role in . . . what happened that night—I wanted to punish you . . ."

I give something that's a cross between a sob and a laugh. "Well, you managed that. Part of me wondered if you might be dead, after all. If you'd done something stupid, when you'd found out what really happened." I feel my mouth move involuntarily, and think that I might be going to cry.

Her eyes open a little wider, alarmed. "Not here . . ."

And then the spell I am in breaks, and I am suddenly aware again of the confusion of the courtroom; people still trying to make sense of what's just happened; the prosecuting lawyer unleashing her frustration on Barnett and Moran, their backs to us; the avid expressions of the reporters already sidling up to us; then I hear a voice over the hubbub.

"But what are you going to do about this, Josh?" Sabrina. "No, I *won't* calm down—"

Nicky touches my arm. "We need to go now. Before they want to talk to us."

And we do, we just walk out of the courtroom, through the lobby and more double doors and into the press of bodies outside, cameras flashing in our eyes.

Someone thrusts a furry mic toward us. "Nicky, what happened?" It is Purple Coat.

She bends toward the mic: "I had a personal crisis, and went away to deal with it. I had no idea all this was happening. It's just horrendous." She grabs my arm tightly, keeping me moving.

Purple Coat keeps pace with us. "Olivia, will you be taking action against the police?"

I hear Nicky say: "We'll make a full statement later, but the police officers will be out soon—I'm sure you'll have very many questions for them. Thanks."

And she keeps pulling me forward, down the steps of the court to a small dark car in a no-parking zone, clicking open the doors. She slides around to the other side, photographers shooting through the windows as we get in, and pulls out swiftly, a cameraman still filming from the middle of the street as we drive away.

Suddenly it is quiet, the people on the other side of the glass; the edges of the town flashing by. I am starting to feel very strange, as my worldview reshapes itself, caught in the emotions washing through me.

"So where should we go now?" asks Nicky. Alexandra. Lexy. I don't know how to think of her. But this, at least, I do know.

"Home."

PART 3

Chapter 64

NICKY

Of course there was no book.

I didn't lie exactly: only left a few things out. I was—*am*—a ghostwriter. It has suited me, taking on other people's lives. And it offered me a way into Olivia's, in the end.

Like I said, I had been thinking about something a bit different: telling a story of my own. I even had an idea . . .

Because I knew something bad happened in this house. Our house.

I just couldn't remember what.

And now I am sitting in the morning room, the rich pale furnishings glowing softly in the rosy evening light. In the hall, Olivia is on the phone to her lawyer.

We were silent on the way back home, by unspoken consent. Then Annie opened the front door to us, twisting her hands. The house phone had been ringing non-stop, reporters knocking at the door, the gates had stuck again, and Mr. Hayes was really no help . . .

She has been told to put her feet up: the two of us have a few things to discuss. From the hall, I can hear Olivia's murmured conversation wrapping up.

"OK," she says, her face thoughtful, when she comes back into the room. "My lawyer has spoken to one of the police officers. And now that the present-day case against me has collapsed for obvious reasons, given the murder victim is alive"—she gives me a look—"their investigation into past events is not going to go any further."

I take that in. "So they don't believe what I wrote?"

"Officially, you are a clearly vulnerable woman who got carried away." She sits down on the sofa next to me. "Unofficially . . . I think those detectives, at least, won't buy that. But they can't prove anything that happened so long ago. All they're left with is a theory. Plus, it's coming from the top now: leave this mess alone. The chief inspector was in court and was furious to be so embarrassed."

"So we're not in trouble?"

"Nadia doesn't think so. They might want to speak to you, but she's heard what you said outside court: that you were having some personal issues, and went away. That's not a crime. It was the police's choice to go so hard on the strength of what you wrote. And, of course, what Josh said about me. They've realized that was all colored by his affair with Sabrina. They're talking about a charge of wasting police time."

"He's their scapegoat," I say, slowly.

She nods. "But Nadia thinks they will let him sweat, then drop that, too."

"So it's over."

"It's over."

I wonder if I should feel relieved, instead of this mess of emotion I am experiencing—anger and grief, mixed with a leaping excitement. How am I supposed to navigate all this?

It was my decision to come back, and I don't regret my mad headlong rush to the court. But that doesn't mean I have forgiven her for what she's done, only that I started to think—hope—that she could be more than that . . .

The door opens and Annie comes in with a tray, sandwiches cut into neat little triangles, as if we were children. "I thought you might want something to eat."

As Olivia busies herself with the food, I try to compose myself. I don't know what I thought it would be like, our reunion. In the courtroom, I saw my sister shocked out of her habitual cool for a moment. But she is retreating behind the ice again.

I shiver, despite the mild evening. Away from the house, I forgot the intensity of my fear before; the cold white panic of the night of the dinner party, before I settled on the course I chose: to punish her. Before I read her message, and changed my mind.

And the more calculating part of me knows that I am safe; she has nothing to fear now I have come back to help her—so neither do I. Yet I put down the sandwich I've just picked up, and swallow.

"Thanks, Annie," says Olivia. "Take the rest of the evening off."

The housekeeper nods in acknowledgment as she takes away the empty tray, leaving the door ajar, and already I can feel Olivia waiting—waiting for me to explain myself. I feel suddenly resentful; it is my turn to be magnanimous, again. I take a breath, trying to get my emotions in check. "I don't know where to start."

Olivia nods. "Start at the beginning."

So I do.

I was nine when I realized other people's memories went back further than my own.

Bored on one rainy Sunday afternoon, I had pulled out a photo album from the bookcase in the front room. I must have sat there an hour, leafing in wonder through wedding photos of my mother and a tall, handsome, vaguely familiar man who had to be my daddy.

When Gran came in, she didn't react, but the next time I looked for the album, it was gone. I knew, even then, there was no point asking for it. But why didn't I remember anything about him?

It wasn't that there was nothing when I thought about it, not exactly. I knew our house had burned down two years before, and we had lost him. Afterward, Mummy and I came to stay at Gran and Granddad's. My sister Livvy didn't come. These were things I knew, but they weren't memories exactly—there were no pictures or feelings attached.

So much was new and strange when we came here, I reasoned, that perhaps it had shuffled the rest out. Before, I was Alexandra, named for my daddy. Now I was

Nicola, once my middle name. We had started afresh, Mummy had told me, that was OK, wasn't it? I remembered that I wasn't so sure, at first. But if I asked Mummy questions, she would cry or get angry. Eventually I stopped.

She wasn't around much to ask anyway, after she met Steve. He was kind, sweeping us up into his big apartment in town, and when they married I became Nicky Wilson. But they went abroad a lot, for his business, so I mostly stayed at my grandparents', my mother passing through to dispense kisses and clothes I had already grown out of.

I was ten when she and Steve went off the road on a sharp bend in the French countryside. My grandparents said I was too young to go to the funeral. The truth was, my life didn't change that much—but as I grew older, I grew more curious about why I never saw my sister. She and my mother had never really got along, and they were both so upset after the fire. That was all my grandparents told me.

So I searched online, "Vane" and "fire" bringing up photos of the wreck of our old house—miles from my grandparents' in the Midlands—and details of the blaze. And I started to learn why I remembered so little from before. Memory loss could be related to trauma, I read. Which made sense: I was only seven when I lost my home, father, sister . . .

At this point they were just vague shifting outlines when I thought of them, like trying to remember a dream on waking. And I didn't like to think of what had happened to him. But I wondered about Livvy. She was six years older than me, Gran said. Now she would be doing exams. Now she would be leaving school. Now she would be . . . what?

I found out in my final year of college, when I walked past my roommate's open door and recognized the house on her screen, gleaming white against a blue sky.

"What's that?"

"Some blogger . . ."

Olivia didn't give her surname then—later, she used Hayes once married—but I knew. This was my sister, Livvy.

All that time, I had hoped she was OK, wondering how she had been doing without us—without me—but she was fine. More than fine. Like a pilot light switching on, my anger started to burn.

I didn't do anything for a long time. I was busy, with work, then dealing with Granddad, then Gran, slipping away in their usual quiet ways.

But as the years passed, I only had more questions. The severed ties, my mother's silence . . . there had to be something more to the story.

And so I started to consider approaching her, seriously. I wrote an e-mail, a practical message about our grandparents' estate, that I never sent. It wasn't what I wanted to say. I thought about turning up on her doorstep. Would she fall on my shoulders, crying? Or turn me away? I couldn't picture either scenario.

In the end, a chance comment from my agent gave me the idea. Whose story do you want to tell next, Nicky?

Chapter 65

NICKY

Olivia has been listening closely. "But you didn't really think I would let you publish it?"

"No," I say, "of course not."

I never planned to publish anything at all: this was for me. I'd show Olivia something bland as a sample chapter, then let the project drop—blaming other commitments. Maybe, if the week went well, I'd tell her who I was . . .

In the meantime, I prepared carefully. I contacted Joey months before I arrived. He wouldn't e-mail me the photos he had taken over e-mail, would only show me them face-to-face, so I'd send the odd friendly text to keep in with him, before I got the call from "Julia"—Olivia—to say she had a week free.

At the house, I played up my nerves and ignorance about its history, wanting to seem like I posed no threat. Really, as I read through the articles I'd collected one last time, before that session where I'd ask Olivia about the fire, I could have recited chunks by heart.

Of course, I had to ask her about other aspects of her life, too; that was no hardship. I wanted to know everything about her. Still, there were real shocks, from the moment I found that marker in the garden, a grim reminder of the past . . .

The biggest shock of all, of course, was yet to come. I had always wondered why Olivia stayed away from us. I never considered that we were staying away from her.

That changed everything. If Olivia hadn't done what she did, everything would be different. I would have my father; my mother, too, perhaps. And a home.

Instead, the bonds tying me to my life seemed as fragile as cobwebs. It was all her fault and she had prospered . . . I couldn't bear it. It wasn't fair.

So I thought for a while, in the dead of that night after the dinner party. I added that final passage to my notes, condemning her, and e-mailed my document to Joey. I let it look hurried, rushed—as if I had written it in fear, a security against what might come . . .

But I didn't have the ending I wanted yet.

I took only what I could carry, my laptop and recorder in my tote bag—I am very careful, but just in case. I left my phone behind, knowing that without it I would be harder to trace. There was nothing on it that mattered.

I let myself out through the dining room, betting correctly that the French windows hadn't been shut properly after the party. On the terrace, I turned back to look at the house, white against the lightening sky. Then I put a hand to my neck and pulled sharply. Nicky, the necklace read. Even my name wasn't my own because of her.

Not any longer. I threw it away without looking where it fell.

After that, I walked to the railway station in the village, along the lane in the silence of the early morning, and caught the first train out of there. I paid cash when the guard went by and as I journeyed across the country, I grew surer that I could execute the plan that had come to me. There was symmetry to it, almost.

Olivia had disappeared out of my life. Now I'd do the same to her.

Because I couldn't prove an old crime. I wasn't confident anyone would believe me. Instead, I would disappear long enough for them to suspect her of a new one and start to investigate her seriously. I wouldn't have to stay away forever: just until they discovered what she'd done to our family. I could give a helping hand from afar, if needed, the odd anonymous phone call.

Then once her role in our father's death was established beyond all doubt, I planned to return, blaming a breakdown, crisis . . . anything. Maybe I could even reveal who I was: explain that the trauma of my discoveries had triggered my disappearance.

After all, I wasn't the criminal here.

Even my destination fit. When I got to the sea, the cottage was just as it always had been, trapped wasps lying on the windowsills, the unopened bills on the hall floor still addressed to my grandparents. I bought bread, eggs and milk, in the corner shop, then went to ground. I slept, a surprising amount.

It was the perfect place to hide, on the edges of a tourist town. My grandparents had kept themselves to themselves. I hadn't done anything about transferring the deeds to my name yet, knowing I would only have to sell if my creditors found out about this asset before I was more stable.

And I knew no one would think to check in some dusty police file for the address where my mother had been found by officers all those years before . . .

It was early on Friday morning that I pulled on a cap and sunglasses to pick up more food, and saw the newspaper outside the shop. A small item had made it to the bottom corner of the front page:

MUMMY BLOGGER MURDER CHARGE

> A 36-year-old woman has been charged over the murder of writer Nicky Wilson, missing for a week. Police sources confirmed the suspect as mother-of-one Olivia Hayes, a popular lifestyle "influencer" . . .

She would appear before Mansford magistrates' court that very day. It was happening, what I'd wanted. Wasn't it? I felt a shiver of panic. I needed to know more.

In the tatty Internet café for tourists, I read the few reports. But I knew they couldn't give more than the barest facts, once she had been charged. So I clicked to the forums, and saw they were full of some post she had made . . . a confession? Some thought so.

I found it on her blog. It was brief, barely an apology, I thought angrily, until I read the final line. She'd signed it Livvy.

I hadn't heard anyone calling her that, not Josh, not Sabrina. But I must have, when we were little . . . that was the name I knew her by.

I went back up the narrow streets, and by the time I was at the little stone cottage it was clear to me what I had to do. I took Granddad's old Rover, still parked in the driveway, and drove as fast as I dared.

In Mansford, I had to get in line to get through the court building security, then it took me minutes to find the right courtroom, I had to fiddle about looking for HAYES on the court lists pinned to a board—I was too late, I had missed her . . .

And then suddenly I turned a corner and saw the suited figures on their phones. "Did the snapper get her in the police van?" ". . . she's up now, I hear . . ."

No one stopped me as I walked straight in.

Because I couldn't do it. I thought I could walk away, but I couldn't. My sister had sent a message to me. And she was sorry—whatever that meant. But if the past was worth anything at all . . . I had one last chance to rewrite our story.

Chapter 66

NICKY

There is a silence, as Olivia absorbs all I've said. "You couldn't have got a new phone from somewhere," she says mildly. "Ring ahead, maybe?"

"I know. But I thought it might speed things up if they saw me, well, in person. Alive."

Then I realize she's cracking a joke. I smile uncertainly, as Olivia looks down at her hands.

"You know, I never even thought about who you could be until I saw what you had written," she says quietly. "Even then . . . I don't think about the past, if I can help it."

"I understand." You were in such massive denial, I think pityingly. "I can't imagine how hard it has been to live with what happened—with what you did that night." I take a deep breath, knowing that there can be no more secrets between us, if we are to move forward. "When you shot our father."

She looks at me, searchingly, and opens her mouth

like she's about to say something—then shuts it again. Because really, what can she say?

"We have to face up to things," I say firmly, but I feel like I am about to jump off a cliff: to be saying this aloud. "I'm sure it must have been a . . . terrible mistake. And I was so angry when I worked it all out—I just wanted to make you suffer. But since then I have had time to think, and I can understand, now, why you and Elsa covered it all up. You were still a child. And you've gone through a lot—you've paid the price."

It takes me a lot to say that, to be that generous, but I can actually see her shutting down as she digests my words: her posture stiffening, her expression becoming still more closed-off, if possible.

"We can't erase the past," she says carefully. "You told me that. But I am sorrier than I can say."

It is not enough. And it is too late. But I lean forward to pat her arm. I don't think either of us are huggers.

"She used to wear that same perfume," I say, recognizing the fragrance, still lingering despite all she's been through. "Elsa."

Olivia looks surprised. "Yes, she did. Shalimar."

"I knew it was familiar. There's so much I want to ask you."

She yawns widely, belatedly putting a hand over her mouth.

"And I need to know," I continue, trying to keep my voice steady, "about that night. I need to know exactly what happened. I still can't remember." You owe me that, I think.

"Of course," says my sister. I can't read her at all, if she is even upset at the prospect. "But would you mind if we talked tomorrow? I'm desperate to get out of this tracksuit. And I haven't slept properly for days. Stay the night. Journalists have been calling my lawyer, too . . . she's working on a statement. And I'll pick Bea up in the morning, but for now, all I want to do is sleep." She is already turning away, getting up.

"Of course," I say lightly, "whatever you want."

I stay there a while longer, trying to sort through the maelstrom of feelings. Some heart-to-heart. I did the right thing, surely, coming back. I know I did.

Yet I feel cheated, confused and, underlying it all, awash with sadness. I don't know what I expected from her, but more than that. Maybe tomorrow she'll be different. But I don't know what to do now, really.

After a while, I start to feel cold: a breeze is making the hairs on my forearms stand up. There must be a door open somewhere: Annie has gone outside. Or maybe that gardener . . . I'd forgotten about Cav.

I walk through to the empty kitchen. On one side is the open bottle of the wine, the condensation puddling around its base.

I steal forward, into the utility room where the door is wide open to the evening—there is someone out there, I register, and my heartbeat accelerates—before the scene resolves itself. "Oh!" I say. "It's you."

It is only Olivia, looking out through the brick arch of the kitchen garden to the lawn and the water beyond it. She turns her head at my exclamation.

"Sorry," I say, "I thought you'd gone up already."

"I didn't mean to scare you," she says. "It was just nice to be outside again."

"I wondered who was out here," I say, embarrassed at my overreaction. "I thought it might be Annie."

She turns fully to face me. "No, it's only us tonight. I told Annie to have a break, she has a village friend she sometimes stays with . . ."

She trails off. But the spike of fear has reminded me of something. And suddenly I have to know what I am dealing with.

I hear myself say: "I know you're tired . . . but one last thing. Those weird things that happened, while I was here."

"Weird things?"

"Little things, really. I found a pin in my makeup . . . and the tile that fell off the roof, it could have really hurt me"—her expression is one of polite interest—"then when I was in the cellar, looking around, I heard someone follow me down . . . Do you think it could have been Josh?"

"Josh?" I can hear the ring of skepticism in her voice.

"Well, at first I thought it was Sabrina, but then I learned she didn't stay over that night. So it can't have been her. So I wondered, if Josh thought I was finding out too much about your past, before he turned on you—maybe he was trying to scare me off." What I don't say: Was it you, Olivia?

How far would you have gone, to keep your secret safe?

She tilts her head thoughtfully. "I suppose it's possible," she says. "I didn't think Josh could betray me in the way he did. But those things you mention could have been accidents. And we've had squirrels get in the cellar before—maybe you misheard . . ."

I don't think they were accidents, or that I misheard anything.

"Well, no harm done," I say, just as politely.

After that I go up the stairs, the house big and silent around me. Olivia would be up soon, she said.

There are pajamas on my pillow, a toothbrush still in its packet: Annie must have prepared the room. I didn't bring anything with me in my mad dash from the cottage. The police will have to give me my suitcase and phone back, there will be people I should contact to let them know I really am OK: my agent, friends. Tomorrow.

As I settle into bed and switch off the lamp, I remember something else—so trivial that I forgot to mention it just now: how the coffee spilled all over me in that first session, after I asked Olivia about our mother.

Could that have been Josh's handiwork, too? I am trying to picture the moment now, because I am sure it was Josh who had his hand on the cafetière, but wasn't there someone's else hand in the frame, too, helping? It's such a little thing, but something is wrong with this picture, with what Olivia is telling me . . .

I feel a hot tear slide down my cheek. It's too late. How can we rebuild a relationship after all this?

I turn over, trying to calm myself, but my mind won't stop remembering new details. She said she never thinks about the past. But footsteps had worn a path right to the stone marker for our father.

Another tear follows, soaking onto my pillow. I did the right thing—didn't I?

But, I think, *but*.

I can admit it now that I'm away from Olivia: I didn't come back just for her. I came back for myself, too. Because I didn't want to do it to myself, in the end; didn't want to make myself a ghost in my own life.

But I still don't trust her. Because she is a killer.

Before I go to sleep, I slip out of bed in the darkness and lock my door.

Chapter 67

NICKY

I can see the tips of the long grass and the clouds in the sky. I am hiding in the meadow, like I always do.

Nicky!

Olivia is calling my name, like she always does. This is the game we play, and I should come out now.

Nicky!

But she sounds angry, and I don't want to come out yet. It is soft and comfortable, here in the meadow. And there are fireflies dancing in the air above me.

No, not fireflies. Burning embers in the air . . .

I sit up and I see. The meadow is on fire. Flames are licking across the long grass, dancing toward me, as the blue sky blackens.

Now I smell it, too—the thick smoke, bitter and so hot, burning my throat.

Nicky!

Livvy is not angry, she is scared, but I can't see her,

everything is going dark, even as I feel the heat on my skin.

Nicky! she shouts again, but I am Lexy, why is she calling me that. I can't think. I can't breathe . . .

I wake up, lifting the damp hair off the back of my neck to cool my skin, as I come back to consciousness.

Then I remember my dream. I was in the field on the other side of the lake, with Olivia. I couldn't see her, but I knew she was looking for me. And there was a fire. It was so vivid, I can almost smell it still—

"Nicky!"

The doorknob rattles, before a dull thud on the wood, but the door stays shut.

I sit up. I *can* smell smoke in the air, my eyes are already starting to water. In one headlong movement I am out of my bed and grasping at the key, then—

I freeze, my hand on the metal. I don't trust her . . .

"Nicky!" Her voice is close to a scream, as I stand there in the dark, my thoughts whirling. Is this a trick? In the cellar I ran, I couldn't face what was in there with me—but I've nowhere to go now—I told Olivia we have to face up to things—

"Nicky!" She starts hammering on the door, shaking it in its frame.

And suddenly, it's as if the decision's already made for me. I have to know. I have to know what kind of person she really is. Whatever happens next . . .

*   *   *

I twist the key and pull the door open—and recoil as the heat hits me from the hallway, but Olivia grabs me by the wrist, surprisingly strong.

"Quick. Come on." She sounds hoarse, as she pulls me forward. How long has she been trying to wake me? She is muffling her face with something, but it's all so dark—darker even than it should be at night—thick black smoke all around us, making my eyes stream. And now I can hear that old familiar roar, the crackling of the fire from farther down the corridor.

"We should stay in here and shut the door!" I shout, bumping into the wall, disoriented. I don't understand why there is so much smoke, it is madness to go through it. "We can't go down there!"

"No," says Olivia, and she starts pulling me down the corridor. "It's everywhere!" Pain flares as I hit my hip on something—the banister—we've reached the main stairs. And now Olivia is trying to drag me down to the floor, and I resist, alarmed, so she moves the cloth away from her mouth to bark: "Get down."

She's right—I need to get on my hands and knees, feeling the carpet prickle through my nightclothes—and I start crawling and sliding down the stairs, under the worst of the smoke and the heat. As we reach the little landing on the turn of the staircase, I twist my head up to the big window, tears sliding from my sore eyes, and *that can't be right*—I can see bright yellow flames, coming from *outside* the house—but I have to keep going. At the bottom of the stairs I clamber to my feet and turn left, for the front door, but again she grabs me, pushing me in front of her. "Too many locks," she shouts, because the alarms are going off now, finally, screaming like sirens.

And she gets us into the narrow hallway, the smoke is not as bad down here, as we burst into the kitchen, me following as she goes for the windows. I hear her wrenching open the lock on the French doors and then she pulls one open, the little bolt at the bottom not holding, and I stumble after her onto the terrace, both of us coughing and gasping. I wipe my streaming eyes on my pajama sleeve, the fabric coming away black and greasy, and look back at the house.

Now I see why we couldn't stay in my room and wait to be rescued. There is fire crawling all over it, the ivy is alight, it is consuming it from the outside in . . .

"Come on," says Olivia, grabbing my hand, and I turn back to the garden, and want to scream. The fire is in the trees touching the house, the shrubs that flank the lawn, we are surrounded by it, whipped up by the wind after the long dry summer. In front of us, I see a line of flames ripple across the grass, making a scurrying run toward us.

But the heat and noise from the house is forcing us forward, and we are already running down the terrace onto the expanse of lawn. Without speaking we are heading for the darkness at the base of the garden, where there are no flaming trees or burning grass, just the cold water of the lake—*Livvy always knows what to do.*

Now there are sparks whipping through the air, and the fire is in front of us, too, long live fingers tearing through the grass before us like something alive, and my lungs are burning. But we are quick, too, we are flying over the ground—*I can always run faster with my sister, like we have wings.* What is happening?

We have done this before, I know somehow, but

now I am the stronger one, I am pulling her along, headlong down the slope where the lawn ends, crashing our way through the thicker grasses and long weeds, blessedly wet and cool.

Still we keep going, desperate for breath and to get away from the flames and the smoke, running faster than we have ever run. And now we are at the edge of the water and I scream: "Jump!"

For a second we are suspended in the night air, hand in hand, then—

Chapter 68

NICKY

The lake is so cold that it clears my mind of all thought.

I can see it is lighter above me, through the dark water, and feel my pajamas swirl around my body, and then instinct kicks in, I am moving up, up with short, fast strokes, and I surface, taking huge heaving gulps of air. I see the stars in the night sky, the black water lit up red and yellow by the fire behind me—*I let go of her*—before thought returns fully and I twist and turn, looking for her, "Livvy!"

I can't see her.

I take a quick panicked breath and kick myself down into the cold, forcing my eyes to stay open. The sides of the lake are steep, I didn't touch the bottom when we jumped in. I can barely see a thing, but I stretch my arms out as far as I can, grasping at nothing. And I reach and reach, and my lungs are burning, and now I am coming up again, into the air, and shout: "Livvy!"

Nothing disturbs the water but me: she hasn't surfaced.

She was coughing more than me, wasn't she, she was out there banging on the door of my room, she has breathed in more smoke . . .

I go under again, using my arms and legs to push down and out, farther into the depths of the lake, heading for the bottom, blind in the water. And as I go, I grasp for something—a hand, an arm—my throat still burning from the smoke and my lungs full of new pain, and now I am out of air once more, I can't stop myself—I kick up again for the surface, and burst into the night, gasping.

I couldn't do it, I can't do it. I was scared of not coming up again.

I scull with my arms to stay afloat, hearing nothing but the rasping sounds of my breathing and, far away, the noises from the house. The alarm is still ringing, tinny and high, but it could be miles away; everything is quiet on the still water.

I have to find her.

This time I take a deep breath, forcing myself to be controlled, then I kick myself up and over again, positioning my body straight in the water to dive one more time, straight down, and yet I don't panic, I let my breath out slowly, so I can sink even deeper.

The water is colder here, unstirred by any current. I swim forward, unseeing, and reach with my hands.

And still she is not here.

She is not here, as I keep swimming, and I am feeling the pressure tighten in my head now, like some-thing is pushing on the bones of my face, I need to go up, but I cannot leave without her—and then my hand brushes something, just weeds, but then I touch them again, and *not weeds it is hair*—and I make a fist and try to kick back up.

I can see light at the surface as I look up, it is brown through the earthy water, but I am so far away. I have Olivia, one hand in her hair and holding a shoulder now, too, but I am fighting the reflex to breathe in, underwater, and I am getting nowhere, as if something is dragging me farther down.

And there is a moment, as I feel myself sinking deeper into the lake, when I know with perfect clarity that I could let go, no one would blame me. No one would think less of me for saving myself.

You mustn't panic, just keep going.

Now my feet touch the mulchy bottom, soft and slick against my soles, I am that deep—and I hear it again, a voice out of the past.

You have to stay calm, and if you do touch the bot-tom, then you KICK.

So I do. I let my legs bend a little more, and then I kick with all my strength, pushing off against the bot-tom of the lake. I kick again in the water, now I have momentum, and keep kicking, up and up, until we have done it, we are at the surface. And I gasp for air, but I keep our heads above the water, wrapping my arm under her chin, as I keep kicking.

The water's edge is just meters away now, we are so close to the meadow and safety, but I am moving by inches. And she is so heavy and still, a dark shape facing away from me, her head knocking against my own, and I feel my feet touch the bottom again, but this time that is a good thing, it is shallower on this side.

Both our heads go under again, water filling my nose painfully—I slipped—but I am being driven now by something beyond fear, and I get us onto the slick steep bank of the lake, half in and out of the water.

I smell the cold earth, feel the muddy ground through my dripping clothes.

But she is not saying anything, is she drowsy? Unconscious?

I heave myself further out of the water, and pull her by the arms, so she is lying on leaves and mud and grass.

"Olivia," I say, my voice hoarse from the smoke and exertion. I shake her shoulder, then again, more roughly. "Wake up."

I turn her over a little, and some water comes out of her mouth. Her eyes glint, half-open, but I can't see her chest moving.

And I am so tired and scared, I am so desperate and so full of wild emotion, that later I think that that must have been what did it.

That is what shakes the first memory free.

I am hiding in the meadow and Livvy is looking for me. When the shouting starts, we play this game. Come out, come out, wherever you are, she calls. It's OK, Lexy, you can come out now . . .

I was right there in the meadow, I felt the grass tickling my skin, but there is no time to think about that, I have to turn her onto her back again, remember what I am supposed to do.

I feel for a pulse in her neck, but my hands are numb, with cold or shock, and I don't know what I am looking for even if I find it. So I lean forward and tilt back her head, and breathe into her mouth, one, two . . .

And at the same time, something else surges up out of the past, *I am running, hand in hand with my sister, skimming across the lawn, cold and wet under our bare feet. Because we heard him shouting, from the garden, and I was scared, but Livvy knew what to do. I can always run faster with my sister, like we have wings. Livvy makes everything right . . .*

But now she is so still, and I put my two hands in the center of her chest, like I am supposed to, and push down, wait a beat. I do it again. Nothing happens.

I keep going, counting ten, twenty, thirty beats—how can that be right? It seems so many—and start to cry. This can't happen. It can't end like this, not for us.

"Come on"—as I push down on her chest—"come on, Livvy."

And then I stop talking, just pushing down, counting in my head, in the coolness of the night, *just keep going.* It's time to breathe again, two strong quick breaths.

I see fat hot tears splashing on Olivia's face below me, as I push down her chest, counting, then breathing for her again, and still nothing is happening . . .

I am sinking, Daddy let go. He says I have to learn, but I can't swim, and I can hear Mummy crying, too, when I come up coughing again, but she is still standing there, on the bank far away. And then suddenly I am going up out of the water, lifted high over the lake, Livvy has got me, her pretty dress all wet and sticking

*to her skin. Don't cry, she says, you mustn't panic, just
keep going. This is important, Lexy, if you ever get out
of your depth. You have to stay calm* . . .

I can't let it end, I can't let her go, not like this. *Just
keep going.*

Because Livvy always looks after me. "Livvy . . ."

I feel it coming somehow, before her body shakes
and convulses, and I help her onto her side as she starts
coughing, making horrible racking noises, water coming out of her mouth.

Afterward she is shaking, and I am shaking, too, and
I hug her close to keep her warm, until the sirens arrive, drawn by the fire and the alarms, strangers running down to the lake with their hoses.

Then I stand and shout, my voice reedy and high,
we are here, we need help.

And through it all, the oxygen masks and the ambu-
lance and the long frightening drive to the hospital, I
keep holding her hand.

Because now I remember.

We are going on vacation . . .

I remember what happened that night.

Chapter 69

NICKY

If at first the memories came in flashes—like a camera going off, its bulb exploding light everywhere, illuminating what I had forgotten—soon they unfolded like a film played at high speed.

These days, I think of it like an old-fashioned cinema reel: at the start, just stray images flickering, then short bursts of action, before it all coalesces into something full of noise and color and life.

I was there in the meadow, feeling the heat of sunshine; I was running across the lawn, my feet flying across the crisp cool green; I was in the lake, my nose and mouth filling with coldness.

And then I was at the house, reliving the day that became that night. Even as I worked by the water, crying over my sister's slack body, my past was hurtling into focus. I didn't know, and then I did: it was there, fully formed in my mind.

The story I have been trying to tell all this time.

*   *   *

We are going on vacation.

Daddy says he can't come, he has work to do, but I cannot be sad, not really. I am so excited, and so are Mummy and Livvy. I am so excited that I was annoying Nanny, who had to close the house up. Away with you.

But as soon as we drive away, the sun shining through the car windows, Mummy and Livvy start arguing. I try not to listen, I am good at that. But it is hard sometimes.

You always think you know best, says Mummy, her voice spiky, and after that Livvy stops talking, she just leans her head against the glass.

It is better when we get off the highway and stop at the service station. I play on the adventure playground for hours. After that, I go to sleep in the car.

When I wake up it is dark and we are moving again.

Are we there yet?

Not yet, says Mummy.

But I keep asking. We have been in the car for so long now . . .

We are going back home, Alexandra, says Livvy.

She must be angry, because she didn't call me Lexy. I don't understand why.

So I listen to them talk for a bit. Mummy wants her jewelry, that is the least she should take away from this marriage, she says. She couldn't pack it before, when he was there.

Livvy thinks we just need to leave.

I don't know why Livvy has to argue all the time. She thinks I don't know things, but I know a lot. She is going to have to go away soon, I heard Daddy tell Mummy. That girl is completely out of hand.

It was after she stole the money. She gave it back, so Nanny didn't get the blame. But she still got in trouble. It wasn't fair, when she only took it to give to Mummy. I heard them talking.

So I told Daddy that. He said I was a good girl to tell him, and to say no more about it, to anyone.

I get a funny feeling in my tummy when I think about it though, because Olivia is still having to go away to Grandma Vane's and her new school.

So I don't think that's the only reason Daddy is angry with her.

I think it's after Mr. Gregory came to talk to him. I watched through the banisters to see his police uniform, but he was just in normal clothes, which was a shame.

Nothing official, said Mr. Gregory, but we can't have a repeat of this behavior, Alex. When your own daughter feels she needs to get me involved . . .

Daddy looked so sorry as they shook hands goodbye. He always knows the right things to say. Everybody loves my daddy. We are a lovely family, everybody says so.

But afterward there was shouting again, then the other sounds. Livvy came in to read me a story, even though I am too big for that now. She always looks after me.

So I think now that I will help her.

I say in a loud voice that Mummy can buy more jewelry when we get to the cottage.

She says, yes, darling, we can do that, too.

I wish Daddy was coming with us, I say, and no one says anything at all.

* * *

The next time I wake up we are home again, but everything is all dark and unfriendly, and it is just me and Livvy inside the quiet car.

She's getting her stuff, says Livvy. She sounds cross still.

But I forget that, when I see Toby coming round the side of the house, his tail wagging.

Look, Livvy!

I open my door so Toby can say hello properly, pushing his cold wet nose into my hands—

What's the matter, Livvy?

Because she isn't pleased to see him. She has gone all white.

Stay here, Lexy.

And Livvy sounds so serious as she gets out that I do what I am told.

She is gone a long time though. Even after I count to one hundred, she still doesn't come. Toby has wandered away somewhere, and I don't know what could be hiding in the dark . . .

So I decide.

And when I open the car door again, I can hear shouting, like sometimes happens.

Think I didn't know . . .

Never going to leave me . . .

You whore . . .

And I am afraid. Because even though I love my daddy, he is different some nights, after his drinks. Never when Nanny is here, or other grown-ups. And he is so good to Mummy the next day. So I know it's not my nice daddy leaving those blue marks. It's someone else.

But then everything goes quiet and somehow that is worse.

The front door is a little bit open, so I can go right inside.

Livvy?

I don't say it loud. The hall is full of shadows.

When I take another step in, I see the door is open to the sitting room, and—

Livvy! I run in to her.

But she just stands there, her eyes all big and wide.

Then I see it. The shape on the floor—

Mummy!

She can't hear me, she's not moving.

Don't look, Lexy. Livvy sounds very stern. She'll be OK.

And I don't say anything more, because I can tell Livvy's listening for something.

Then I hear it. A thud, like something big is being dropped.

My heart is beating very hard.

When the noise comes again I know it is not outside, it's inside. With us.

We locked him in the cellar, says Livvy. He's very drunk.

In my head I can see the door in the kitchen wall, the thick painted wood.

Then the banging starts to come faster and faster, like whatever it is won't stop.

She was all right, says Livvy, we almost got out of the house, but she collapsed. I think she's . . .

She says words I don't know. Con Cussed.

Livvy runs over to the desk and looks for something in the drawer.

We need to go now, I say. Livvy! Mummy needs to wake up . . .

But Livvy is not listening, she is whirling around and now she has one foot on the metal sticky-out bit round the fireplace so she can reach up, and pull it down from the wall.

We are not to touch that thing, ever, Nanny says. Daddy keeps it for squirrels.

But Livvy knows how it works. She knows everything. She holds it in her hands, and she is putting the things from the drawer in it.

Come here, Lexy, she says. Stand behind me.

I do what she says. Because Livvy always looks after me.

But I wrap my arms round her, my head pressed in her T-shirt, just to be extra sure, as we listen to the bad man trying to get out of the cellar.

He lost it, Livvy says, he didn't care how much he hurt her—her voice is small and hard. I don't know what that man is capable of, I'm not letting him near us.

And I know her words are meant to come out brave, but I can feel Livvy shaking, and that's the worst thing of all.

Now she moves the gun up against her shoulder and does something to it—a movement I feel—and I know she's ready.

We breathe in and out, and we listen to the banging noises, and it feels like we are there a very long time, just me and my big sister together.

Then there's a crash louder than anything before.

That's the cellar door down, Livvy says.

I know Daddy wouldn't hurt us. But it's not my nice daddy here now, and I am very scared.

The footsteps come heavy and fast through the corridor to the hall. Then they stop.

He must be deciding where to go. It's darker in here, and we're hidden by the half-closed door. Maybe he will just go out the front . . .

The door swings open.

We see that big shadow in the doorway, and I know he sees us.

Livvy, I whisper.

She's breathing even quicker now, like she does when she is scared but won't say so.

Livvy, do something!

The bad man takes a step toward us, and I know he'll hurt her—

Livvy!

When the bang comes I feel the kick through her whole body. It throws her back against me, but I keep holding on.

And we stay like that, until everything is quiet again.

Chapter 70

OLIVIA

I thought, when she returned, that she finally understood the truth about that night.

But as we talked in the sitting room, that evening after court, it hit me. She still didn't remember. Not what had happened. Not what our family was really like.

She thought I was the one in denial. But it was her. I just couldn't face telling her right then. Not when I'd just got my sister back. It took all I could not to break apart again.

Because of course, I still feel guilty.

I know it was not my fault. Sometimes—more and more often, these days—I can *feel* the truth of that, too.

I know also that moment can be the most dangerous time for victims of domestic abuse: the moment they decide to leave. Maybe I sensed that even then, at thirteen.

He was getting worse: drinking more, angrier, unpredictable. I knew we would have to leave this way, clandestinely. My mother and I had talked it over, and an end-of-the-summer vacation offered our opportunity.

He thought the Cornish vacation cottage was too suburban for words. He might join us there later, he said, and my mother agreed that would be lovely. She didn't tell him we wouldn't be there when he turned up. That we didn't plan to go there at all.

Instead, as soon as we set off, the three of us, my mother, Lexy and me, would head straight to her parents' Midlands home hundreds of miles away. From there, she could safely let him know it was over between them.

Of course, the plan went wrong. We had been slipping money away, to amass a little fund, but he noticed cash was going missing.

I said it was me. I couldn't let Nanny get the sack.

We didn't know Lexy had told Alex the truth about who took the money, stoking his suspicions about my mother's plans. So when Elsa insisted that we go back to get her valuables, the things she hadn't been able to pack with him there watching her, he was waiting. It was a setup—forcing her return and a confrontation.

He was worse than I'd ever seen him before.

In a way, my naivety helped cover our tracks.

I didn't think of cans of petrol, leaving the gas on.

The ashtray was full: he must have been waiting there hours, drinking, as the night drew in. I just picked up the box of matches propped by it, lit one, and dropped it in the wastepaper basket in the corner.

I took bits of an old newspaper, once they had caught, and scattered them around the room. The flames flickered in the darkness, reflected in the shining wood, as I went out again, past the body under the blanket. I'd put that over him.

We had already got Elsa in the back seat. She was groaning by then, but not really awake.

I'd only ever been allowed to drive down to the gate before; but I went very slowly along the empty roads. I didn't think anyone saw us: Annersley was dark, except a light still on in one of the pub's windows.

When Elsa woke up, not far from the village, I stopped the car. It's hard even now to think of her sheer naked terror and distress.

It just went off in my hands, I said, I didn't mean it, I was so scared. Yet in a way, she understood: I always protected Lexy in that house.

I told her she had to drive us to the cottage now, just as everyone expected, for an ordinary family vacation. Eventually, she did.

There, we had a few days' reprieve: time to think, so that when the police did arrive, we knew what we had to say. We didn't consider telling the truth. It was a different time, even twenty-some years ago.

And Alex—I don't think of him as my father, not anymore—was so careful. Everyone thought that he could do no wrong, even Nanny. They thought my mother was wild, spoiled, with him for his money.

He had made sure of that, isolating her, spreading rumors. Nanny was always bringing little pieces of gossip back from the village, even in those blurry muddled days after the fire.

Then one time, she came back and told us that my friend Paul Bryant had seen our car leave, on the day of the fire. I knew that to be a lie, of course. He could only have seen it go by after midnight.

I walked over to his parents' pub. Paul said that when he'd told his Uncle Pete that he had seen our car leaving in the dead of night, the policeman had guessed at what happened: a fatal accident, or worse; then a cover-up.

They thought—must still think—my mother did it. And so they helped us hide it.

But not for money, like Nicky thought. *They* owed *us*.

Because I had confided in Paul, told him how my family wasn't like everyone else's, that sometimes my father would hit my mother, and worse. So he went to his Uncle Pete in the police, thinking he would fix it. Pete Gregory spoke to my father and . . . nothing happened. He carried on.

At least people believed this story from the start. The body was too damaged to show the true cause of death—the lead shot must have melted away in the heat. If they found traces, I was ready to blame the house's old lead piping. But no one did.

And no one thought to look for the vintage shotgun

that once hung in the sitting room, or the cartridges kept in a drawer of the desk. Pete Gregory, after all, had never bothered Alex about a license for that antique. He wasn't going to mention it now.

After a few weeks, we left. Elsa just wanted to get away, whisking Lexy off to her parents'. I went to my new school, just a bit later than my father had planned—only, now I wanted to go. The friends we had been staying with kept the dog.

Afterward, I didn't want to talk to Elsa. Grandma Vane, never a fan of her daughter-in-law, didn't help. But my mother didn't try that hard to keep in touch. I suppose she blamed me, for picking up the gun, and I blamed her, for not being able to keep us safe; both of us were trapped in our guilt.

When, years later, the letter arrived from my grandparents to tell me she had died, I didn't feel much. But I wondered about Lexy. Maybe I realized, if not then, when? So I wrote back, telling them I could not make the funeral, but I would like to see my sister.

They replied quickly: they were very sorry but they didn't want me stirring up the past. She had forgotten what had happened. It wasn't a good idea to open old wounds.

Over time, I decided they were right. Focus on what I could fix.

I suppose there's one more thing I should mention. The other morning, we were in the park, near the hotel in Mansford where we are staying since the second fire. Nicky—we agreed she's not Lexy anymore—was asking me what Bea was like as a baby, her first words, when she started to walk, all the things she's missed.

And what's her middle name? she asked.

She's Beatrice Alexandra, I said, without really thinking. For you, of course.

It was just the truth, but she got all happy and teary. She said it meant something important—that we were always thinking about each other, in some way, even if we weren't being sisters like we could have been.

I suggested we go and feed the ducks, it was such a nice day. I don't think I'll ever be quite as, well, *mushy* as she is.

Although, when you think about it—and I did, after-ward—she's right.

That's all I want to say. That's my story.

Chapter 71

NICKY

They traced the latest fire to a room up on the attic floor. In the end they decided it must have been the bright afternoon sun, reflecting on a mirror, that had set an old wooden dresser alight. It must have been smoking all evening, before the fire caught.

Neither Olivia nor I have spoken publicly about our ordeal, other than releasing a blandly worded statement via her lawyer requesting privacy and time to heal. It drew a veil over the circumstances around my sudden departure from her house, citing long-standing personal issues that predated my visit. Not quite a lie.

Although there have been lots of MANSION CURSE headlines, the reports have held nothing to alarm us. My ghostwritten document was never made public. The police knew better than to leak it and give the whole embarrassment more publicity.

Of course Joey has been in touch with me, desperate

to know what happened. I met up with him and said I'd had a kind of breakdown, sticking to the official line.

I am sure he did not believe me, but he was surprisingly good-tempered about it: if there is one thing more delicious to him than a cover-up, it is the idea that the mainstream media has missed the real story. He has been distracted, though, by his burgeoning photography career: Olivia had the bright idea of getting him to take photos for her. She is used to finding a way through things. It is strangely reassuring—familiar, even.

The other day we went to look at the house, for the last time. The building was wrapped up in tarpaulins, but Olivia wanted to walk around the garden.

Josh won't contest the sale, it seems, as the divorce is settled. Local reaction to him abandoning his wife in her time of need came as a serious shock; he is even going to anger-management classes to work on his tendency to break things when he's in a temper. Sabrina is back at the farm with Leo, keeping a very low profile.

The damage to the house is much less than it was the first time—thanks to the state-of-the-art alarm system Olivia had linked up to the station. But she wants a fresh start.

Annie won't go with her. She is moving abroad, to be closer to her brother and his family. Which is maybe just as well.

The grass at the bottom of the lawn was scorched in a few places but was already growing back when we visited. It was growing back, too, over the earth path worn to Alexander Vane's stone marker.

I had already asked Olivia about it: Alex's mother had insisted on it, while she tried to forget it was even there. So it wasn't Olivia's frequent footsteps that had worn away that path. But someone's had.

"You know," I said then, "I thought it was Cav, who had been with you since before the fire." I explained how I'd heard her and Josh arguing about it, or so I thought.

"Cav?" she said, smiling but puzzled. "No . . . *he* didn't work for us before. Don't you remember Annie?"

I did. Details are still coming back, even now.

Nanny, we had called her then—Olivia's mispronunciation, from when she was little, that had stuck. Annie wasn't a proper nanny, really. She just came in from the village to help out.

When Olivia came back to Annersley years later, she sought Annie out. Annie had been working as a housekeeper in Devon, and was thrilled to come back.

Annie, I also realized, was the link between the house and village. The rumors about Elsa that Marie Crompton repeated to me—Marie would have heard them straight from the source: her friend Annie. And, more recently, their chats would cover all the village gossip; how the writer who'd come to stay at the big house had been asking some questions of Marie's grandson Joey . . .

And Annie didn't drive. Which means when I thought I was alone in the house, no cars parked outside, Annie could have been in there with me: watching me.

I think she just wanted to scare me off: she must have guessed that there was something to hide—and that Elsa had done it. Until . . .

I remember what I saw over Olivia's shoulder as we talked after court: the door left ajar by Annie. I think Annie was waiting, listening, and heard our secret. That Alex Vane had been shot by his own daughter.

It must have been a tremendous shock. Everybody loved Alex, after all. Perhaps she just wanted to punish us a little, with another scare. She had her own key to let herself back in that night. And there are all sorts of ways you could start a fire, then slip away. Maybe she didn't think the house would burn so fast.

I cannot be sure. I hope that Olivia is right, that it was just an accident. But sometimes, at night, I wonder if a house might be haunted by its past, after all.

I think of that fire returning, that we almost didn't escape . . .

But what's most surprising is how much we have to look forward to. We have been talking, Olivia and I, about the future. She is looking for a different kind of influence: she has it all worked out.

"Design school, then no more licensing my name out—I'm going to do it all myself. I want Olivia Vane to be a household brand. Everything you need for the perfect home. But with rather less of me in the photos."

I smiled at her determined expression. I know she will do it.

"And what about you?" she said then.

"I don't know. I might go traveling . . ." I didn't really fancy another ghostwriting job. Unsurprisingly. And I will get a slice of the house proceeds, she told me the other day—although I wasn't sure, she says it's only right—so for once I have no financial pressures, right now.

"Aren't you going to finish our book?" she said.

I pulled a face. "Are you joking?" I still can't always tell with her. "You know we couldn't put that out there."

"Why?" she said. "Change names, tweak a few details. Don't they say truth is stranger than fiction?"

"I don't know . . ."

"I'd help," she offered. "Think about it."

So I did think about it.

Of course, it would be difficult. We would have to spend a lot of time together, Olivia and I, examining old wounds. We would have to build a whole new relationship, as the women we are today, not the children we once were. And we would have to find a way to tell our story, without repercussions for us, or Bea.

Who knows if it wouldn't all be too much? If the past would not be better left alone?

After all, we are very different people, and very different, too, from those two little girls who ran across the lawn hand in hand, and felt like they were flying . . .

But as I say, who really knows?

Maybe we could make it work, somehow. Maybe

we could be sisters again. Maybe one day you will see our story on a shelf, pull it down, check the cover, hold it in your hands. Turn the page, then another, to see what happens next.

Like I said: details are still coming back, even now . . .

Epilogue

And now it is time to go.

Livvy is concentrating, driving slowly. But I keep watching through the back window of the car.

I see something moving in a window near the front door and wonder if he has got up again, after all. But then the curtain flickers once more, and this time the window must break, because fire comes out.

Next to me, Livvy makes a sound, like she can't catch her breath.

Shh, Livvy. I slide back down in my seat so I can reach to pat her arm. Shh.

After a second she says: Seat belt on, Lexy.

It is her loud voice again. But I know it makes Livvy feel better when she can tell me what to do, so I do what she says.

She did it inside, too. Come here, Lexy, she said.

But I know Livvy, even when she acts grown-up. I knew she was scared. That was the worst thing of all, knowing how scared she was underneath.

And no one was trying to stop it, and no one was coming to help.

They never did.

So when he came toward us I knew what to do. I got all shaky and hot, like fire was inside me, and I did it. I put my fingers over hers and I stopped him. I stopped him from hurting us.

And I can't feel sad, even now, because Livvy always looks after me. It was my turn to look after her.

But one day, maybe, I will forget what it was like to be so little and scared, and forget what I had to do.

I hope I do.

ACKNOWLEDGMENTS

Thank you to John Scognamiglio and to everyone at Kensington for your creativity and hard work. In the UK, thank you to Lucy Frederick, Ben Willis and the Orion team, and to Clare Hulton for all your support. Thank you to first readers Helena Curran, Liz Rowley, Zoe Rowley, Rowena Mason, and Jennifer Twite. Thank you to Sarah Przybylska and Graham Bartlett for your expertise. A very big thank-you to all the family, friends, and colleagues who have cheered this book on—and to all the readers who have supported it now that it is out in the world. (And lastly, ER. For helping to get our story out there.)

Connect with

Us

Visit us online at
KensingtonBooks.com
to read more from your favorite authors, see books
by series, view reading group guides, and more.

for sneak peeks, chances to win books and prize packs,
and to share your thoughts with other readers.

facebook.com/kensingtonpublishing
twitter.com/kensingtonbooks

Tell us what you think!

To share your thoughts, submit a review,
or sign up for our eNewsletters, please visit:
KensingtonBooks.com/TellUs.